SPECIAL MESSAGE TO READERS

THE ULVERSCROFT FOUNDATION
(registered UK charity number 264873)
was established in 1972 to provide funds for research, diagnosis and treatment of eye diseases. Examples of major projects funded by the Ulverscroft Foundation are:-

- The Children's Eye Unit at Moorfields Eye Hospital, London
- The Ulverscroft Children's Eye Unit at Great Ormond Street Hospital for Sick Children
- Funding research into eye diseases and treatment at the Department of Ophthalmology, University of Leicester
- The Ulverscroft Vision Research Group, Institute of Child Health
- Twin operating theatres at the Western Ophthalmic Hospital, London
- The Chair of Ophthalmology at the Royal Australian College of Ophthalmologists

You can help further the work of the Foundation by making a donation or leaving a legacy. Every contribution is gratefully received. If you would like to help support the Foundation or require further information, please contact:

THE ULVERSCROFT FOUNDATION
The Green, Bradgate Road, Anstey
Leicester LE7 7FU, England
Tel: (0116) 236 4325

website: www.foundation.ulverscroft.com

Sarah Butler lives in Manchester and runs a consultancy which develops literature and arts project that explore and question our relationship to place. She has been writer in residence on the Central Line, the Greenwich Peninsula, and at Great Ormond Street Hospital, and has taught creative writing for the British Council in Kuala Lumpur. *Ten Things I've Learnt About Love* is her first novel.

TEN THINGS I'VE LEARNT ABOUT LOVE

Alice has just returned to London from months of travelling abroad. She is late to hear the news that her father is dying, and returns to the family home only just in time to say goodbye. Daniel hasn't had a roof over his head for almost thirty years, but to him the city of London feels like home in a way that no bricks and mortar ever did. He spends every day searching for his daughter; the daughter he has never met. Until now . . .

SARAH BUTLER

TEN THINGS I'VE LEARNT ABOUT LOVE

Complete and Unabridged

CHARNWOOD
Leicester

First published in Great Britain in 2013 by
Picador
an imprint of, Pan Macmillan
London

First Charnwood Edition
published 2013
by arrangement with
Pan Macmillan
a division of Macmillan Publishers
London

A catalogue record for this book is available from the British Library.

ISBN 978–1–4448–1694–5

Published by
F. A. Thorpe (Publishing)
Anstey, Leicestershire

Set by Words & Graphics Ltd.
Anstey, Leicestershire
Printed and bound in Great Britain by
T. J. International Ltd., Padstow, Cornwall

This book is printed on acid-free paper

For Anne and Dave

‘so here I am homeless at home and
half gratified to feel I can be happy any where’

John Clare

Ten things I will say to my father

1) I met a man in Singapore who smelt like you — cigarette smoke and suede.
2) I remember that holiday in Greece — endless ruins, and you having to explain the difference between Doric, Ionic and Corinthian columns again and again.
3) I wish you'd talked about Mama. I wish you'd kept something of hers.
4) I still have the book you bought me for my tenth birthday, when I wanted to be an astronaut — *A Tour Through the Solar System*.
5) I know you always hoped one of us would be a doctor, like you.
6) I have a recurring dream. I am standing outside your house. There's a party; I can hear people talking and laughing inside. I ring the doorbell, and it takes you for ever to answer.
7) It was me who stole the photograph from your study.
8) I used to spy on you — watch you gardening or sitting in your armchair, or at your desk with your back to the door. I always wanted you to turn around and see me.
9) I'm sorry I haven't been about much.
10) Please, don't —

My father lives on his own in a haughty terraced house near Hampstead Heath. The houses round there are smug and fat, their tiled drives like long expensive tongues, their garden walls just high enough to stop people from seeing in. It's all bay windows and heavy curtains, clematis and wisteria.

I queue for a taxi outside Arrivals and smoke three cigarettes while I wait. When it's finally my turn, I duck into the car and find myself dizzy and sick with the nicotine. The driver plays Mozart's Requiem. I want to ask her to turn it off, but I can't think how to explain, so I stretch my legs into the space where my rucksack should be, rest my head against the door frame, and close my eyes. I try to remember the exact colour of my bag: it's a sort of dirty navy blue — I've been carrying it around for years; I should know what colour it is. Inside there are jeans, shorts, vest-tops, a waterproof coat. Ten packets of Russian cigarettes. A pair of embroidered slippers for Tilly. Mascara. A lipgloss that's nearly finished. An almost perfectly spherical stone, which I'd picked up to give to Kal, and then cursed myself for crying. An unused *Rough Guide to India*. A head-torch. A photograph of all of us, including my mother, from before I can remember: that's the only thing I'd be sorry to lose.

We arrive too soon. I pay the driver and step out onto the pavement. As she pulls away from the kerb I want to hold out a hand and say, stop, I've changed my mind, let's go somewhere else, anywhere else, and then sit in the back seat again with time on hold, and watch London through the window.

There are eleven steps up to my father's house. At the bottom, two sickly-looking trees stand in chubby blue-glazed pots. A huge bay tree obscures most of the front window, but still I look for him, sitting on the sofa, a cigarette curling itself into ash in one hand. He's not there. My stomach aches; my mouth tastes of sawdust and sleep. I pull a leaf from one of the trees in the pots — freckled a pale yellow-green — and tear along the length of its spine.

My father's front door is painted a dark red-brown, like blood that's been left to dry. Two tall panes of wrinkled glass — bordered by delicate green ivy — reveal nothing much of what's inside.

When I was thirteen he sent me to school in Dorset. I remember coming home after the first term. He'd had to work, so Tilly picked me up, her fingers nervous at the wheel, her crisp new driving licence stowed in the glove compartment. I stood on the top step, looking at the same brass doorbell I am looking at now, while Tilly scrabbled about for her keys. I thought how the door didn't look like our front door, and pressed the bell to see what it sounded like from the outside.

I take a cigarette from my pocket, even though

there's no time to waste. The lighter scratches at my thumb. I inhale too quickly, and cough — a thin, smoker's cough — my hand against my chest.

Ten ways other people might describe me

1) Tramp.
2) Bum.
3) Homeless.
4) Down on my luck.
5) Rough sleeper.
6) Dispossessed.
7) Scum.
8) Marginalised.
9) Misunderstood.
10) Lost.

I'm an old man with a dodgy heart, there's no two ways about it. And the truth is I'm more at home here — at the edge of the river, where's there's mud and mess — than in fancy squares like that one by the Tube, with its flashy screens and security guards.

I move around. It's as close as I get to any kind of a strategy. Each place, I imagine you. I don't have much to go on, though there are things I can guess — hair colour, height, age. And I know your name; I could call to you and watch you turn. We'd stand here and let the cyclists hurry by, listen to the barges knock together like bells, and we'd talk.

Last week, when I thought I was dying, all I could focus on was you. It's not easy to focus on anything when you feel like there's a grown man sitting on your ribcage, but you pulled me through — you always have.

It happened upstream from here, on the Embankment, opposite the Houses of Parliament: the bit by the hospital, with the high wall, where the ends of the benches are carved into birds' faces, sat up on piles of bricks so you can see across the river. I was walking west, with a vague plan to go as far as Albert Bridge, find a place for the night in a quiet Chelsea corner. The police are tricky there, but if you tuck yourself away, sometimes they'll leave you be. I was just walking. The doctor said emotional upset can bring it on, but I'm not sure I was upset that day, not particularly.

I stood against the wall and held both hands to my chest, tears in my eyes like I was a kid, not a man approaching sixty who can survive on the street. I hope if you'd been there, you'd have stopped and asked if I was OK, but you weren't, and anyway I'm used to people paying no attention. I stood and looked at the river, and I thought about you, and how for all I know you're dead already. The world's full of danger, after all. Car crashes. Knives. Blood clots. Cancer. I carried on looking at the river, thinking about what could have been, and scared I was going to drop dead any minute. I suppose it's not surprising that I lost it; I don't mean screaming and shouting — that's not my way, and in any case when you live like I do it's what they call circumspect to keep your head down. No, I just blubbed like a baby.

Don't get me wrong, I'm not always like this. I like a drink and a banter. I like lying on the pavement and looking up at the stars. It's just that I thought I was having a heart attack; I thought I was going to die without finding you.

I thought about her too, with her scarlet name. We went away once — a weekend in Brighton — snatched time; perfect. We ate ice-cream, and fish and chips. We — it feels wrong to say this to you — but we made love in a run-down hotel with a view of the sea.

I'm lying when I say it was perfect. It was grey and dreary. I let myself get angry: hard words in a borrowed room. That way her eyes would click shut and her lips would harden. I suppose it was difficult for her too.

Once I've fallen in love, I find it almost impossible to get out; I've learnt that about myself. It doesn't make for an easy life.

* * *

I'm not one for doctors, but after all that, on the Embankment, I made myself go. The surgery smelt of new carpets — sweet and sharp. I sat next to a woman in her forties and she stood and moved to the other side of the room. I try not to let things like that bother me. I picked up a pile of newspapers and started to look for you. Nothing.

The doctor's name was the colour of sun-warmed sandstone. She had kind eyes, and her hands, when she touched me, were soft and cool. It's natural to be upset, she said, it's frightening; the first time, everyone thinks they're going to die. I cried again, there in her tiny room with the bed with a paper sheet stretched across it. She smiled, and gave me a tissue. It was as much her touch as the business with my heart, or the woman in the waiting room, that got me, and I suspect she knew it. She asked me all the questions doctors ask of a man like me, which, I find, are never the questions that matter.

She gave it a name: angina, ice-cold blue, beginning and end. She showed me a tiny red bottle and told me it would help — a quick spray underneath my tongue and I wouldn't be left pressed against a wall, clutching my chest. I took the prescription and left. And I carried on doing what I've been doing for years. I have written your name more times than I can remember. Always, at the beginning, I write your name.

Ten things I know about my mother

1) Her name was Julianne — pronounced like she was French, except she wasn't.
2) She was beautiful (I found a photograph in my father's study, of the two of them and the three of us. I'm holding her hand and gazing up at her. I took it when I went away to school and he never mentioned it. It is in my rucksack, which is lost).
3) I have the same colour hair she had.
4) My father loved her — he's never found anyone else.
5) She didn't always think before she acted. I know this because when I was fourteen I climbed a tree on Hampstead Heath wearing flimsy shoes with no grip. I went too high, fell, and broke my leg. On the way to hospital, Dad said, 'You're just like your mother, Alice. Can you not stop and think for five minutes about what might happen?'
6) After she died, Dad packed everything that had anything to do with her, including the turquoise and gold cushions Tilly and Cee loved so much, into big black bin bags and drove off with them in his car. He didn't bring them back.
7) In summer she got freckles on her cheeks and shoulders, the same way I do (my father

told me this, and then blushed, which I'd never seen him do before. I didn't know what to say).

8) She and Dad argued a lot (according to Cee; Tilly says she can't remember, but she's always been one to sit on the fence).
9) She was driving a Citroen GSA. She'd had her licence for five months and twenty-one days. The verdict was accidental death, which sounds too much like incidental for my liking.
10) If it wasn't for me she wouldn't have been driving at all.

The cancer is in my father's pancreas. Cee told me over the phone — me standing in the hostel reception in Ulan Bator, her in Dad's hallway, the line full of static. I'm still not even sure what a pancreas is, though I'd never admit that to Cee.

Cee thinks I'm a lost cause. You're wasting your talents, she tells me, flying off to the other side of the world at the drop of a hat. Time will catch up with you, she tells me — by which she means I should get on and have kids before my ovaries dry up. You did the right thing with Kal, but you need to start thinking about settling down, she says. Dust settles, sediment settles — but I don't say that. What was wrong with Kal anyway, I ask. She just sighs, the way she always does, the way that makes me feel five again.

I stub out my cigarette and ring the doorbell. It's Tilly who answers, and I'm thankful for it. She's wearing tapered jeans, and a voluminous orange T-shirt. Her face is tired and pale. The hall stretches in black and white chessboard squares behind her, and I remember the two of us chalking hopscotch marks, laughing at the chill of the tiles on the soles of our feet.

'Alice.' Tilly opens her arms. She is marshmallow soft. I lean my forehead, for a moment, against her chest, and smell the soft, summery smell of her perfume. Cee is coming down the stairs. Neat white slip-ons, black linen trousers, and a sleeveless turquoise shirt. Her hair looks recently cropped — dyed a chemical shade of red. She has our father's eyes, a deep brown the colour of garden compost. I'm told I have my mother's.

I won't cry. I step away from Tilly. Cee stands with an empty water glass in one hand, her skin puffed red beneath her make-up.

'You should have called,' Tilly says. 'I'd have picked you up. I've got the car here, and it's miserable sitting in a taxi getting your ear chewed off.'

'It's fine,' I say. We stand, awkward, silent. I glance towards the stairs.

'He's sleeping,' Cee says, and I feel a familiar flare of anger. We are all too close together. It's not a narrow hallway, but I am finding it difficult to breathe.

'How was your flight?' Tilly asks. 'I looked it up — four thousand, three hundred miles. Isn't that amazing?'

The thing I loved more than anything about Mongolia was the horizon — wider than I've ever seen; endless land and endless sky. I push the front door closed. I'd forgotten how it sticks.

'You've got to — ' Cee starts.

'I know.' I pull it towards me, shove the handle upwards and slam it shut.

Cee looks at my bag — a small black day-pack — and then looks behind me. 'Is that all you have?'

I picture the baggage hall — fluorescent lights, rows of trolleys, the scratched black rubber of the conveyor belt. I had stood and waited for my rucksack to appear. People snatched up their bags and scurried away. I waited until there were only four things left, circling: two hard cases, a long package wrapped in newspaper and packing tape, and a pink holdall with fraying straps. I waited until the screen flashed up a different flight number and city and a new group of people clustered round. A new consignment of bags began to appear. I thought about just picking one and walking away with it, but didn't.

'I'll go up,' I say, and walk past them, keeping close to the wall so our bodies won't meet.

'Alice, he's asleep.' Cee puts her hand on my arm.

'I'll stick the kettle on — we can have a cup of tea.' Tilly's fingers fuss at the hem of her T-shirt.

I step out of Cee's grasp. 'I won't wake him.'

I am four steps up now. The stairs are painted white, the red carpet running along the middle pinned down by thin brass rods. Kal joked about it, the first time he came here — an interminable Sunday lunch. I feel important every time I go up to the bathroom, he said, and I laughed, because I'd never thought about it like that before. I wish he was standing next to me, holding my arm. I still have his number in my phone. Sometimes I just sit and look at it.

'Alice.' It's Tilly's voice. Her face is scrunched into a frown. 'Just — ' She squeezes her hands together. 'Just be prepared, honey.'

* * *

My father's room is at the front of the house, on the first floor. It has two tall windows which look out onto the street, over the top of the red brick wall opposite and into the courtyard behind. I open the door as quietly as I can, and step inside. The thick green curtains have been pulled shut against the day, and the floor lamp by the sofa casts a warm yellow circle onto the carpet. I don't want to look at the bed. I stare instead at the wardrobe: the miniature triangles of paler wood inlaid around its edges, the oval mirror, the dull metal hinges. I look up at the ugly ceiling rose and its pauper's chandelier, six fake candles resting in dusty holders.

Cee once told me that before I was born, in the other house, her and Tilly were allowed into our parents' room on Saturday mornings. They used to sneak in between Dad and Mama and demand to be told stories. After the stories, if he wasn't working, our father would get up, put his dressing gown on over his blue pyjamas and go downstairs. Tilly and Cee would roll about in the warm space he left behind, waiting for his footsteps on the stairs and the clatter of a tray. Saturday morning stories and breakfast stopped once they moved here and I came along. When I asked why, Cee just pursed her lips and shrugged, as though somehow it was my fault.

The room smells of skin and sweat. It's too hot. I rest my hands on the sofa back, and I listen: a gentle tick from the water pipes; a bird chirruping to its mate outside; the sound of my father, breathing.

The last time I saw him was a couple of days

before I flew to Moscow. We had dinner at a new Spanish place in South End Green. Tapas; a rich red wine. There's a recession coming, Alice, he said, I'm not sure it's the best time to abandon your job. It's just temping, I said, and I've got savings. I need to get out of here. You always need to get out of here, he said, why is that? I told him about Kal, but that didn't explain all the other times. I'm trying to think now if he'd looked pale, or thin, if he'd seemed ill, or worried. I don't remember.

The man in the bed does not look like my father.

My father has a strong face, a square jaw, thick bushy eyebrows. He is a big man: tall, not fat, but bulky. His shoulders are broad, his chest solid. When he hugs you — which isn't often, but isn't never — you can feel the strength in his arms. This man is too small to be my father.

On the floor to the right of the bed is a slim white-and-blue box. A thin tube runs from the box, underneath the sheet that covers the man in the bed. A second tube ends in one of those plastic bags you see in hospitals, half full of yellow liquid.

The man in the bed is breathing like an old person. His face is gaunt, the skin tight against the shape of a skull I don't recognise. There's a chair at the left-hand side of the bed. Someone must have brought it up from the dining room. It looks wrong in here, with its high slatted back and narrow cushioned seat. The dining room, too, must look out of sync, one man down.

As I lower myself onto the chair it creaks

loudly. I hold myself still. He doesn't wake up. I want to touch his hand, but it's underneath the sheet, and so I sit and look at my own fingers — stacks of silver rings, nails bitten to the quick.

'I just got in,' I say. My voice sounds thin, off balance. 'From Mongolia. I just got in now.' I feel a sudden sweep of fatigue. 'I'm not even sure what day it is.' I laugh, but it sounds wrong, and so I stop. 'I came as quick as I could, I didn't have mobile reception for a week — more than that.' His hair is roughed up against his pillow; his lips are dry and cracked. I can feel the breath high and shallow in my chest. I want to cry. I want to lie down on the floor and close my eyes. I want to run away.

'I came as soon as I got the messages.'

I remember sitting in the back of a jeep in Mongolia, with a couple from Sweden and a guy from Palestine, my mobile phone useless and forgotten at the bottom of my rucksack, the road — it was hardly a road — jolting us back and forth, and all around us: nothing. Just miles and miles of nothing. The joy of it.

'It's so gloomy in here, Dad. Don't you think it's gloomy?' I stand up and pull the curtains apart. It has started to rain, thin lines of water on the other side of the glass. 'I see England's having another great summer, then,' I say.

'Alice?'

I spin around. 'Dad?' I stay where I am, one hand on the edge of the curtain. I wish I hadn't opened them. The light picks out the shape of his face, casts deep shadows where the skin caves in. His skin is the wrong colour — too much yellow.

'Dad. How are — '

'Terrible.' He sounds like he's got a cold — phlegmy and hoarse.

'My phone didn't have reception,' I say. He coughs and I see his face tense with pain.

'What can I do? What can I get you?'

He moves his head to the left.

'This?' I walk to the bedside table and pick up a wooden stick with a pink cube on the end.

'Dip it — in the glass,' he says.

The glass holds a shallow layer of pink liquid. I dip in the cube and hand it to my father. He dabs the sponge to his mouth. I can see every bone underneath his skin. Maybe we did learn about the pancreas at school. I have a feeling it's a dark, purply red, that it tapers to a point at one end. I can't remember what it does.

'I'm sorry — to ruin — your holiday,' he says. He takes shallow, rattling breaths every few words. The pink sponge falls onto the sheet and spreads a wet stain across the cotton. I pick it up and put it back onto the bedside table.

'It wasn't a — ' I stop myself, sit back on the dining chair and wrap one leg over the other. I don't know what to do with my hands, so I shove them underneath my thighs. The edges of my rings dig into the backs of my legs. 'Do you know, in Mongolia, no one owns the land? There are no fences,' I say.

'Did that man — go with you?'

'Kal?'

'The Indian — chap.'

'He's British. I told you, Dad, we split up. I

told you that.' I stand and walk to the window, lean my head against the glass. It's cold on my skin. I imagine sitting with Kal outside a yurt, watching the sun turn the earth a rich orange-pink. 'There were eagles too,' I say. 'Massive eagles just by the side of the road — when there was a road. They had these huge claws. They could kill a mouse just by picking it up.'

I hear him shift, and I turn back. He's staring at me. The whites of his eyes are dull yellow.

'You know — that I love — you,' he says. 'As much — as the others.'

I close my fist around a handful of curtain and squeeze hard. It's like there's a weight in my stomach, bigger than my stomach even. I listen to his breath rasp in his throat. The water pipe has stopped ticking.

'It's important. I always — told — your mother — it was important.'

'What do you mean?'

'For you — to know, for — you to know — that.'

He used to buy me a peppermint mouse from Thorntons every Friday afternoon. I don't know why I remember it now, but I do: the crackle of plastic wrapping, the glee of biting off the nose — dark chocolate and sweet green mint beneath.

Neither of us speak. His eyelids flicker, then close, and his breath pulls in in a faint snore. I walk towards the bed and look down at him.

'Please don't,' I whisper. 'Please don't.'

There's a knock on the door. I expect it to be Tilly or Cee, but it's a nurse, a short wide woman wearing blue trousers and a loose blue shirt.

'You're Alice,' she says. 'Mr Tanner's been telling me all about you.'

'He has?'

She bustles past me. 'Sleeping again,' she says. 'Let's be getting this changed, shall we?' I back away from the bed. She picks up the plastic bag and lifts the sheet. 'You've got the curtains open today, Mr Tanner? That's nice, isn't it, a bit of light on the proceedings. And your daughter's here, that is special.'

'What did he say?' I ask.

'He's sleeping now.' She doesn't even lower her voice. I can see my father's body — thin beneath cotton pyjamas.

'I mean about me.'

She turns a valve on the bag and starts to pull it away from the tube. I watch the yellow liquid slosh against the sides.

'I've got to — ' I wave my arm in the direction of the door.

She doesn't even look up. 'Right you are, dear. It's good you're here, he's been looking forward to it no end.'

I close the door behind me. The corridor smells the same as it always has — wood polish and a hint of wet plaster. I head up the stairs, aiming for the attic, but Tilly intercepts me.

'You met Margaret?' she says.

'The nurse?'

'She's good.'

'Right.'

'Cee's made some tea.'

Kal used to call Tilly and Cee 'the Terms and Conditions'. How are the Terms and Conditions, he'd say when I got back from any kind of family gathering. Anxious and unreasonable, I'd say, and we'd laugh, every time.

'I'd quite like to — ' I look towards the attic stairs.

'Oh, Alice.' She hugs me, my arms pinned tight to my sides.

'He understands, doesn't he? About my mobile. About not having reception. Tilly? He doesn't think — ' I step away from her and stare at the woodchip wall in front of me. It looks dirty and old. 'I just don't want him to think — '

'I made biscuits,' she says. 'The oat ones.' They're Dad's favourite. I imagine him lying in bed, listening to Tilly in the kitchen, the smell of baking drifting up the stairs and into his room.

'Lead the way, Captain.' I touch my fingers to my forehead in a mock salute. Tilly gives me a weak smile, then turns and walks in front of me down the stairs.

Ten things I've found that spell your name

1) A book in Newington library with a cover the colour of glacier water.
2) A row of mugs glazed metallic gold, in a shop window, Camden Town.
3) A child's magenta-pink plastic headband, on the concourse of Euston station.
4) A school jumper with its arms tied around a tree on Southwark Bridge Road — navy blue.
5) Thin slices of grey slate, by that new office block at the Angel.
6) A shard of pale-blue glass on the river wall, Cremorne Gardens, Chelsea.
7) A fake gold bracelet, the paint chipped around the edges, outside Battersea Park station.
8) A burst balloon — bright pink, the rubber soft as skin — on the ramp up to the Tate Modern.
9) A flake of dark-blue paint from a hoarding on Elephant Road, near the station.
10) The end of a charcoal-grey leather belt, the stitching frayed, in the car park outside Waitrose, Balham.

Today, my heart is strong. I follow the shape of the river, looking for colours. As long as I'm discreet, no one will take too much notice of an old man filling his pockets with rubbish. There are people in my situation who stick to the same place, who draw an invisible line around themselves and won't go outside of it, but I don't know where you are, so I keep moving.

Each letter has a colour. I'm not sure if it's the same for you. I'm not sure if you will understand, but I don't think on that too much. Here, by the flood warning sign — a pale-blue sweet wrapper still sticky with sugar. The letter A is the colour of glacier water. Here, by the windowless wooden building with its whirling top, a single gold hoop earring. L is gold. And by the abandoned jetty, a pink ribbon and a glossy blue flyer. I is magenta pink; C is navy blue. E is charcoal grey — I pick up a tiny stone shaped like an arrowhead.

There's a yacht club, not quite new any more, which sits out on the river like a woman lifting her skirts away from the water. I arrange the colours as best I can, on the path just by the entrance gate, and then move on. Around the corner, there is a beach full of treasure.

I'd like to meet you here, stand next to you with the city's junk at our feet. It's a good place for colours. Here: a sun-bleached orange belt; a scrap of plastic just the right shade of purple; a piece of material so pale the blue is almost white; a length of bright-green string. Lower down there is glass and ceramic. A burnt bottle, the glass turned black. Lower still there is stone and metal and broken bricks. Nails rusted up so thickly they lose themselves. If you hit them, hard — like this — you can break off the warm-orange rust and see the shape underneath. I find flint, the corner of it bulked out like a knuckle. Magnolia, amongst the scraps of torn-up paper.

The first letter of each word gives it its colour; you can still see the rest, only they're fainter. So it's good that the pale-orange belt is the largest; it's not always so easy to get the balance right. Five holes, rimmed with metal. I make another two. There is more cotton and string in this city than you'd credit — I use it to tie the words together. I collect it as I walk, roll it into a multicoloured ball which lives in the right-hand pocket of my jacket; not the same pocket as the picture — I have learnt to take care of the things that matter.

I walk down to an old inlet for unloading boats, past a leather boot, cowboy style, with stitching up each side, a chunk missing from the heel like someone's taken a bite. The water is the colour of steel. The red light blinks mournfully on top of Canary Wharf, and the mirrored blocks reflect back a blank, colourless sky. It's been a wet summer: I can feel the rain stored deep in my bones; my boots have suffered.

I close up the belt, careful not to snap the

strings, then bend down — something it gets harder to do, you'll find that out one day — and place it onto the water. For a moment, I think it will sink and I'm ready to fish it out, even if it means a day or more with a sodden boot. It hesitates, then catches the current and it's away. I watch it, and think of a picture I saw once, a frenzied pattern of thin black lines: a map showing twenty-four hours' worth of journeys made by buses in the square mile centred on Waterloo Station — or at least that's what the label said. It was more beautiful than you might imagine.

As I turn away from the water I see a coconut, with hessian skin, up by the wall. I picture a boy standing on the deck of a ferry, tossing the coconut between hands that will one day be scarred by wind and salt and life, but right now are as soft as the skin just below his ear. I picture him throwing it from palm to palm, feeling the scratch and the satisfying curve of its shape. He has run up from the bowels of the ship, away from the roar of gas hobs and the slap of meat against chopping boards, the flash of knives and the hard, clipped words of his co-workers. The wind whips the sweat from his forehead, plays with his hair the way his mother used to, and he has a sudden memory of a scratched wooden sideboard, red plastic roses in a brass vase, dust tucked into the creases between the petals. He should be in the kitchen raising a hammer to smash the coconut into pieces. Instead, he fixes his eyes on the horizon — a shimmer of blue, almost merged with the sky, lifts his right arm and throws the coconut in a high, wide arc.

I balance the coconut on a flat stone and break it open. I've never been one to save things up. Perhaps it's an inheritance from my father. Even so, it serves me well these days — hesitate, and someone will take it from you. I don't like coconut much, but I eat the lot. Flakes stick between my teeth and I have to dig them out with the edge of my fingernail. When I'm done, I walk back to the shore and place each piece of husk on the water. They float like tiny boats out to sea.

⋆ ⋆ ⋆

The problem with cities, or at least with cities like this one, is that they're near enough impossible to write on. That's not to say I don't try, just that it isn't simple.

As a rule, I don't tell people about you, or the writing. The last time I spoke of it was to a man I hadn't seen in a long time, a man who drank cheap cider out of thin ring-pull cans. He asked how I knew you were even here, in London. How do you know she's not in Milan, or Dubai, Paris or Tokyo, he said, Manchester or Rotterdam, Barnsley or New York? He went on for some time, listing the name of every city he could think of, shifting his eyes upwards as if looking for places hidden amongst the grubby ceiling tiles. She might not even be in a city at all, he said. I asked him to stop, but he wouldn't, and so I stood up and walked out of the church hall, with its laminate floor and felt-covered noticeboards, its long foldaway tables and hard plastic chairs.

* * *

I send you a birthday card each year. I don't know the exact date, but I can make a good enough guess. The hardest thing is the envelope: all that blank white. I write your name — I have that at least — but I don't have an address. I drop it into a postbox, and dream, those nights, of the envelope pushed through a letter box, and you, walking along a hallway towards it.

Ten foods that stress me out

1) Any kind of shellfish you have to crack open or pull apart — all that fuss for so little reward.
2) Chinese mushrooms — slick wet balls in your mouth, they give me the creeps.
3) Kal's prawn curry, not because I don't like it — it's delicious — but it's his mum's recipe and so he'd always mention her, and then I'd have to make a comment, and then we'd fight.
4) Glacé cherries, because they're nothing like cherries.
5) Watermelon, because I feel like I should eat the seeds, but I can't, and so I end up spitting them into my hand and not knowing what to do with them.
6) Anything that I have to cook, if it's for more than one other person.
7) Birthday cake. Ugly candles. Fondant photographs. Crappy icing handwriting. They're never right.
8) Breakfast cereal. Sugary or wholesome, it is boring as hell. I'm a toast and Marmite girl.
9) Tilly's double-cream, sugar-fest sherry trifle. She spends so long making it look perfect you don't want to touch it, and then she gets upset when Cee says she only wants a spoonful.
10) In fact, eating pretty much anything in the company of my sisters stresses me out.

I wake early, in the single bed I used to pretend was an ocean liner, and it's like someone's dumped a skipful of rubble right on top of me. My stomach's growling, but I don't want to see anyone, and so I creep up to the attic. It's stuffed full of rejected furniture and old cardboard boxes. The rocking chair still sits underneath the skylight. I used to curl up in it and rock, faster and harder, hoping for disaster. Usually Dad or Cee would shout up the stairs and tell me to stop. Sometimes they weren't around and I'd rock until I felt sick, or bored. I sit in the chair now and let the weight of my body move it back and forth. It's dusty up here, and warm, despite the rain and the cool edge of the air outside. The carpet is the same carpet — an ugly, too-bright green. It's worn underneath the wooden supports of the rocking chair. The rain taps Morse-code messages onto the skylight. I always loved sitting here, listening to the rain; I used to find it calming.

Kal calmed me down, even Cee must have recognised that. Every time we went out, for drinks or dinner with friends, there would be a moment when I'd look over at him — waving his arms about, telling some story or other — and feel a kind of stillness. I miss that.

I stretch out my legs and think about my

rucksack. I'd intended to tell someone about it, but there was a queue at the desk. I hate queues. And anyway, there wasn't time. I wonder if they'll ever bother trying to trace me, or whether my rucksack will just sit in a room somewhere. What will they do with it? Unpack it? Give the stuff away to charity? See if they fancy anything and then chuck the rest of it in the bin? I suppose a bag can just get lost in a system. Though it would have to be *somewhere*. Even if you don't know where a thing is, it is still somewhere.

I've forgotten whether the straps are the same blue as the body, or black. I screw up my eyes and try to remember. I tell myself it isn't important, but it bothers me.

Downstairs, the front door bangs shut. Cee. She lives in Berkhamsted. Husband. Three kids. A part-time job in HR for an engineering firm. They've given her time off. Compassionate leave, and he's not even —

I decide to go downstairs voluntarily. I don't want her marching up here.

The kitchen smells of baking. There are twelve fat brown muffins on a cooling tray next to the sink. Cee is sitting at the heavy pine table, pulling her laptop from its case. Tilly is faffing with the cafetière.

'They're bran and honey,' Tilly says with a forced smile. 'It's from *Good Food*. Do you want coffee?'

I nod, and sit opposite Cee, who flicks me a glance and then starts to unwind her laptop cable. She is the sort of person who winds the cable around the adapter every time she's finished using it.

'Cee wants to draw up a plan,' Tilly says.

Cee turns the computer on and it whirrs and chirps to itself. 'Now you're here, we can divide up duties.' She's wearing jeans with a white shirt tucked into the waistband. Her face looks pinched.

I rub at my jaw and fix my eyes on a thin scratch on the tabletop — it's about the length of my little finger. I wonder who made it.

'I've been doing some research,' Cee says. 'I think we should talk to the doctor, about his mouth. It's terribly dry.'

'Hasn't he got that pink thing, on the stick?' I say.

Cee's lips twitch. 'I think we need to look at other solutions. And then I've been reading about this transdermal background pain relief.'

I could ask her to explain. Instead, I stare past her at the fridge, which leers, big and white and ugly, in the corner of the kitchen. I remember when Dad bought it, and none of us dared ask what on earth he'd do with so much cold space.

'Alice?' I tune back in. Cee's glaring at me. I smile. 'The chime,' she says, and I know from her tone that she's repeating herself, 'is right here.' She points to one of those portable doorbell receiver things, perched on the end of the table like some kind of incendiary device. 'Dad has the bell push by his bedside,' Cee says. 'In case he needs us. That was Steve's idea.' She juts her jaw forward a little, the way she does when she's trying to prove a point. 'If you're the only one in, you might want to take it around with you,' she says. 'There's a clip on the back. Now, Margaret comes three times a day, takes care of the catheter and all that.' She wrinkles her nose when she says catheter. 'Tilly's got a whole load of food in. And now you're here' — she smiles; it looks more like a grimace to me — 'I'll be working mornings and coming in the afternoons.'

'I came as quickly as I could,' I say. 'Ulan Bator's a fuck of a long way away, you know.'

'I didn't suggest for one minute — ' Cee says. 'I'm just saying that now you *are* here — '

'I thought maybe you could read to him, Alice.' Tilly puts three plates, the top one stacked with muffins, and three cups of coffee onto the table. 'He'd like that, and you're so good at reading aloud.' She sits down and looks at me, imploringly.

'The important thing is to keep him company, make him feel loved,' Cee says.

'He is loved.' I break off the top of a muffin and bite into it. I glance around my father's kitchen. It's old, 1970s at a guess. The oven stands on its own, the grill hood reaching high over the hobs. The cupboards are white chipboard, edged with pine. It is not the kind of kitchen my generation aspires to. No granite work surfaces imported from Italy, no Portuguese wall tiles, no double sink with a mixer tap you can pull out to sluice down the corners. The floor is lino — the kind that never looks clean, however much bleach you use. It's an old man's kitchen. I can't stop thinking about the colour of his skin.

'How's he got this bad in two weeks?' I say.

Cee's hand moves over the plate of muffins, then withdraws. 'We called you as soon as he got the prognosis, if that's what you mean,' she says.

'He'd been losing weight before that,' Tilly says. 'But not so much as you'd notice, and then a couple of times I was here he seemed tired.' She shakes her head. 'The next thing we knew he was calling us from hospital.'

'Surely he must have known something was wrong?' I say. Tilly takes a second muffin and pulls off the paper. I stare at the surface of my coffee. 'He's a doctor, for God's sake. He's a surgeon. He knows about — about health.'

Cee drums her fingers against the tabletop. 'He smokes, Alice. And drinks.'

'Alice, why don't you tell us about your trip?' Tilly says.

'Not now.' I sip my coffee. It's too weak, so I walk to the sink and throw the rest of it away. The kitchen window looks over the garden, an uninspiring oblong of grass, the flower beds around the edges overgrown with weeds. My father is more of an indoors man. When I think of him I think of wood-panelled walls, books, the snap of a newspaper shaken straight. I watch a blackbird hop across the lawn, and stop to dig its beak into the soil. I can hear my sisters shifting their weight in their chairs and imagine them exchanging looks, Tilly silently urging Cee to keep her mouth shut.

'They live in tents,' I say, still facing the window. My voice comes out louder than I had intended. 'In Mongolia,' I say. 'They live in tents. And every three months they pack everything up and put it onto their camels and they go off to somewhere else.'

'Why do they do that?' Cee asks.

'I like it,' I say. 'I like the idea of always moving on.'

Cee starts to say something but Tilly cuts in. 'How do they decide where to go?'

I turn then, and shrug. 'I don't know,' I say. 'I suppose where there's water.' I lean against the edge of the sink and bite at my fingernail.

'So why don't they just stay in the first place they get to?' Cee asks. 'If there's water there.'

'How long will it take him to — ?' I say.

Tilly crumbles the remains of her muffin onto her plate.

'They said three to eight weeks,' Cee says at last.

'And that was two and a half weeks ago?'

'That's right.'

* * *

The rain carries on all morning: that shitty, English kind of rain — thin and soft, the sky flat and white and boring. I leave after lunch. I tell Tilly and Cee I need to buy clothes, which is true, and perhaps I slam the front door and walk down the steps with the intention of doing just that. I get on the Tube though, and I stay on it, past Warren Street, Goodge Street, Leicester Square.

At Charing Cross a woman with wide, Slavic

eyes gets on with a pushchair. Her baby wears a pink cord dress and white, wrinkled tights, and stares at me, unblinking. I stare back. The mother looks over. She is expecting me to smile, coo, wave. Instead I just hold the little girl's gaze — and feel strangely comforted.

I get off at Kennington and take the stairs instead of the lift. At every corner there is the possibility of meeting him — polished black shoes, trimmed beard, the umbrella I left behind held away from his trousers so it drips onto the floor. I meet no one. It's been six months. More. I could work it out but I won't.

It is all achingly familiar. The whiteboard by the station entrance; the bin overflowing with crisp packets and takeaway wrappings; the metal grille on the newsagent's windows; the pavement narrowing against the high brick wall, and then the stretch of Alberta Street down to Penton Place — a half-finished tower block creeping up above the horizon; the graffitied hoardings and flapping blue tarpaulin at the end of the row of flats, where there used to be another building.

When I get to the corner of Amelia Street my hair's wet against my scalp and I'm not sure what to do with myself. The odds are he'll be at work. But even if he's not, I can hardly just knock on the door: excuse me, Kal, I'm back from Mongolia, I was just passing by and was curious to know if you'd got married. And, by the way, my father's sick and I can't bear it. I lower my head and speed up, walking on the opposite side of the road, next to the gardens. I run my palm across the railings and listen to the wind push-pull the leaves. If he looks out of the window he'll see me. I straighten my shoulders and lift my chin. It's a beautiful street: a long line of arched red doorways and neat cream-painted window frames. The Victorians gave a shit about detail, Kal would say proudly, you wouldn't get any of this in those newbuilds they chuck up in a couple of months. He took me onto the roof the first time I visited. I was wearing something too short and too thin for the time of year. He stood behind me, wrapped his arms around my waist, and we turned 360 degrees, from Big Ben round to Crystal Palace and back again. I pointed out the constellations: the ones we could see, and the ones we couldn't. You're happier outside than inside, aren't you, he said, and I looked up at the stars and realised he was right.

I find our bedroom window. His bedroom window. The geraniums are still there, with their cheery red petals. It was always him that looked after the plants, so it's hardly surprising they're thriving, but still I'm disappointed by it.

The gardens are more of a park, really, open to anyone. We never used them — we preferred the roof, lying on the slope above the stairs, watching the clouds. I duck into them now, the gate screeching out my presence, and follow the gravelled path, thick with weeds, which twists around a semicircle of grass. I choose a bench — splattered with bird shit and lichen, fingernail scratches across its wooden slats, green metal arms. If it wasn't summer I would have a clear view of the flat, but it's the entrance to the communal stairwell I'm more interested in.

From here I can see who goes in and who comes out.

We were together a year before I moved in: hardly unconsidered, despite what Cee would say. I knew it would be hard, we'd talked about it. There would have to be rules, he'd said — I wouldn't be able to answer the phone, there might be times I'd have to leave suddenly. We didn't talk about how he'd gather up all my things and shove them into the wardrobe, how I'd come back and feel like I'd never lived there in the first place, but I should have been able to imagine that. When I left, Tilly was the only one who didn't look relieved. Which makes sense, I guess, considering she's the invisible woman in her relationship too.

The month before, we had decorated the bedroom. Nothing fancy. Pale-blue walls, oak laminate floorboards, a new chest of drawers. I sit on the bench, bite at my little fingernail and picture each detail of the room: the chips in the skirting board, the built-in cupboard with its scuffed steel hinges, the mark on the wall from the headboard. Kal used to water the geraniums every morning in his dressing gown, his legs sticking out the bottom like a wading bird. I guess he still does.

He'll disappear off to India and marry someone he's never met, and then where will you be? Cee used to say, hands on her hips. I would roll my eyes and accuse her of being racist, and yet, all the time, there was a bit of me — however much I didn't want there to be — that felt a frisson of panic every time she brought it up.

I stand, stretch my arms above my head and leave the gardens. I intend to walk past the stairwell, but instead I turn into it, and walk up, because why shouldn't I? No harm done. I run my finger over the tiled walls. My feet leave wet prints on the concrete, but he won't notice. There's a new mat outside his door — muted rainbow stripes. He wouldn't have bought a new doormat himself. But the label I made — *no junk mail please* — is still taped to the letter box, the blue felt-tip writing starting to fade. Any new girlfriend, any wife, would have taken that down, surely. There's no doorbell, just a cheap brass knocker, shaped like a fox. I reach up a hand and stroke its head, then turn away and run down the stairs and onto the street before I can do anything stupid.

Ten things I own

1) A ball of cotton thread, every colour you can think of.
2) A small penknife, the blades almost blunt.
3) My mother's wedding ring — I wear it around my neck, on a piece of string.
4) A wax jacket.
5) A pair of brown cord trousers, a little too short.
6) A pale-blue shirt.
7) A pair of brown leather shoes, which almost fit. There's a hole in the bottom of the left one.
8) Eleven pounds and thirty-six pence.
9) A white plastic bag.
10) A picture I drew, years ago, of your mother.

On days like this it's important to keep moving. I cut across to the other side of the peninsula, past blocks of flats with brightly coloured balconies, over wide empty roads, past endless hoardings, to where the machines belch aggregate and the air is bitter with burnt sugar. I would like to bring you here. We could sit in one of these concrete cylinders, layered with graffiti, and we could talk. Maybe I'd tell you that when I was twelve I found a tin of orange spray paint with just enough left to write my initials on the wall in our local park. D.W. The W tucked inside the loop of the D. It stayed there for months, and I got a thrill every time I walked past.

* * *

I worry about you. I worry you aren't happy, I worry you're hungry, I worry you're ill. I worry you aren't in this city. I worry you are here but hate it. I worry you are dead.

* * *

I carry on into Greenwich proper, find a lilac scarf screwed up beneath a fence by the Royal Naval College. When I spread it out, I see a thread has snagged through its middle. In the busy square by the *Cutty Sark*, I pick up the silver back of an earring. I see a man drop a half-eaten pasty into a black bin. Beef and onion. Still warm. As I bite into it, I try not to think of my mother, red-faced in the kitchen, glaring at the pastry which never turned out right, however many times she tried.

On the corner of Evelyn Street and New King Street I find a snapped grey shoelace, one end still squeezed into its plastic coating. It reminds me of school — short trousers and cold calves.

In Rotherhithe, I walk the long, silent road which bends to fit the river. The buildings on my right — with their private river views — turn their backs to the road. On the opposite side, there are St George's flags and tea cloths tacked across windowpanes. The likelihood is you would live on the river side. I imagine you have a job which requires a suit. I try to picture you, short like her, with her red hair, your heels clipping the pavement. A skirt, cut to fit; the neat pressed lines of a cotton blouse. My picture of you flickers and fades; I can't see your face.

I don't remember buying the last suit I owned, but I can see the bulk of it on the plastic coat hanger, on the clothes rail in the corner of my room. I remember the feel of it — the weight of the jacket, and the belt I had to start using to keep the trousers from sagging around my waist. I remember destroying it. If the scissors had been sharper, it would have been more satisfying.

Beneath a bench in a tiny cobbled square, where the light sneaks through the leaves and moves across my skin, I find a child's hairgrip, the colour of gold. Is that what it's called? A grip? It worries me, sometimes, that I'll become someone who has forgotten the names of too many things. I've considered making some kind of litany in my head, a list of words to keep repeating in case I lose them. I don't do this because of you; because the thought of you turning away from a mad old man mumbling nonsense to himself is worse than the fear of losing words.

Sometimes, holding an object can make your hands look like a stranger's. The hairgrip — well, you'll see, but the two fingers are actually a single piece of metal folded back on itself; and where the metal bends there is a tiny flower with five gold petals and a red plastic centre. I hold it between my finger and thumb and I see how tired and old and hardened my skin is. I see the dirt ingrained into the lines. I see that my nails are thick and yellow, the area around them flaked and sore where I have pulled off thin strips of skin with my teeth — a habit from childhood.

It would be better if the scarf was gold and the hairgrip lilac, but I can't hope to always be exact. I leave them on the kerb at the corner of Mill Street. I lay the scarf flat. I turn the shoelace into a circle and I put the silver earring-back and the gold hairgrip inside it.

* * *

This, as you probably don't know, has been going on for some time. Not as many years as you've lived, I'll admit that. There was a long time, most of your life if I'm honest, that I packed up my knowledge of you and locked it away with the rest of the things I have decided, for many reasons, not to dwell on. I imagine the inside of my head as a catacomb — a maze of dark corridors with the memories rotting in their sealed stone caskets, shelves and shelves of them.

I was twenty-seven when I first knew of you. It might have turned out differently — I wanted it to, but your mother was insistent, and I couldn't find the right words to make her change her mind. I left London, limped off to Leeds and tried to pretend I'd never loved her in the first place. I drove a courier van. I walked around the city and thought about limestone and brick. I spent a night, once, on a bench in Roundhay Park; no one bothered me. I met a group of artists who'd just left college. We smoked pot and stayed up all night. I had a relationship with one of them: Melissa — she had hair shorter than mine and a line of tiny stud earrings up each ear. It didn't end well. And all that time you were growing, and I had to work hard to stop myself thinking on that.

And then my dad fucked up. I spent the winter in Preston. Wet tarmac. Bare trees. My mother's jaw so tense I thought she'd grind her teeth down to nothing. I lost my way after that.

* * *

Don't listen to my grumbling. I mustn't bore you. I met a Buddhist once — he sat on the raised triangle of grass where Stamford Street meets Blackfriars Road, his eyes closed, meditating. This is it, he told me. Here and now, you and I, these streams of traffic: this is it. This is the only time and the only place we have to make the changes we need to make in our life. I'd like to say I took it on board. I didn't. But it comes back to me — the freckled dome of his scalp, the pale pale blue of his eyes, like the sea reflected back from rain-filled clouds. Here, now. This is all there is.

* * *

Tower Bridge is split in half, raised up towards the sky. The cars tail back to Druid Street. Drivers tap impatiently on their steering wheels. Tourists exchange gleeful looks; they take pictures of their friends pointing at the white bulk of the ship and the tipped-up miracle of the broken bridge. I catch a curl of cigarette smoke from an open car window. The man reluctantly hands one over when I ask, a flash of fear at the back of his eyes. He lights it before he gives it to me. I breathe in cool grey. I find they calm me down, cigarettes. Kill you too, the doctor told me. I shrugged and said something has to, which is true enough, except the truth is I'm not ready yet.

The bridge heaves itself back into place. A cluster of motorcyclists, crowded right up to the barrier, rev their engines. The city crawls back into action.

After the art gallery job, I starting driving a taxi. Not a black cab. My car had tired blue seats and a boot with a dodgy catch. I had a radio on my dashboard, its lead twisted like a telephone wire. A disembodied voice reeled off pickups and destinations.

I worked nights. The traffic was better, the money was better, the passengers — mostly — were worse. I looked for you, I scoured every inch of the city, out to Heathrow, up to Golders Green, across to the Westway; every second I was looking for you. I'd watch the people who sat in the back of my car, fragments of their faces reflected in my mirror. I took comfort from their stories: a long-lost school friend sitting in the same Tube carriage, a former colleague discovered in a suburban café. London, passengers would say, it's an amazing city: millions of people and yet you manage to bump into someone you know.

I wait until the crowds along each side of the bridge disperse. I stop halfway across and lean my body into the railings, drop my head down towards the water. I'd be lying if I said I've never thought about it: stepping off the pavement into the hurtling bulk of a lorry; lying naked in the snow; sitting for a moment on the edge of a bridge, taking in the world one last time before letting myself go. But there is always the thought of you.

I watch the water slip past beneath me. My father took me fishing once. I couldn't tell you where or when, only that the sun was hot enough to burn my cheeks, that I hadn't yet grown taller than him, that we ate sardine sandwiches from a yellow Tupperware box, that I caught a single, puny fish to his five, and that for once he didn't seem to be disappointed in me.

On Whitechapel High Street, men dismantle market stalls — a grate of metal against metal. They fold green and white covers into familiar squares, stack battered boxes into white vans parked half on the pavement with their hazards flashing orange. I pick up an apple, and two bruised bananas. I find an olive-green leather glove, the stitching loose where the thumb meets the first finger. A silver pen dropped outside the library. I pull a piece of chestnut-brown bark from a tree. Half a torn envelope, black writing on maroon paper.

I cut up Vallance Road, by the brown concrete building lapped by green tarpaulin, and then into the park. In the central circle I choose a bench that looks towards Derbyshire Street; beyond that, Bethnal Green Road; beyond that, Hackney and the canal. I lay the glove on the seat and use the pen to weigh down the envelope, snap the bark in two and place the pieces on the green leather. I sit with it next to me.

I would like to buy you a cup of tea, somewhere they have proper mugs and sugar in bowls on the tables, and I'd like to sit across from you and tell you everything.

* * *

Time to move. I leave the glove on the bench and walk towards Hackney. At the entrance to London Fields, at the end of the stretch of shops where the road widens out like an estuary, there is a square of paving, with a low brick wall and two wooden benches. By the benches are three trees: two small ones with slender trunks, and one large — a sycamore, still thick with leaves. In one of the small trees, in the crook where the trunk splits in two, I see a terracotta Buddha, about ten inches high. In the sycamore, barely visible amongst the leaves, I see a clock. Its batteries are finished. I know because I stand and watch it and the hands don't move. Right now, I guess it's about five hours fast, or seven hours slow. I imagine you walking past at the exact moment in the day when it is telling the right time.

I sit on one of the benches and look up at the clock, and I wonder if there are other people, like me, who leave messages across this city in the hope that someone will understand them. I wonder what the clock and the orange, fat-cheeked Buddha mean. When I stand, I find an oyster shell, of all things, on the floor beneath the bench. I run my fingers over its perfect, pearl-white inside. It's easy after that — a plastic bag with a hint of blue; a green cigarette lighter; a child's sock, creamy white beneath the dirt; a length of charcoal-grey wire; a chestnut-brown hair-tie.

I picture my father, standing at the window of the room he used as his study — as though he was some kind of aristocrat with a library, except the PVC windows gave him away. I just don't know what to do with you, Daniel, he said. I was twenty-two, I'd just lost another job. You need to build foundations for yourself, Daniel, he told me, over and over. You need to have a stable base. You need to be able to provide, for yourself, for your family. He was a fucking hypocrite — I said as much to my mother after she found him in that same room, vomit congealed across the carpet, his skin as white as the stack of bills on his desk. She looked at me as though I'd slapped her.

The clouds have grown heavy with water. They throw shadows down onto the streets. I can smell rain. There's a shelter in Angel open tonight; I should be able to get there before it starts in earnest. I pull off a tiny square from the plastic bag, stand on the lighter until it breaks into pieces, and choose a triangle of green. I unravel a stretch of wool from the sock, curl the wire into a tight coil, and tie the hair-band in knots until it is a hard brown ball. Each colour sits neatly in the pearl-white cup of the oyster shell. I go back to the paved space at the edge of the road and reach up to where the third, empty tree splits its trunk in two. Then I balance the shell and its contents between the branches, closing off a tiny triangle of space. It will catch the rain when it falls. Perhaps, walking home, you will look up and see.

Ten reasons to hate my sister (Cee)

1) Her bathroom tiles have pictures of dolphins on them.
2) If she did *Desert Island Discs* she'd choose Foreigner, 'I Want To Know What Love Is', as her can't-live-without record.
3) She has given her sons names starting with the same letter.
4) When I used to ask her about Mama she'd look so pitying, and at the same time so smug, I could barely listen to what she was telling me.
5) She buys eggs, takes them out of the box and puts them into a ceramic bowl shaped like a chicken, which sits on top of the fridge.
6) She used to tell me our house was haunted.
7) She makes me feel like I've done something wrong.
8) She reads the *Daily Mail*. So you can imagine what she thought about me and Kal.
9) She thinks I'm a fuck-up.
10) Hate is maybe too strong a word. I remember her reading to me, when I had a cold or an upset tummy. She would do all the voices, pull funny faces to make me laugh.

It's a warbling, electronic sound, less shrill than my father's doorbell, but all the same, when it rings, I head for the door. It's only once I'm halfway down the hall that I realise it's him, ringing from upstairs. My heart rams against my ribs and I run. When I get to his room, I find him propped against the headboard, a pillow behind his back, his eyes open.

'Oh, Alice,' he says, as though he hadn't expected me to be there.

'What's happened?'

'Well, I'm not — dead.' He manages a weak smile. 'I wanted to — talk — to Matilda — and Cecilia.'

'I can help.' He looks at me like I'm a child — too young to understand. 'Tell me what you need, Dad, I'll do it.'

He shakes his head. 'I just — have something I need — to say — to your sisters.'

'Tilly's at the supermarket.' My oldest sister has already cooked enough for an army. The fridge is packed with Tupperware containers of soup, chilli, frittata, risotto, and Dad's battered-looking cake tins are crammed with biscuits and lemon slices and muffins. There's no need at all to shop, but when I said as much she looked so hurt I didn't push it. 'And Cee's at work. She'll be here later,' I say.

'It doesn't matter — another — time.'

I am standing by the narrow sofa, with its tired-out rose-patterned upholstery. 'I don't understand, Dad.'

He shakes his head again. My Seamus Heaney anthology sits at an angle on his bedside table. I've been reading him my favourites: 'The Peninsula', 'The Salmon Fisher to the Salmon', 'Bogland'. Dad's hardly a poetry fan, so maybe it isn't fair, but he hasn't protested.

'Do you want me to read to you?'

'I'd kill — for — a cigarette,' he says.

'*Dad.*'

'You sound — like your sisters. Always — sensible — your sisters.'

Not like me.

'It's hardly going — to hurt — now, is it?' he says.

I get my cigarettes from my room.

'Better — open the window,' he says. 'Or there'll be — trouble.' He grins, but I can't smile back.

I light one for him, and pass him the ashtray from the table by the sofa. He draws in a shaky breath, coughs. I sit and watch him, twist the ring on my middle finger round and round. He meets my gaze.

'Let me — enjoy it, Alice. Have one — with me.'

I remember Cee's campaigns to stop him smoking. She'd cut out articles with graphic pictures of blackened lungs. She'd cry at the dinner table. She'd steal his cigarettes and cut them into pieces. Maybe that's why I started — to be closer to him. I shake out another from the packet and light it.

He smokes half of his and then drops it into the ashtray. I stub it out for him, take another drag of mine and then stub that out too.

'What are you — going to — do?' he says.

'About what?'

'With your — life. You'll go back — to — Malaysia?'

'Mongolia. I don't know. I'll decide once — ' I press my fingers to my lips. 'Dad, didn't you know something was wrong? I mean, these things take time to get this bad, don't they?'

'Don't bite — your nails — Alice.'

I slide my hands underneath my legs. 'But you're a doctor,' I say.

'I need to — lie — ' He struggles beneath the covers, trying to lever himself down.

'Wait, I'll help you.'

He feels like a child, fragile and light. I wrap my arms around his chest and lower him onto his back. It takes no effort at all. I stay sitting on the edge of his bed and stare at the ink drawing of an anvil on the front of the poetry book. I listen for birdsong, but I can't hear any, only my father's breathing, rough as sandpaper.

'Do you remember the peppermint mice you used to buy me?' I say. 'I haven't eaten one of those in years.'

He takes my hand. I watch his yellow thumb stroke the line of flesh in between my thumb and forefinger.

'Will you tell me what it is?' I say.

His thumb stops moving.

'I can tell Cee and Tilly later.'

'You — remind me — of your mother,' he says.

He almost never talks about my mother. I have no idea what to say.

'Your — hair,' he says. 'Your sisters — were always jealous — of that.'

I shaved my head when I was seventeen, in the school holidays. I stood in the bathroom, the sink full of auburn curls, and stared at my pale scalp and the unfamiliar shape of my skull in the mirror. That will show them, I'd told myself. Exactly what I thought it would prove I can't really remember. It was just me and Dad in the house, though, and when I went down for dinner, psyched for a fight, he just looked at me, barely raised his eyebrows, and continued as if nothing had happened.

'What was she like?' I say. I try to keep any hint of desperation out of my voice.

He is staring up at the ceiling. I'm not sure he's heard.

My mother died when I was four. She was supposed to be driving to pick me up from a ballet class. I remember standing in a church hall holding a pink bag with a ballerina embroidered onto the front, listening to the music of the next class and the girls' feet on the wooden floorboards, waiting. It blurs then, except for Dad's face, white and frightened — the way he looked at me as though he didn't know who I was.

It was Ella Summers from ballet who told me Mama had been buried in the ground with the worms, all nailed up in a dark box, and that I'd never see her again. I cried, screamed, held my hands clamped against my ears and told Ella Summers I hated her, but I knew, by the way the triumph faded in her eyes, that she was telling the truth. I had nightmares for weeks afterwards. Tilly and Cee took it in turns to lift me from my bed and into theirs, hold my hot shaking body and whisper soothing words into the top of my sweat-stained head, until I fell asleep again. Ssshh, don't upset Daddy. Ssshh, Mama's safe. It's not your fault — no one thinks it's your fault.

'Dad? I asked you about Mama.'

'Difficult,' he says. 'She was — difficult.'

Like me.

'I wasn't — fair — maybe. I promised — ' He frowns. 'I promised her — love you — just as much — Alice.' His eyes droop closed. His mouth turns slack. I feel a swoop of panic. How do you tell if — And then I see the sheet rise just a fraction, and fall again. I want to shake him awake. I put my hand on his shoulder, but he's so thin and so tired, I can't do it. I sit a while longer, and then I close the window, collect the ashtray and our half-smoked cigarettes, and leave.

* * *

My father's house is not small; there are plenty of rooms to wander through, and settle in, but I can't seem to stay in one place. I pick up Tilly's newspaper, flick through it, and put it down again. I start the washing-up and get bored halfway through. As soon as Margaret arrives I grab Dad's keys, slip my feet into flip-flops and scribble a note for Tilly. As I wait to cross East Heath Road I consider lifting my hand to the next cab I see. I could go to Heathrow, find a ticket desk and ask the clerk to pick me a destination. I imagine it — the hustle of the airport, the dead time of the flight, then walking down the steps into the smell of a new country, excitement pushing at my throat. My passport's in the house, I tell myself. My father's sick. I cross the road, through the car park and onto the Heath. I march along the path in between the two ponds, and then up towards the trees. An old man wearing a red waterproof coat and leather boots walks in front of me. I turn right, along a narrow, untarmacked path, because I can't bear to look at him. I kick off my flip-flops and feel tiny stones stab at my skin. It is better than crying. I walk faster, stamping my feet into the earth.

At the top of Parliament Hill, three women wearing tracksuits stand by the sign detailing the view. A man dressed in black is packing away a huge orange kite. Another man, with wild hair, lies on the grass with his hand shading his eyes. There are maybe eight other people, a couple of dogs sniffing at each other, a kid wearing a green jumpsuit, strapped into a buggy. I sit on one of the benches that perch on the slope overlooking the city, pull my thighs up towards my chest and stare at London. A million panes of glass mirror the sun. I pick out St Paul's, the Gherkin, Canary Wharf. When I travel, I always say I'm from London; it never feels quite true.

I brought Kal here, after that first Sunday lunch. We sat, maybe even on this bench, and tried to locate his flat amongst all the other buildings. Your family seem lovely, he said, I don't know why you were so worried. I didn't say, because Cee thinks you're a terrorist, because my dad doesn't trust you not to bundle me off to India and lock me in the kitchen, because none of them get it. I just shrugged and smiled, and said I was looking forward to meeting his family. I still hadn't realised, at that point, how things were going to be.

I take my phone out of my pocket and scroll down to Kal's numbers — mobile, work, home. There's a phone in the hallway of his flat. I imagine it ringing, and a woman, barefooted, walking towards it. He used to paint my toenails for me, a different colour for each toe. Maybe it's not too late. Maybe we could find a way that would work.

I hold my finger over the call button and look out at London, but I don't press it. I've been through all this already, and there's no point. I know that.

* * *

When I get back, the house smells of onions, tomatoes, beef. Spaghetti Bolognese. Dad loves Tilly's spaghetti Bolognese. I find a pan of pasta and one of sauce on the kitchen table, but no sign of my sisters. I imagine the three of them upstairs, talking, but when I get up there it's just

Dad and Tilly. The door's open. Tilly's sitting on the chair by his bed, a plate of spaghetti in her lap.

'Just a mouthful, Dad? I chopped everything up as small as I could,' she's saying.

He shakes his head.

'But it's your favourite. Isn't it your favourite?'

Dad's eyes flick towards me and Tilly turns. There's guilt on their faces.

'He won't eat,' Tilly says. 'He's so thin.'

'Don't fuss, Matilda.' He coughs, a thin rattling sound that makes my heart ache.

'Where's Cee?' I ask.

'She's gone home. She brought this.' Tilly holds up a small bottle with a pump spray. 'It's fake saliva.'

I fold my arms. 'You told them what you wanted to tell them, then, Dad?'

'Alice, what have you done to your feet?' Tilly says.

I look down. They are covered in dirt, and maybe dried blood, too, it's hard to tell.

'Where are your shoes?' she says.

My father is looking at me as though he can see through me. I feel five again.

'There's loads of food downstairs,' Tilly says. 'Why don't you get some? I'll be there in a minute.' As I leave the room she shouts, 'You might need to heat it up.'

I go into the bathroom, lock the door and run hot water into the sink. The water darkens as I rub my hand gently over my right foot. I have to try hard to stop myself from crying. Not because it hurts. It doesn't hurt. I clean my left foot in a fresh basin of water, and then walk damp footsteps downstairs.

The spaghetti's stuck to itself. I get a clump of it into a bowl and spoon on some sauce. Tilly comes down. She shovels Dad's food into the bin and glances at my bare feet.

'You look exhausted,' I say.

'He wouldn't eat anything.'

'I'm not sure he can. Tilly, I didn't heat the sauce.'

She shrugs, serves herself and sits opposite me.

'What did he say?' I ask.

'He's not hungry, he'd rather have a cigarette, will I stop fussing.' Tilly tips her head from side to side as she speaks.

'I mean before that. He had something to tell you and Cee.'

I watch her trying to arrange her face into a neutral expression.

'What's he got to say to you that he can't say to me?'

Tilly twists her fork into her pasta. 'It's nothing.'

'Don't bullshit me. Not you, Tilly.'

Her eyes widen and she rubs at her nose.

'Why are you lot always so fucking secretive?' I can hear the whine in my voice, like a kid.

'I don't think that's fair, Alice.'

'It's his will? I don't even care about his will. Is that what it is?' I pull at a hangnail on my thumb.

'It's nothing that matters.' Tilly looks at me with the same pity I'd seen in Dad's eyes. I want to scream. 'He's an old man, Alice, he's — ' She presses her fingertips together. 'He's dying, Alice. The doctor came while you were out. He said it won't be long. It could be any — '

'This is driving me insane.'

'Alice, Alice.' Tilly strokes at my arm. I brush her away. 'He loves you, Alice,' she says.

I want Kal. I want him to massage the soles of my feet and paint my nails. I want him to bring me a beer from the fridge and tell me about his day. I want to put my arms around his neck and hold on.

Ten reasons to hate my father

1) Lying.
2) Gambling.
3) Giving up.
4) Breaking my mother's heart.
5) Having me.
6) I get my nose from him.
7) He was a bully and a coward.
8) I wake up some mornings and think the whole thing was my fault.
9) All that talk about making an impression, being a man.
10) It's confusing: loving and hating someone at the same time.

I don't sleep in shelters every night. If you go too often they try and fix things — which is fair enough, but I've made the choices I've made, and it's not always as simple as you might imagine.

This shelter's in the crypt of the church on Duncan Terrace. A young man with a ponytail and orange shoes told me about it back in April. There's food, he said; sometimes they have toothbrushes, socks.

By the time I arrive it's raining hard. Along Essex Road, people lower their heads to their chests, hunch their shoulders and quicken their pace. As a kid, I loved the rain. I used to sit at my window and watch it move in the spaces beneath the street lights. I'd watch the drops chase each other down the glass. It always made my mother nervous. She would fret about us getting wet, as if we might somehow be ruined by water. I remember her hovering around my father when he got in from work, trying to brush the water from his shoulders. He would shoo her away, shrug off his coat, and leave his shoes, like two empty beetle cases, soaking dirty water into the hall carpet. Now I share her anxiety. I worry about rotting material, about the rain seeping into my bones, which already feel older than they should. I worry about the picture in the inside pocket of my coat, even though it is wrapped in plastic, even though it has lasted this long already.

I would rather sleep in the church itself, with the street lights bleeding through the stained glass, and the statues watching from the corners, but the heavy front doors, with their hinges like giant flowers, are locked. You have to know to walk through the side door, into the hallway, where a stone Mary frowns at you from an alcove, then through a second door and down the stairs.

The crypt, with its whitewashed walls and beige lino floor, is divided up by low brick arches. Rows of foldaway metal beds occupy the main space. They look stranded, high and leggy, the edges of sheets and blankets escaping from their thin tubular frames. A kitchen has been squeezed into one corner; it's the only space with windows — two narrow strips of grimy glass peering onto the street. The place smells of tea bags, just-turned milk, and body odour.

I don't ever want you to come to a place like this. I try to comfort myself that you were brought up with money, but I have met men who used to live like lords sleeping on the streets, so it's no guarantee of anything. I sign my name in the book, and scan up the list, looking for you. When I'm feeling like this — a little worried, a little unsettled — I see the colours before I see the words. Only one frosted blue name sits amongst the magnolias and dirty yellows, purples and chestnut browns; it isn't yours.

A cluster of people sit on and around a low black sofa facing a flickering television screen. I recognise Lady Grace, her pram at her side, and lift a hand to greet her. Usually she sleeps in the park opposite Smithfields. She complains about the noise, but says the butchers are kind to her and she feels safe with them around. In the pram is a tiny camping stove, a burnt saucepan, and a plastic knife and fork begged from a café. I camp, my dear, she said to me, the first time we met, I'm a camper at heart. Her dream, she said, was to live in the countryside. I want to sleep under the trees, she told me, and listen to the birds.

I'm not in the mood for talking to anyone, so I take a seat on a second sofa, at the far end of the room. There are four newspapers. I work my way through each one, but I don't find what I'm looking for.

I don't feel good. I can't pretend I do. It's like there's something slowing me down, making me ache all over. If I died, no one would know to tell you.

Dinner is pasta with broccoli and lumps of chicken. I queue up, smile at the woman who's serving, dipping a huge metal spoon into an oversized saucepan. I sit at the end of the table with my head down. My plate has a thin blue line around its edge. It makes me think of my mother's plates — each with a drawing of a blue boy and a blue girl standing on a blue island holding hands. There were eight of them, displayed in a dark wood cabinet in the dining room. She cleaned them every Sunday with a feather duster. As a kid, I begged to be allowed to help. But by the time I was old enough to do so, I had changed my mind. How stupid to have plates and never use them, I said, even though I could see how my words made her flinch.

I wonder, sometimes, how she lived with all my father's lies. I suppose it was easy enough when she didn't know, and maybe once she saw them for lies they were so tightly knotted into the pattern of her life, it was simpler to keep on going than try to unravel them.

* * *

'I may join you?'

I look up. He has broad shoulders, muddy brown hair beginning to recede, a round, pale face, hazel eyes. His nose is broad and stained red by drink. I don't say anything, but he sits on the chair directly to my right all the same.

'We eat together. It is better.' He's from Russia, or Poland, somewhere east. 'I am Anton.' He holds out his hand. His is the ice-blue name from the register.

'Daniel.' His hands feel rough with work. It's been a long time since I shook hands with someone.

He takes a mouthful of pasta and eats it noisily, his mouth open, his head nodding.

'What do you do today?' he asks. When he speaks I can see bits of food lodged between his teeth.

'What did you learn today?' My father would ask it every dinnertime, whether I had been to school or not. He would lean on the word *learn*, so it splashed gold across the table-cloth. If I failed to provide an answer that satisfied him I'd be sent upstairs without any afters. The nights he went out, my mother would call me back down and I would eat cold apple crumble, or ginger sponge and congealed custard, or Bakewell tart. I suppose she was trying to apologise.

'I walked,' I say.

Anton nods, still chewing. 'Where to?'

I shrug. 'Just around. And you?'

His face clouds. 'I wait for work this morning, but they no pick me.' He slams a fist into the table. My glass of water trembles. 'They take young ones,' he says. 'I strong as ox. I tell them, but they no hear.' He stabs a piece of chicken with his fork and waves it at me. 'No work, no money.'

'That's why you're here?' I ask.

'I here because my bastard friend say I no stay in his house. He say I drunk, I no good.'

I lift my eyebrows in sympathy, and bite into a piece of broccoli. It's been cooked to a dark, soft green, and oozes water between my teeth.

'I only drunk because of daughter,' he says.

I chew slowly. I don't trust myself to speak.

'My daughter,' he says, and I see his eyes brighten. 'She is pretty girl.' He nods vigorously. 'When she is two years, she say my name.' He lays his fork down and folds his arms, leans back in his chair. ''Tato, tato,' she say. Tato. It is father.' He points his index finger towards his heart. 'She clever, no? I say word, she say word.'

* * *

I don't even know what you look like. I don't even know where you are. I tried to find you, you must believe that. I went to her house and rang the bell, but no one answered, and when I looked through the window I saw the marks on the carpet where the furniture used to be. I waited. And then, eventually, I went home and sat in my flat, staring at the phone. The only people who rang wanted to sell me something — double glazing, electricity, God. I listened to the salespeople stumble their way through their scripts. Once they stopped, once there was a space on their piece of paper for my input, I asked if they knew where she was. They never did.

* * *

'Is she OK?' I ask. Anton frowns. 'Your daughter? You said you were drunk because of your daughter.'

His face closes down like your mother's used to. He picks up his fork and eats.

I eat too. When I'm done I see the pasta has left smears of starch across my plate. 'I'm sorry,' I say. 'I didn't mean to pry.'

'Pry?' When he frowns, a deep line digs into the space between his eyebrows.

'To interfere, to be nosy,' I say. 'I didn't mean to.' I don't think he understands.

'Her mother, she is bitch. You say bitch, no?'

I shrug.

'I love her, the mother, she is my wife, but she is not answering phone. Now I call and there is nothing but the ringing. She has a man, I know this. She is slut bitch, same as all women.' He lets out a long sigh. 'But my daughter, my Sylwia.' He rubs at his left eye with a knuckle. He has dirty fingernails, the same as the rest of us. A thin gold band cuts into the flesh of his wedding finger. 'There is the one time I phone and I have beers and she no let me talk to Sylwia. I have to talk to her, I say, but she no let me.' He rubs his eye again. 'Then she ask for money. I send you money, I say. It is no enough, she say, you are keeping the money. I get angry. I say she no understand.'

The woman in the kitchen calls us over for seconds. I'm full but I take more anyway. Anton lets her pile his plate as high as the first time. We sit back at the table and neither of us talks until the food has gone.

'I think it is just one fight,' he says, clattering his fork onto his empty plate. 'Man and wife they fight, no? But then the next time she ask if I have beers. I say no, but she say Sylwia is at friend's house. And the next time Sylwia is sleeping. And the next time, Sylwia no want to talk to me.' His fist batters at the tabletop. 'She no want to talk to me,' he exclaims. 'She my daughter. She my beautiful daughter. She no want to talk to me?'

* * *

I know that once we meet, it won't matter it's taken me so long to find you. Once we meet we will have all the time in the world to say everything we need to say.

* * *

'See?' Anton is holding a photograph towards me. Its edges are slightly curled. 'Only touch side,' he says as I take it. I balance it between my fingertips like the people at King's Cross station who lift their repeated image, still wet, from the passport photo machine.

She is maybe three years old, I always find it difficult to tell. She has her father's round face, dark-blonde hair tied up in pigtails. She stands with her back to a white-painted wall. To her left is a closed door. At the far right of the photograph is the corner of a windowsill. She wears a blue cotton dress, the skirt flaring out from a white belt and ending just above dimpled knees. Her eyes look above and beyond whoever is holding the camera. She isn't smiling, but she looks content.

'How long?' I ask.

'Since I see her, four years, two months, sixteen days. Since I speak with her, one year, twenty-five days.'

I look at the photo, try to add the years onto her image. He holds out his hand, and I find I am reluctant to give it back.

The man who asked me to write down my name shoos us away from the table. We take two cups of tea from the counter — doused with milk and sugar — and sit on the sofa by the newspapers. Anton tells me about the day his daughter was born, how she held onto his finger and looked into his eyes. He tells me how he met his wife, at the wedding of his cousin. She let him kiss her, but when he tried to touch her breasts she slapped his cheek, and he knew then that he wanted to marry her. He tells me about a trip to Middle Pomerania on the Polish coast when Sylwia was a year old. They took a picnic to the beach every day. He carried his daughter into the sea, sat her high on his shoulders, and listened to her laugh at the spray of water on her toes. He combed the beach for amber, found a lump of it with an ant inside, perfectly preserved. He doesn't ask about me, and I am happy to sit and listen. The television blares — tinny sounds and primary colours. A man slumps in a chair to our left; he's about my age I reckon. His leg is bandaged all the way to the knee. His beard has yellowed around the circumference of his mouth. He mumbles to himself, a soft string of words, before falling asleep. We are all dying too quickly.

'It is better she forget me, no?' Anton says. He turns to me and I look at his pale watery eyes and his battered skin. 'It is better to have no father, than to have a father like me, no?'

I shake my head, but I know what he means, and it makes my insides hurt.

* * *

Anton would have talked until the morning, I think, and I'd have been happy to let him, but these places have rules, and timetables. Just before ten thirty we choose beds next to each other, and try to settle down. Even while the lights still glare white, the snoring starts. It's a problem with shelters. I'm a light sleeper anyway

— I've learnt to be — and even when I'm somewhere safe, like here, my sleep is always fractured. I lie and look at the hump of Anton's back beneath his blanket until someone clicks out the light.

* * *

I stop breathing. I must have done, because I wake up gasping into the dark, like a man almost drowned. I was dreaming: walking across Waterloo Bridge, towards the advert curved around the cinema. There were white letters, the size of men, on a lemon-coloured background, but I couldn't make out the words. I kept walking and walking but I never got to the end of the bridge.

I pick out five layers of snores, from thin and rasping to rich and sonorous. Beneath the noise is the faint touch of rain against the narrow windows. The air is fetid with sleep, and farts, and unwashed skin. One of the volunteers shifts in his chair. Sometimes they read with a torch, or put the television on with the sound turned down, but this one sits in the dark. I wonder what he thinks about. I wonder why he does it. I wonder if he has spent nights sheltering from the rain, if he has stuffed sheets of newspaper underneath his clothes to keep out the cold, if that is why. I wonder if he's lost someone.

* * *

When my mother called to tell me, I couldn't make sense of what she said. I could hear her. I could hear the words, and the tears, but I couldn't get any of it in order.

People call it different things. I've experimented over the last twenty years, most often inside my head. Sometimes, when I had the cab, I chose to talk to passengers, if they had the right kind of face, or if the night was particularly long and dark and lonely.

My father committed suicide.

My father took his own life.

My father died.

My father killed himself.

My father took a mix of diazepam and diamorphine. We never found out where he got it from.

He didn't know what else to do.

He was in too deep.

He was a miserable lying bastard and I don't care that he's dead.

My mother found him. I'll never forgive him for that.

* * *

There was a heatwave the summer I finished university. My parents came to my graduation, my father sweating in a new suit and tie, my mother self-conscious and excited in a wide-brimmed hat. I had avoided every lecture and tutorial I could, had spent my time and energy marching against the war, against racism, for women's rights; seducing women and persuading them to pose nude, eking out expensive tubes of oil paint, drinking beer, smoking pot. It was a miracle I even passed. My father accepted my Third with pursed lips. You'll just have to work twice as hard from now on, he said, though he knew as well as I did that I'd fucked up and no practice would accept me.

Maybe we are more alike than I'd care to admit. He hid his gambling for as long as he was able, and then when it got out, he got out too. Maybe I'd have done the same.

I remember sitting with my mother in the dining room, with the rows of untouched plates behind the cabinet's glass doors. The table was covered with pieces of paper. Letters, invoices, bills. Well, I'm sure there must be some kind of explanation, she kept saying, over and over. There's bound to be some kind of explanation.

Her hair turned white the year he died. It had been laced with grey before, but that autumn, after she found him and all those bills, it faded until there wasn't an ounce of colour left. There were times she tried dyeing it — a virulent orange, a washed-out purple; eventually she gave up and let it be.

Time to move, but there is nowhere to go. I turn onto my side and the bed creaks beneath me. I hear someone cough on the other side of the room. I think about Anton's daughter, imagine her riding high on his shoulders, her hands in his hair, laughing. I want to wake him up and ask how he could have left her, how he could have lost her.

Ten things about my father's house

1) The front door sticks.
2) There's a painting of Tilly and Cee in the hallway. They are seven and five. They wear matching pink dresses and white socks.
3) There is still a faint stain on the living-room carpet, underneath the coffee table, where my mother spilt a bottle of red wine, thirty years ago.
4) My father's study smells of cigarette smoke.
5) There are four bottles of malt whisky in the cupboard under the sink: Talisker, Ardmore, Jura, Laphroaig. The Talisker has a couple of centimetres left, the rest are more than half full.
6) When I was eight I pulled my bed away from the wall and wrote my name in red biro on the wallpaper. It is still there.
7) There's no Internet connection or computer.
8) There are three squeaky floorboards on the second landing: one a third of the way across, just outside Cee's room; one directly outside my room; the other at the bottom of the stairs up to the attic.
9) If you stare at the wallpaper in the utility

room for long enough, the pattern starts to look like hundreds of tiny people standing on hundreds of tiny islands.

10) It's not somewhere I've ever really felt at home.

I know as soon as I open the front door that he's dead. It's like the house is squeezing its eyes shut and holding its breath and hoping, praying even, that what has happened hasn't really happened. I stand in the hallway with the door still open and consider turning around and going back out.

I don't remember how many times I ran away when I was a kid. The returns were never fun: strangers insisting I tell them my address; policemen eyeing me suspiciously whilst speaking into telephones — skinny, short, red hair, green eyes: yes, that's her. Teachers got flustered, or shouted; either way they kept repeating themselves over and over, like I hadn't heard it all before. Dad always looked disappointed and slightly pained, like he'd eaten something that hadn't agreed with him. Cee slapped me once; I slapped her back.

I loved the beginnings: the thrill of sneaking outside into the cool night; the smell of frost on the school playing fields, the yellow glow of street lights, the quick hushed pad of foxes. I imagined myself a cat burglar, a detective, an assassin. I crept away from the building — school or home — and then turned back and looked at it: the blank, darkened windows, the heavy silent bricks. Sometimes I literally ran, sprinted until I felt the burn in my thighs, my heart like a trapped animal in my chest. I was never going anywhere in particular, just away.

I slam the front door shut, take off my jacket and hang it up, over the top of his summer coat. My father. I try to picture his face, but can't. There was no need to go out. I had nowhere to go and nothing to do, just wandered the streets trying not to panic. I should have talked to him instead, told him it didn't matter — whatever it was with him and Tilly and Cee; it was his business. I should have told him I loved him.

'Alice?' Cee appears at the living-room door. 'Alice, he's — ' She presses her lips together.

'Did he — ?'

'We tried your mobile.'

I had left it in my bedroom.

'The doctor's just left.'

I nod.

'I've called Steve. He's going to tell the boys.'

I stare at the raised pattern repeated across the walls — the same arrangement of flowers inside a square border that must be on the walls of a thousand other hallways, in a thousand strangers' homes.

'You'll want to go and see him,' Cee says.

I have never seen a dead person.

'Where's Tilly?'

Cee angles her head towards the living room. 'They say it helps,' she says. 'To see the body.'

My mind balloons. I try to imagine him, one floor above us. I hope someone's opened the curtains, and lifted the sash window. I hope it's not gloomy and hot in there. Did it just happen without warning, or did he know? Did he lie and stare at the ceiling and feel his heart about to stop? Did it hurt?

'We've both said goodbye.'

I walk past her, into the living room. Tilly is sitting on the sofa, her hands clasped in her lap, her face white.

'We tried to call you,' she says.

'I'm sorry.' They are waiting for me to cry. I am waiting for me to cry.

'Did he — ?'

She lowers her gaze. 'He wasn't really with it, Alice. At the — ' She twists her hands against each other and looks up at me.

I want Kal. I want him to stroke my hair and sing to me. He used to make up songs, silly nonsense songs with meandering tunes: *Alice, Alice, Alice. Don't run down the rabbit hole, I can't bear to see you go. Stay here with me, Alice, Alice, Alice*. I want to feel his lips on my skin, the vibration of his voice in his chest. I could call him, but it would just make things more complicated.

'Honey.' Tilly holds out her arms. If I let her hug me I don't know what will happen. 'I'm going to — ' I gesture towards the hallway, and Tilly nods.

But I don't go into his room. I walk straight past it and up to the attic and I sit in the rocking chair and rock, back and forth and back and forth, digging my nails into the palms of my hands. When my sisters work out where I am and call to me I can't answer. And when Cee comes up the stairs and stands in front of me with her arms folded I can't look at her. Eventually she gives up and goes away.

Kal and I had a fight about avoidance. It was towards the end, when the problems were getting harder and harder to ignore. He told me I was passive-aggressive. I told him he was a coward. We're stuck, I told him, we can't move anywhere, because you refuse to tell your parents I even exist. They don't rule my life, he said, they're not everything. You could have fooled me, I said. Sometimes I think you're jealous, he said. Are you fucking joking? I threw my coffee cup on the floor for effect. It didn't even break, just rolled a little way and dribbled its dregs onto the thin dark-brown carpet we both hated.

* * *

I hear the shrill of the doorbell, then voices. This is what they mean by hushed tones. Four sets of footsteps on the stairs.

They will put my father in a coffin and nail the lid shut. I press my face into my knees and squeeze my hands around my bare feet. I can feel myself shaking.

I try not to listen. When they've gone, I go down to my room and turn on my phone. It takes a while — a network of conversations and connections and fragments of hold music — to get to the lost-luggage section at Heathrow airport. I sit on my bed, open and close my fist around the edge of the duvet. The sheets are plain, navy blue, the kind of thing my father buys; the kind of thing my father used to buy. I ache, as though someone has dug out a hollow from the bottom of my chest and filled it with lead.

'How can I help you?' The man on the end of the line has a rich Nigerian accent. I would like him to read me a story. I would like to lie in my bed, with the duvet tucked around my chin, and have him read me a story.

'Hello?'

'Sorry, yes, my rucksack.'

'Do you have the identification code, Ma'am?'

'I'm sorry?'

'The code to identify your bag, Ma'am. It should be on a sticker — on the back of your passport, or it might be on any papers you had at check-in.'

I stare at the wallpaper — pink roses reaching their thorny stems up past my bed. 'Ma'am?'

'No. No, I don't think I have that.'

The man on the end of the phone sighs, quietly, but loud enough for me to hear. 'Well, perhaps we could start with you telling me your flight details.'

I remember the seats were dark blue, with little napkins over the headrests. I remember the meal was chicken with tomato sauce, and rice. I remember the woman sitting next to me wore a yellow jacket with buttons that looked like chocolate coins.

'Have you ever argued with someone and then they've — I don't know, gone?' I say.

'Ma'am?'

'And then when you think about it, you realise you never really did anything except argue with them. Or at least you never said what mattered.

Not really. And then they've gone, and there's nothing you can do, is there?' I trace my finger around a rose. I try to remember choosing this wallpaper; it's horrible.

'Ma'am, if you could give me your flight details, and a description of the bag, then I can — '

'It doesn't matter.'

'But, Ma'am, I can — '

'Really, it's fine, thank you. You've been very helpful, very patient. Thank you.'

I walk down the stairs and along the corridor towards Dad's room. The door is closed. It's painted white, with four recessed panels. I've never really looked at it before. I put my hand on the brass doorknob. There's a red line where I've pulled off a strip of skin by my thumbnail. I need a cigarette.

You know you shouldn't smoke, Alice, Dad would say every time I was home. I would laugh and point at his own cigarette. He'd say, I know, one rule for me, one rule for everyone else, but seriously, it's bad for you. I know, Dad. I just don't want to have been a bad father, he said once, and I laughed it off. I should have told him: You're not; you weren't.

I open the door and walk in. The curtains are closed, which makes me angry. I march from the doorway to the window, the one by the sofa, and yank them open. Golden afternoon light. Suddenly I'm not sure about opening the others, but it is easier than looking at the bed. A large black car, studded with chrome, sits in the courtyard opposite. Mrs Williams' cat watches me from next door's windowsill.

The bed is empty. Someone has stripped off the sheets. I wasn't expecting that. The duvet is bundled just off centre, like a child's impression of a cloud. The mattress reveals its stitching, the thick beading around its edge. Six pillows lie, coverless, by the bedhead. What did he want with six pillows? One has a yellowed stain at its edge. I can't move.

When they took him away, did they lever him onto a stretcher, or put him straight into a coffin? I don't know why I want to know. I don't want to know. I want to know. They must have marked the door frames, chipped the paint on their way down the stairs. I don't want to look.

I am standing right by the bed now. If I bend my knees I can feel the hard edge of the frame. When I lie down, the springs press into my spine. I can see a black speck on the ceiling right above me. I can't tell if it's a fly, or a spider, or just a mark. I watch to see if it moves. It doesn't, which could mean it's just a mark, or that the spider or the fly is dead.

Ten things I'm frightened of

1) Turning out like my father.
2) Not being able to explain it all to you.
3) The sea. I can cope with it at the shoreline. I can take my shoes off and paddle. It's further out, where it gets cold and black, that it scares me.
4) Being locked up.
5) Not having the right words.
6) Sleeping.
7) Dying.
8) Dogs.
9) Never finding you.
10) Finding you.

Anton is staring at my scar. I turn my head so he can't see it — a thin mother-of-pearl line that stretches from the corner of my right eye down towards my ear. There are maybe ten of us dotted around the table. A couple of people are still sleeping. Lady Grace has left already. I am halfway through a bowl of cornflakes, which are starting to bloat with milk.

Anton sits opposite me. He has a mug of tea, a bowl piled high with sugar-sprinkled cereal, and a plate stacked with white toast. He points at my face with his spoon, spattering milk across the tabletop.

'What is this?' he says, touching his own cheek with his free hand.

'An accident,' I say.

He takes a mouthful of cereal, raises his eyebrows.

'I used to drive a cab,' I say. 'There was an accident, about five or six years ago.' What I don't say is that I nearly killed a man. What I don't say is that it happened because I was looking for you.

'You get insurance, yes?'

'I got sued.'

He slurps his tea and pulls a face.

My memories of that time are all broken up. Even the crash: I didn't have the slow-motion awareness people talk about. I was looking for you. I thought I'd found you. A woman with red hair just like your mother's walking down the street, and then nothing, a yawning white blank, until I woke up with my body turned inside-out by pain.

Anton digs his spoon into the bottom of his teacup, retrieves a mound of half-dissolved sugar granules and sucks them into his mouth. Behind him I can see sunlight creeping in through the kitchen windows. The glass is streaked with water, but I can't hear rain.

'What you do today?' he asks.

'Walk.'

He frowns.

'And you? You'll look for work?' I say.

He shrugs his heavy shoulders. 'I don't know. Three days now and they no take me.'

'If you want, you could — ' I stop myself. It's been a long time since I got involved with someone else.

'Where you go?' Anton asks.

I consider telling him about you, but decide against it, even though — perhaps — he might understand. I recognise how his eyes flick away from whoever he's talking to, and I know that I do the same.

'Where do you want to go?' I say.

Anton spins his cup on the plastic tabletop. 'Buckingham Palace.' Buckingham — a rich mahogany word, the colour of an old-fashioned dresser — sounds unfamiliar when he says it. 'I want to see Buckingham Palace.'

We beg sandwiches from the volunteer clearing up the kitchen. She gives me a toothbrush and toothpaste. The bathrooms here have a single urinal and a single cubicle. I stand at the sink and brush my teeth until my gums bleed. I try not to look in the mirror.

Anton wears white trainers. His jacket looks like an old army sleeping bag, a puffed-up, shiny olive-green, the colour of his daughter's name. I pull on my boots and tighten the laces from the bottom.

At the top of the stairs, Anton turns right instead of left. I follow him into the church, which has the feel of a school hall about it, and look away as he crosses himself, then kneels in the back pew. I am not a religious man, but as I wait for Anton, I look at the painting of Christ on the far wall, encased by feathered gold flames, and I let my prayer — words that sit on my lips all day long — drift up towards the arched ceiling.

Outside, the day is already bright. It's still cool from the rain, but I can sense the heat, waiting. It will be a day I have to walk with my jacket tied around my waist; I have a way of doing it that doesn't crease the picture in the inside pocket.

* * *

I used to meet your mother in a flat in Bloomsbury. It belonged to a friend of hers, Marina, who worked in Paris, but kept a place for trips to London. Maybe you don't want to know this; I can't help but tell you. It was small but perfect. We locked the door and it was just me and her in this tiny bubble, the world babbling away outside without us. She made me laugh. She'd tell me stories about her girls, and the other mothers she knew; she had a way of seeing the absurd in everything. When she laughed, really laughed, I felt happiness as solid and real as cut glass. Sometimes we'd go out — afterwards. I remember walking through Woburn Square Garden, just as the daffodils were opening up into yellow, deciding which of the elegant terraces we would choose to live in. But she'd be nervous about being seen, and sooner or later we'd argue and she'd say she had to go.

⋆ ⋆ ⋆

'This place is rich, no?' Anton twists his head left to right, taking in the black-fenced squares, the haughty rows of brick houses, students pouring in and out of university buildings: flocks of fashionable shoes, careful hair, and serious textbooks. I can almost hear the click of her heels on the pavement, the touch of her hand on my arm, the light in her eyes.

Anton stops on the corner of Gordon Square and watches three girls cross the road. He nods.

'Sylwia, she come here,' he says. 'Me? I am probably dead, but she come here. She study. She speak English already, better than me. She come here.'

We carry on walking, along Torrington Place towards Tottenham Court Road. I could listen to him all day. I like to know that Sylwia's hair curls when it's wet, that her skin smells like warm milk, that she mumbles in her sleep. I have missed all these things.

When I ask him if he writes to her, he twists his face away from me.

'What is to say?' His skin colours, a sharp red reaching up from his jawbone, and I know, as clearly as if he'd told me, that he cannot write.

He wants to buy beer, but I shake my head and he doesn't push it. When we walk through Soho, his eyes widen at the sex shops and he chuckles to himself. As we cross Mayfair the two of us shrink towards each other, saying nothing.

I've never been impressed by Buckingham Palace, but Anton loves it. He loves the gold-topped statue. He loves the soldiers in their furred hats. He loves the families who take photos lined up against the fence.

'Four years in London, Anton,' I say. 'And you've never been here?'

He shrugs. 'I here for work, for money, for daughter,' he says, and his eyes flick away from me. 'I wish for camera,' he says. 'I wish for camera to send picture for Sylwia.'

We stand in silence. The soldier on the right could be carved out of wood. I wait for him to move, to give himself away, but he stays absolutely still. I wonder if he is thinking about someone he loves.

'My scar,' I say. 'It was from the car door. I don't remember anything.'

He is listening.

'I thought I'd found someone,' I say. 'That's why I lost control. They tried to make out I was negligent, I hadn't got enough sleep, I'd been drinking the night before, I hadn't had my eyes tested in five years, anything they could think of, but it was because I thought I'd found someone.'

We watch a young boy, maybe eight years old, hold a camera in both hands as though it might explode, and point it towards two women, their arms interlocked, their eyes smiling.

'Who?' Anton asks.

I can feel my heart strain against my chest. There aren't any benches here. I lower myself onto the steps, by a group of students — French, I think — who flirt and play with their phones and squeal at their own jokes. One of them — a boy of maybe seventeen — catches my eye and looks quickly away. I see him lean in towards the girl next to him and whisper to her. She glances at me and blushes. The day is heating up and I can feel a prickle of sweat across my back. My mouth tastes bitter, despite the toothpaste.

Anton sits next to me. 'I think you are very sad man,' he says.

I shift on the stone step. 'Sometimes.'

He nods. 'My mother,' he says, 'she sad like you. It is difficult.'

'You're angry with her?' I ask.

Anton shakes his head. 'Not angry,' he says. 'No, not angry. She dies, maybe ten years now.'

'I can write a letter for you,' I say. 'If you'd like me to. To Sylwia.'

I don't look at him, and he doesn't speak. I can see his right leg dance a frantic rhythm against the step.

'It would have to be in English,' I say. 'But you said she can speak English?'

After a time, his foot stops its jig. 'You are kind man, Daniel,' he says. 'I like for you to write letter.'

I nod.

'Not here, though, not here,' he says.

* * *

We walk towards the Angel, because it's his patch, and because I know a place there. It's set back on a wide breadth of pavement. They don't welcome you with open arms, but they wouldn't turn you away. There was a time I tried to look for you there — on the computer. A woman who smelt of my mother's perfume helped me. It said there were 432,000 results, but I couldn't find one about you.

Anton walks too fast for me.

'You must slow down,' I tell him, holding a hand to my chest, feeling my heart swell against my ribs.

He frowns. 'You are ill?'

'Just walk slower with me.'

He eases his pace. I prefer to walk this way anyway, to look up and down as well as along.

* * *

I took a man and his son in my cab once. I picked them up from an unlit house in Tooting at four o'clock in the morning. The boy couldn't have been more than five. The man carried him cradled in his arms, a sports bag lodged over his left shoulder. He spoke to the boy in fast whispered sentences, in a language I couldn't understand. Heathrow, please, he said to me. I sneaked glances at them in my mirror, caught their faces periodically lit by street lights: the boy's eyes drooping, the man's hand stroking his son's hair. I doubt they were running away, but I wanted them to be. It was a quiet night. I pushed down the accelerator and the car swallowed up the miles to the bright glare of the airport. By the time we arrived the boy was asleep; the man's face was tense with worry, a muscle tic just above his jaw. He gave me a big tip and a terse nod, heaved the bag out of the boot, picked up the sleeping child and vanished between the glass doors of the departures hall. I imagined an anxious wait at check-in, a determined stare straight ahead at passport control, a moment of relief as the plane lifted its nose into the sky.

* * *

'Would you go home, if you could?' I ask Anton, as we dodge the tourists clamouring around the British Museum. He's distracted by the smell of fried onions from a hot dog stall. It's not until we turn the corner, following the long line of the black fence, that he speaks.

'It is difficult,' he says.

'Of course.'

'I have no money for plane. And then if I go, maybe I cannot come back. And I say yesterday, maybe it is better to no have father than have me. There is drink in my face, no? I have no money for her.'

I picture my father, sitting at his desk, adding up the debts, the bottle of pills in his briefcase on the floor.

'But surely — ' I realise I don't know what to say to him.

We walk without talking. I send silent reassurances to my heart: it's OK now, it's OK, nearly there, nearly there.

I find a tiny sock in Myddleton Square, pink, with a thin ribbon threaded around the top. I stop and pick it up, put it into my pocket. Anton doesn't notice, or if he does he says nothing. As we walk, I trace its outline with my fingers. There's a little bow at the front, held on by a single stitch. I can feel the raised seam at the toe end, and a patch of mud, perhaps, or something else, dried on. I imagine a girl in a pushchair, fidgeting her feet against a plastic rain cover. The woman pushing the buggy has bags underneath her eyes. She's rushing to get to the doctor's surgery. Last time they were late for their appointment and had to wait for hours. It's raining and chilly, but she can feel herself sweating beneath her clothes. When the sock falls, the child lets out a wail, because the air is cold and the rain cover feels wrong against her bare toes. The mother doesn't see the sock fall. She is tired out by her child's crying. She pushes her hair back from her face and keeps on walking.

We stop in front of the library. It is a large, curved building, the stretch of wall underneath the windows packed tight with tiny blue tiles.

Anton looks longingly at the pub across the road.

'We have no paper,' he says.

'I'll ask.'

Anton shakes his head. 'I no want bad paper, no bad paper.'

I step towards the entrance. The glass doors slide open. Anton stays on the pavement.

'We don't have to — ' I turn back to him. The doors start to close but sense my presence and hiccup open again.

'Yes, yes. I want — ' Anton squares his shoulders. 'What is this place?'

'A library,' I say. 'You choose somewhere to sit.' I wave towards the tables positioned in between metal shelves of books, then walk towards a sign that reads 'Information'. The man behind the counter has a patchy red beard and a stubby nose. He raises his eyes to me and I can see his thoughts mapped out on his face. I don't look bad, don't think that, but clothes wear out quickly when you're in them all the time, and London's a dirty place — your skin holds onto it. If it was raining, it would be easier — people are more forgiving when the weather's against you and you're drenched to the skin. I smile at the man, not enough to show the broken tooth on the bottom row, but enough to show willing.

'I want to ask for your help,' I say.

He eyes me suspiciously, but I plough on. 'I need to write a letter.'

He takes a step backwards, tiny but visible.

'Could you give me two pieces of paper?' I ask. 'And lend me a pen?'

'I'm not — I mean, we don't — '

'I would very much appreciate it.' I put on the poshest accent I can find; it's rusty — those kinds of vowels don't do you any favours in my world.

He frowns. The phone to his right burrs softly and flashes red. He pushes his thumbs and forefingers together. His colleague answers the phone. I wait.

'Well, there's — ' He takes two pieces of paper from the printer behind the desk and holds them out to me. 'And I suppose — ' He takes a biro off a computer keyboard. It has no lid. There are bite marks around its base.

I do my best not to look like I'm snatching them. 'Thank you.'

He looks bemused. I offer another smile.

'And an envelope,' he says. 'You'll be needing an envelope.' He stops himself. 'Unless you have one?' I shake my head. He turns and bends to open a drawer. His navy-blue jumper lifts to reveal the crumpled edges of his shirt, the bulge of flesh at his sides.

'You're very kind,' I say, taking the envelope. He makes a slight movement with his head — a jerk to the side.

Anton lets out a whoop when I approach with paper, pen and envelope. Heads snap up, and I press a finger to my lips. He has chosen a table near the window, hemmed in by shelves. Newspapers are strewn across it. I stack them into a pile for later, and lay the blank white paper in front of him.

'This one for practice,' I say, separating the

sheets. 'This one for best.' It has been a long time since I wrote anything.

We are in the fiction section. C — the same navy blue as my old school uniform; D — a pale orange, like powdered sherbet; E — dark charcoal grey; F — white with a faint pearly sheen. My mother had a string of pearls, one of my father's many gifts. Guilt, I suspect, but she would say love. We lined them all up on the dining-room table — rings and bracelets, necklaces and brooches. Choose two, I said, just two. I had to keep my voice hard because she was crying and I've never been any good with tears. She picked the pearls, and a gold locket in the shape of a heart. His picture sat opposite hers, cut not quite the exact shape of the space. I made myself hold my tongue.

Anton dictates for me. I had expected to ask him questions, to help him decide what to write, but the words fall ready-made into sentences. This letter has existed in his head for a long time.

My Sylwia — 'With a 'w', with a 'w', Daniel. You English — '

I write you from London, England. Here is very big with many people. I miss you. Every day I wake and think of you. I see your face. I think every day, how beautiful you are. I sleep in house that is very big.

He looks at me with guarded eyes. I nod encouragingly.

It has garden with two line of flowers, and tree that has apples. You like it here. You like to dig in garden with little spade and make flowers grow.

I think, sometimes, you forget me. It is OK, Sylwia, if you forget. People's faces hard to keep inside head when not there. I don't forget you. I want — 'No, no, I wish' — *you to remember me.*

I write, and I think about you. I have never seen your face. When things are difficult, I worry that when I do find you I won't recognise you. I worry that it was you on the street that time, and I've screwed up the one chance I had. Usually, though, I know that I won't be able to miss you.

* * *

You can't miss someone you've never met. But I miss you.

* * *

It is difficult to explain. Maybe when you older, I tell you. But soon, I come home. We take trip to mountains. Your legs longer now, you are faster than me. You can tell me all the things from after I go.

A man with blond dreadlocks squeezes past our table. I can see him looking at us, and pretending not to. He selects a book with orange flames on the front cover, and hurries away.

My daughter. I want to show you London. I want to watch your eyes light up at the green of Hammersmith Bridge, the green you see when you get so close to the paint you can smell it. I want to show you my places, the spaces I put things into. A fading yellow daffodil held between the slats of a gutter. A silver coat hanger on the outstretched hand of a tree. A cinnabar-red button tucked into the space between time-eaten bricks.

Rubbish, you will say.

Not rubbish. Look.

I want to tell you about the word cinnabar: how it is a mineral and also a moth. It's such a bright, plastic red you'd think man had made it, but it starts beneath the earth, and exists in the sky.

I have many question for you, Sylwia. I want to know every second from when I go. I hope there is no hate for me going. It is to help, I come here to help. Sometimes things work out a different way, it takes time to get back where I need to get.

I love your mother, Sylwia. Sometimes grown-ups fight, but I love her, and you.

I make you promise, Sylwia, I come home. It take time, but I come home and when I come home I lift you up and you see over heads of all the people, high so you see over houses and talk to birds. If you angry, I can wait.

My friend Daniel write this letter for me. He is kind man.

I love you Sylwia.

Tato

My handwriting has never been good. I watch it crawl like a tired insect across the paper, leaving a blue trail in its wake. When I write my own name it looks unfamiliar. I glance up and see the man at the counter, watching us. I wonder if he likes working here, whether all these words feel like a burden or an opportunity.

'I'll write it out again, neat,' I say. Anton and I both look at the ragged edges of my letters.

He nods. 'And then I draw for her.'

The neat version is not so different from the first one, but Anton doesn't comment. He takes the paper and the pen from me and starts to draw a border around the writing. I watch him, his eyebrows knotted together, delicate interwoven leaves and flowers emerging from the end of the pen. Even at my age, people can still take you by surprise.

I turn to the newspapers, because there is always a chance, and the day I give up might be the day I find what I'm looking for.

* * *

Here's the strange thing: I nearly didn't see it. I mean, I saw it, and then I moved on, because when you've looked for something for as long as I've been looking, the idea of it is so strong, so clear in your mind, you struggle to recognise a variation of it in the real world.

I have been looking for your name all these years, ever since I found out what it was. Not just in newspapers, but on the radio, book spines, computers, even gravestones.

I find his name, not yours — his black name with its whisper of silver and gold. The newspaper is *The Times*, which is hardly surprising. I am onto the next page when the name connects, like a punch to the windpipe. My heart scrambles inside my chest and I have to close my eyes and breathe. When I open them, Anton is still drawing, an intricate version of a rose; the man behind the counter is typing away at his computer. A woman walks past the window, her phone held to her ear. The newspaper lies on the table in front of me. I turn the page.

It is his name, not yours, but when I manage to focus on the smaller print beneath, I see that you are there, ice blue at the end of a line.

The date is tomorrow, a crest of the hill, shimmering green Thursday.

I think about how sad you must be, and it makes my heart ache. I close my fingers around the tiny child's sock in my pocket.

They might have printed the wrong date, the wrong time.

I mustn't panic.

I rip around the text in tiny, quiet movements, so the man behind the counter won't hear. Anton looks up, but I don't meet his eye. I fold the paper and place it in my inside pocket, along with the sock, the ball of cotton and the spray for my heart. I know what it says, but I can't bear the thought of losing it.

⋆ ⋆ ⋆

I wore a jacket with a stain on the lapel to my father's funeral. I didn't want to go at all, but my mother rapped on the door of my room until I opened it, and stood there until I got dressed. It was a bright day, like this one, the air warm, the sky a flat summer blue. I hadn't washed my hair for days. My scalp itched. My eyes hurt.

There were ten people at the funeral. I didn't know six of them. One man had Florida-orange skin and wore a sharp grey suit. I imagined him in a room with blinds pulled across the windows and a green table patterned with upturned cards, smiling as he watched my father lose money he didn't own. The vicar mumbled his words, stumbled over my father's name. Afterwards, outside the church, the sharp-suited man shook my hand and said he was sorry to hear the news, my father had been a friend, a good man. His voice was low, rich and confident. His nails looked manicured. I didn't say anything.

⋆ ⋆ ⋆

'Daniel, you are ill?' Anton's voice sounds distant, like I'm underwater, or carrying a cold in my ears.

'I need — ' I stop, start again. 'There's a — ' I shake my head. 'I have to — '

He narrows his eyes.

'Look, the envelope, and then we need to write the address.' I pull the envelope from beneath the letter and shove it towards him. 'And a stamp, you'll need a stamp.' I see fear flash across his face. 'There's a post office on Rosebery Avenue, near the market, just up the hill. You have some money?' I shouldn't have started this. I have things to do.

A breath, a breath, a breath. Without Anton I would never have known. I don't want you to think I am a man without honour. I fold the letter in half and half again. He has made it beautiful, despite my handwriting.

Anton pulls a creased piece of paper from his pocket. I can't make sense of it, but I recognise the shape of an address, and copy the letters one at a time onto the envelope. We stand up. The man behind the counter watches us. I make myself approach him.

'Thank you,' I say, though I need to be outside, walking towards you; I need to be there, waiting. 'Thank you. My friend wanted to write to his daughter, in Poland. Thank you for helping.' I put the pen on the counter.

Anton nods, pats the envelope and smiles. We are almost out of the door. We almost don't hear him.

'Do you have money for a stamp?' the man says.

I look back. There's a self-satisfied quality to his smile. It happens, sometimes, when people feel they're doing something good. I never begrudge it, though there are those who do. I watch Anton. He shakes his head.

'Hang on.' The man dives his hand into one trouser pocket, then the other. He holds out a pound coin. 'That should be enough for a letter,' he says. His voice rises, like he's asking for something.

Anton takes the money. His nails are long, like a woman's. He nods, shortly, and looks at the floor. The man behind the counter pauses, and then shrugs us away, turns to serve a young woman with a pile of textbooks.

* * *

The post office queue is long and slow. We shuffle forwards with the rest of them. People take surreptitious steps away from us. At first I don't care, because the thought of you is almost close enough to touch, and I can't think past the race of my heart. But then I worry. I am used to the smell of myself. I am used to the way the ends of my clothes fray into thin lines. I try to still the panic.

Anton kisses the envelope, and drops it into the red mouth of the postbox. 'You have to go. Thank you, Daniel.'

'I'll see you,' I say.

He moves his head from side to side. 'Maybe, Daniel.'

He's right. You never know what might happen.

Ten inappropriate thoughts during my father's funeral

1) How the hell do aeroplanes fly when they're so heavy?
2) He loved Tilly and Cee more than me.
3) There's a bag of unwashed underwear in my lost rucksack.
4) Kal looks well. He's found someone else, I'm sure of it.
5) There's something ironic, surely, about a doctor dying.
6) I don't believe in God.
7) How much would the machine that closes the curtains in front of the coffin cost?
8) What if I told Kal I'd changed my mind?
9) The vicar looks a bit like Sean Connery.
10) I'd like to go back to the house, line up the whisky bottles, and drink the lot.

I am cold; ever since he died I've been cold. Outside, the sky is a tasteless blue. I'm wearing the clothes I bought yesterday: skinny black trousers; a black top with a bow at the neck, which I don't like much. I examine myself in the bathroom mirror, a toothbrush between my lips. The cold is stealing the glow from my skin, pinching my mouth thinner, narrowing my eyes.

When I get downstairs, they are all standing in the living room, even though there are enough seats for everyone. Cee's boys loiter by the fireplace, awkward in dark suits that look brand new. Tilly's wearing a long black jersey dress that clings to the curve of her stomach. Cee is neat in a black linen suit. She's wearing blue eyeshadow, like she's going to a party. I stop in the doorway, and feel for just a moment that they are simply a bunch of strangers, that they are somebody else's family and I have nothing to do with them. Everyone's eyes keep straying towards the window; the room shifts each time a car goes by.

'They should be here at eleven,' Steve says. He has thick lips that always look wet. He pulls up his sleeve to look at his watch. It's expensive, I can tell by the way he touches it. 'About ten minutes.' He swivels his head, as though looking for approval. Cee squeezes his arm.

'I'm just going to have a cigarette,' I say. 'Out the front.'

Cee tuts audibly and I see her and Steve exchange glances. 'They'll be here any minute, Alice,' she says.

My hand shakes as I light the cigarette. I pull smoke into my lungs, but it doesn't make me feel any better. The front door opens behind me and I brace myself for a lecture from Cee, but it's Tilly. She perches on the wall next to me.

'Can I have one?' she says.

'You don't smoke.'

'I'd like one though.'

'They're terribly bad for you.' I light her one. She takes a shallow drag, and starts coughing. She smiles at me, sheepishly, and I smile back.

'I can't help thinking about Mama,' Tilly says.

I flick my cigarette and watch the ash drift down towards the steps.

'You were so young,' she says. 'I remember you were so young and I felt I should be like Mama for you and I didn't know how to.'

I stare down the road. The trees cast hard shadows onto the pavement. I think about the bag with the embroidered ballerina. I wonder what happened to it.

'You did OK,' I say. 'You did fine.'

Tilly smiles weakly.

'You must have all blamed me,' I say.

'What?'

'For Mama. For her driving that day.'

'Oh, Alice. Don't. You can't think that.'

We smoke in silence.

'Alice?' There's an edge to Tilly's voice.

'Yes?'

'I wanted to — The thing is, I told — '

‘Look, they’re here.’ I point to the black hearse moving slowly down the road towards us, followed by two long black Mercedes.

‘They’re here,’ Tilly echoes and stares at her cigarette like she doesn’t know what it is.

His coffin sits on the low bed of the hearse. It’s made of rich red wood, polished so that the flowers on its lid have their white petals reflected back to them. The front door opens as the cars draw to a stop. There’s a scurry of movement behind us, Cee fussing with the boys — tissues, mobile phones off, ties straight. Tilly takes my hand and squeezes it.

‘It was like this with Mama,’ she says. ‘It doesn’t feel real.’

A sombre-faced man climbs the steps with slow deliberation. ‘Cecilia, Matilda, Alice.’ He shakes our hands and nods as he says our names. His hand is large, his skin cool: comforting. ‘You’re ready?’ he asks. His eyes meet mine, and I want to say no, I’m not ready for any of this. I am really not ready at all. Instead, I lower my gaze and follow him. I am wearing a pair of heels I found in my old room; I can’t remember leaving them there. I watch my feet on the steps — black patent with pointed toes — and I remember, too late, that the last time I wore them was the night Kal and I went for dinner, when I told him I couldn’t do it any more, not unless things changed, not unless we could stop pretending. It’s not pretending, he said, we’re not pretending. Well, it’s starting to feel like it, I said.

I let the man herd me into the back of one of

the cars and sit squashed between my sisters. They have always made me feel even smaller than I am.

I know that if I looked up I'd see Mrs Williams at her window, her cat cradled in her arms, watching. Instead, I stare at the hearse. From here I can see the word *Granddad*, spelt out in red carnations, framed in the back window. I look across at Cee. She is staring straight ahead. I don't say anything.

We drive as though we are moving against a steady headwind. I catch glimpses of light and shade and colour through the windows, but I keep my head down, fix my gaze on the polished fittings around the gearstick.

'I wish we didn't have to do the whole thing twice,' Tilly says.

'It's what he wanted,' Cee says. Her words are clipped short. 'He wanted family there at the crematorium, and then a church service afterwards.'

Tilly sighs. 'Did we do this with Mama too?'

Cee coughs, her hand pressed against her mouth. 'I'm not sure I remember,' she says.

'Did she kill herself?' I say it without thinking.

'Alice, for Christ's sake.' Cee glares at the back of the driver's head. I watch Tilly's hands fidget in her lap.

'I'm just asking.' I fold my arms across my chest. 'Wasn't she going in the wrong direction?'

Neither of them answers me.

'Maybe she was running away,' I say.

I think I hear Cee mutter 'just like you' under her breath, but I'm not sure.

We get there too quickly. I attach myself to Tilly, lace my fingers through hers. We walk between two fat pillars into a carpeted room with wooden pews down both sides — like a church. Four men I don't know carry my father's coffin in front of us. They place it carefully on a narrow table. They have done this before. The curtains are yellow velvet. The coffin sits on rollers. My father is —

The woman leading the service has a soft, irritating voice. She keeps saying 'a celebration of life'. The boys sit behind me, shuffling in their seats. I wish Kal was here, his arm around my shoulders.

I should have gone back and talked to Dad. I don't know what I was thinking, trying to punish him, when there was no time left. I picture him that evening in the tapas bar, before I left for Moscow, sitting across from me at the small, circular table with its red cloth, a crowd of half-glazed terracotta dishes around the candle. Are you sure this is the best thing for you to be doing, he asked me. I thought the job was going well. It is, I said, it is, but I have to get away. Leaving isn't the only option, Alice, he said. Sometimes it's worth sticking around and trying to make things work.

If I'd stayed, I'd have had more of him. If I hadn't —

The woman has stopped speaking. Tilly squeezes my hand, hard enough to hurt me. The curtains twitch, and then draw themselves together into a yellow wall. Someone must have set up a business selling self-drawing curtains, to make a coffin vanish at the flick of a switch. I hear the hum of another machine, the rollers beginning to move. I imagine him, inside the box, moving towards the heat.

He took us to the ballet every Christmas, for years. Him in a suit, the three of us in new dresses and polished shoes. The hustle and excitement of it. A box with red velvet seats and a view of the wings. Everything gilt-edged and glowing. The lights lowered and that moment of silent anticipation before the curtains parted, as though by magic, and the whole thing began. I loved watching the dancers when they got off stage, how they changed into real people out of the spotlights.

It's over. We're standing up. There's music playing, Fauré, I think, tinny through their speakers. We are sliding ourselves out from the pews and walking the carpeted aisle to the door. It's done. He's gone.

The hearse has gone too. I wonder if it's already on its way to another funeral. The red-carnation *Granddad* has been put on the back shelf of one of the cars. He wouldn't have liked it. He would have thought it was tacky.

We turn off Hampstead High Street, and slow to a stop outside the church. Trees hang their branches, heavy with leaves, over the top of a black iron fence, dapple sunlight onto the concrete paving slabs. It is not until I have stepped out of the safety of the car that I see Kal.

My stomach presses itself back against my spine and adrenalin shoots through my legs. He stands by the arched entrance into the churchyard, looking at me. Dark eyes. Wide mouth. I turn away. I scan the street — a line of trees down the centre of the road; a white wood-panelled house with a yellow door; a graveyard behind a tall fence; a man wearing an old waxed jacket, his hand raised like he's greeting someone. I can feel my heartbeat.

Tilly's standing close next to me. I glare at her.

'I tried to tell you. Alice, he'd have wanted to know. I know Dad could be — But they got on, didn't they?'

The two of them, drinking whisky, talking about the cricket scores, some article in the *BMJ*, doctors' politics.

'You had no right to,' I hiss.

She lays her hand on my arm, and I have to force myself not to push her away. I set my shoulders and turn to face the church, to face Kal. He is wearing a suit. I always fancied him in a suit. Stop it. If he'd just move, just step to one side, or go into the church, that would make it easier. He stays where he is, looking at me. Those eyes. Stop it. I curl my fingers around Tilly's arm and squeeze.

'Don't leave me,' I whisper.

'I won't.' She puts her hand over mine.

I walk straight past him. I try to walk straight past him.

'Alice.' That's all he says.

I almost stumble. I nod my head in his direction, but I can't look at him. I stare at the church. The door and window on the right aren't straight; you can see where the wall's been re-mortared along the cracks. There must be something wrong with the foundations.

Tilly leads me inside. The ceiling rises into white arches above us. Twisted gold lines reach up and over, like painted ropes. We arrange ourselves along the front pew. I fix my eyes on the altar and think about the yellow velvet curtains in the crematorium. I think about Dad's bed, stripped of its sheets, and then I think about my mother at the wheel of a car, the bonnet crumpled like a piece of paper, the wind-screen shattered. There was barely a scratch on her, Tilly told me once; I don't believe it.

The church is filled with subdued noise: footsteps, whispers, people fussing with the order of service, shuffling with the prayer cushions, making themselves comfortable. I allow myself a single glance around. Kal sits on the other side of the aisle, a few rows back. He is wearing the green tie I brought him back from Vietnam. It was the first trip I'd been on since I'd moved in with him. I remember standing in the shop and running my fingers over the colours, waving away the over-attentive shopkeeper. It's the colour of your eyes, Kal said, when I gave it to him. Hardly, I said. He said, I'll think about your eyes every time I wear it. Stop it.

Hugo Wells does the first reading. He worked with Dad. He has cropped white hair and a neat white beard. His hands are slender. Piano player's hands, I remember Dad saying, best surgeon I've ever worked with. His voice is strong and certain. *Why should I be out of mind because I am out of sight? I am waiting for you, for an interval, somewhere very near, just round the corner. All is well. Nothing is hurt; nothing is lost.* The light falls golden through the stained glass, glints off the brass, pretends the world is beautiful.

I can't concentrate on the sermon. I twist in my seat. Kal's head is lowered. He doesn't see me. Maybe I was wrong. Maybe we could have carried on the way we were. Maybe we could try it again.

Tilly gets to her feet and walks clumsy steps up to the lectern. She lifts her head and gives a nervous half-smile. I will her on.

'Our father was a very special man.' Her voice wobbles, rights itself again. 'We were lucky to have known him.' People shuffle and nod. 'He was quiet, serious, hard-working, but he also had a real sense of fun.' She glances at Cee and me and I find myself smiling and nodding. 'When I was ten, and my sister Cecilia was eight — this was before Alice came along — we went on holiday to Normandy.'

All I can hear is the roar of blood in my ears. Before Alice came along, everything was fun. Before Alice came along, Dad wasn't so distracted, so withdrawn. I remember Cee, once, her eyes black with anger, her fists locked onto her hips, declaring I should never have been born in the first place, I was a great big mistake and Mama and Daddy were cross when I came along. I ran crying to Dad. I must have been six, maybe seven. He lifted me onto his lap and smoothed the hair from my eyes, rocked me until I was calm enough to speak through the sobs. He denied it, of course he did, told me I was beautiful and wanted, a gift to him and Mama. He said he loved me and there was no accident involved, and that he would have words with Cecilia because it was a cruel thing to have said. Even so, I left his study with a lingering sense of uncertainty, lodged like a sea-worn pebble at the base of my throat.

I close my eyes and force myself to remember: eating ice-creams on Westminster Bridge with Dad trying to teach us about politics. Christmas mornings — one of Dad's socks at the end of each of our beds, an orange at the bottom, because as a boy he had always had an orange at the bottom of his. My graduation, when he held both my shoulders and I could see the pride in his eyes.

I watch Tilly's lips move. I try to tune back into her speech. 'I remember him lifting Alice onto his shoulders to see over the crowds,' she says.

It was some kind of parade, the streets packed with people. I was too small to see; too big, really, to be picked up. I remember holding onto his hair, my feet against his chest — tottering, but safe; on top of the world.

'We always felt very loved by him. We knew he was someone who would have laid his life down for us had it been necessary.' Tilly takes a shaky breath; it is magnified by the microphone. 'We will miss him very much.' She bows her head and stumbles down from the lectern, back to the pew. Once she's seated, she crumples into tears. When we stand for the last hymn, I put my arm around her shoulders and try to hold her upright. *The Lord's my shepherd*, I sing, though I don't believe a word of it.

* * *

'You're lucky,' Kal said to me once, 'to have a dad like yours.'

'What, one who was never around?'

'That's not true.'

'Speaks the fellow surgeon.'

'I like him.'

'So do I.'

'He's not — '

'What?'

He shrugged, his eyes closing up the way they did whenever we got anywhere near talking about his parents.

I picture Kal sitting behind and to my left. If his father died, no one would even think to tell me. I used to fantasise about his family. When he went over for dinner I would drink a bottle of wine on my own in the flat and imagine his parents' house — from the blue carpet in the hallway to the marble-effect tiles in the bathroom. I'd act out their dinner conversation. Have you met a nice girl yet, Khalif? Not yet, Ummi. You want to get a move on. Mrs Abad's daughter's just graduated from Cambridge, you know. I can get a picture for you.

* * *

It is all done, again. I walk with Tilly down the aisle and feel people's gazes snag against us. Someone is playing the organ, not particularly well; they falter over the complicated passages. Dad wouldn't have been impressed. Not with that, not with the flowers which have been positioned on a bench at the back of the church, not with any of it.

Cee corrals us into a line by the door. I let people take my hand and say what they need to say. I don't know who all of them are.

I am waiting for Kal. As soon as I see him, my heart quickens and I feel that burst of adrenalin; I am ready to run. Maybe he will walk straight past. He doesn't. He takes my hand and the shock of it stops my breath.

'Alice, I'm sorry — '

I swallow hard. I can't speak.

'He was a good man.'

Dad got used to Kal, quicker than Cee did. They'd talk about the NHS, and the cricket. Kal bought him a bottle of malt whisky every Christmas.

'How are you?' he says.

I raise my eyebrows.

'I'm sorry. I — I heard you'd been away.'

I think about Mongolia: the colour of the earth as the sun dipped towards the horizon; a couple of yurts, a scattering of horses, miles and miles of emptiness.

'I should let you get on,' he says, glancing behind him at the raggedy queue of people.

'We're having drinks.' The words come out in a rush. 'At the house.' I look down at my black patent shoes and wonder if he remembers them too.

He hesitates, just for a second, and then says, 'That would be nice. Thanks. I'd like to raise a glass to him.'

I bite at a fingernail.

'It's good to see you, Alice.'

I hold it together until he's almost at the road and then I turn towards the wall of the church. The sobs come from the very centre of my body, double me up. I feel a hand rub a line along my spine. It is not his hand. There are more people coming out of the church. I don't care.

'Alice. Come on, let's go.' Cee leans towards me. There's a man I don't know standing by the church door. He looks uncertain. He needs a shave, and a shower. I let Cee lead me. When I get back, I decide, I'll go to bed. I'll hide under the duvet. I'll barricade the door.

But the house is filled with people and I am swept into the living room. Two trestle tables covered with white cloths stand in front of the bookshelves. I have no idea where they came from. One table holds rows of wine glasses, some already filled with red and white. On the left-hand side, short stubby glasses cluster in front of the remains of Dad's whisky collection. The second table is heavy with food. It feels somehow disrespectful.

Kal stands by the fireplace; he has a glass half filled with honey-coloured whisky and is talking to an old man who must be in his eighties, his skin dry and wrinkled as a walnut casing, thin drifts of white hair across a freckled scalp. I realise I will never know what my father would have looked like as an eighty-year-old.

'Sandwich, Alice?' It's Steve, clutching a plate of sandwiches with two slices of cake teetering on the edge. He's taken off his jacket to reveal a pale-blue shirt with patches of sweat beneath each arm.

'No, thanks.'

'It'll do you good. Grief's tiring, you need to keep your strength up.'

'Why do you think he painted this room red?'

Steve looks around, frowning. 'It's rather grand.'

'Don't you think it's dark?'

'Well, if you trimmed back the bay tree a bit.' He nods towards the front window, biting into a prawn sandwich. A blob of mayonnaise falls onto his wrist and he licks it off. 'How about a drink?' he says.

'Red, please.'

He smiles, scuttles away and returns with a glass full to the brim. Our fingers brush as I take it.

'Thanks. I should mingle or something,' I say, but before I can escape, Cee descends.

'Can you believe that bastard isn't even here?' She brandishes a celery stick. 'Why she doesn't get rid of him, I do not know.'

Cee has never liked Toby, Tilly's man. Who officially isn't Tilly's man on account of being married to someone else. He's a nice guy, attractive, too, in a classic way I've never really gone for. But the fact remains that he is married, which makes him an undeniable bastard. I hadn't even noticed his absence.

'Apparently,' Cee continues, 'he said he'd be here and then something came up. What could possibly come up? She spends her entire life making excuses for that man. She pretends it doesn't bother her, but I can see it in her eyes.'

And her hands. Tilly's hands have always given her away. I picture them, tight white knots as she brushes off the latest disappointment.

I confronted her about it once.

'What am I supposed to do?' she asked. 'I've made my choice and it's him.'

'Why doesn't he leave her?' I demanded.

She shook her head sadly. 'We don't live in a Hollywood film, Alice,' she said.

In the end I concluded she liked it this way. She's always the treat, the cherry on the top, the favourite chocolate from the box. She gets weekends away and illicit presents. There must always be an air of subterfuge. It's not what you'd expect from Tilly, but I get it. Cee thinks the whole thing's insane, but then her idea of a romantic night is a Chinese takeaway, a box of After Eights, and a rom-com DVD while the children are asleep upstairs.

'You girls have got a big job on, then,' Steve says. Cee glares at him.

'What do you mean?' I say.

'It's a big house,' he says.

'Been doing your sums?'

Steve frowns.

'Alice, he's just saying there'll be a lot to sort out,' Cee says.

She's already started. I found her in Dad's study yesterday, surrounded by piles of paper, half-filled black bin bags, cardboard files. Her face was flushed a deep pink, her shoulders hunched forwards and the tip of her tongue caught between her lips. She snapped her head up when I opened the door, then looked down to a blue box file by her feet. She shifted it closer to the chair, and hooked her leg over it. Her hands danced at the edges of the pile of paper in her lap. I imagine her and Steve discussing it over breakfast. What we'll keep. What we'll junk. How much we'll sell it for.

'I'd better go and talk to people,' I say, and force a smile. I look up, and through the window I see the man from the church — with the stubble and the greasy hair — standing on the front doorstep. Someone else will let him in. I start to push my way towards the door. It's like moving through glue. I keep my head down, don't make eye contact.

But I am caught, just as I reach the hallway.

'You must be Alice?'

The woman is tiny, even compared to me. Her eyes are fierce blue, her hair resolutely dyed. 'Heavens, you're like your mother.' She looks me up and down. 'Last time I saw you you were just a nipper, and it's always hard to know if the resemblance will last. I'm Marina, pleased to see you again.' Her handshake is firm. There's a Highland lilt to her voice. I instinctively like her, but I don't want to talk to her.

'You're wishing us all away to our own homes no doubt.' She nods. 'That's fair enough, but it's good to see you. They tell me your father always talked about you with real pride.' She smiles, a little falsely, I think. 'That's nice to know, isn't it?'

I stand and stare at the space just above her right shoulder. She's about to turn away. 'You knew him, how?' I say, despite myself.

'Oh.' She coughs, cherry-painted nails pressed to narrow lips. 'I knew your mother. We were close.' She holds up two fingers, twisted around each other. Her eyes shift to one side. 'I hadn't seen your father for a long time.' She pauses. 'Your sister wrote to me about Malcolm. I was surprised to be on the list, to be honest, but I wanted to come and pay my respects, to all of you.' She looks hard at me. 'We didn't always see eye to eye, but he was a good man, a decent man.'

'You knew Mama?'

'Since school.' She touches my forearm. 'I still miss her,' she says, and sighs.

'Do you know where she was going?'

'I'm sorry?'

'That day. When she — In the car.'

Marina frowns.

'She was supposed to pick me up from ballet,' I say. 'But when they found her, she was on the wrong road.'

She hesitates, just for a beat, and then she lets out a soft breath. 'Heavens, she'd have just got some idea into her head.' She looks at me, her head on one side like a bird. 'She had whims, your mother,' she says, and smiles. 'She'd have been driving to get you and seen a sign to somewhere she'd always wanted to go, or a road that looked pretty, and she'd have just turned off and gone. She was like that. She'd have been daydreaming, driving too fast, not paying attention, and then — ' She stops herself and our eyes meet. 'I've never known anyone else quite like your mother.'

A silence settles. I finish my wine and twirl the empty glass between my fingers.

'I was wondering,' Marina says. 'Did you meet someone called Daniel this afternoon?'

She's right, I want her to leave. I want all of them to leave. I shake my head and gesture as though I have somewhere important to go. She opens her mouth as if to say something else, but I turn and walk away from her. Tilly's in the kitchen washing glasses. She looks up and takes my glass, but says nothing. Outside, I lean against the kitchen wall and close my eyes. The sun is warm on my face, but I still feel cold.

'He was never much of a gardener, was he?'

Kal's voice makes me jump. I push myself upright, feel my top catch against a brick. 'He did a bit,' I say. 'He'd come out on the weekends, listen to the radio, do some weeding.'

'Summer's a bastard though, isn't it?'

He's right. Everything is overgrown. The grass needs cutting. The weeds are choking the flowers.

Kal and I met at a mutual friend's fancy-dress party. We'd both cheated. I'd just got back from Nepal and wore a gold-trimmed sari I'd bought there. He was dressed in blue hospital scrubs, splattered with fake blood.

'Ah, a Hindu goddess.' I was terrified he was insulted. 'Don't look so worried,' he laughed. 'You look gorgeous.'

'And you — er — '

'Look like a murderous surgeon? I had an axe, but I seem to have lost it.'

He was easy to talk to, interested in where I'd been and where I was going next. He didn't ask what my job was, or what I was intending to do with my life. He was older than me by almost six years. At the end of the night, when the Roman soldiers and Lycra-clad superheroes were making a dash for the last Tube, I leant over and kissed him, and he kissed me back.

I reach one hand back towards the wall and push my palm against the bricks. He's trimmed his beard, and had a haircut. I can smell his aftershave.

'Are you home for a while?' he says.

'I have no idea.'

I want him to touch me. I want him to kiss me so I can forget about everything else. 'Are you with someone else?' I say.

'Alice.'

'That means yes. I bet you're engaged, aren't you? Cee always said — '

He sighs, and shoves his hands into his trouser pockets. 'With all due respect, your sister knows nothing about me.'

'Sorry.'

He shrugs and scuffs his right foot against the ground, stares down at it. 'I tried to call. I even wrote you a letter,' he says.

I know too much about him. I know how he presses his thumb into the centre of his chin when he's thinking. I know he likes cooked tomatoes but not raw ones. I know what he looks like when he's asleep.

'I called your dad and asked for your address, but he said you'd gone away. There wasn't anywhere I could send it to,' he says. 'I didn't want to email. It felt — '

'Do you still have it?'

He looks at me then, and I see he's tired. The skin around his eyes looks worn and soft.

'The letter?' I say.

He shakes his head and lowers his gaze, and I wonder if he ever wrote it. I want him to put his arms around me. I want to tell him that I wake up angry every morning, because Dad should still be here, because I never said I loved him, even when I knew he was dying. I want to tell him that the house freaks me out, that it's darker than it should be; that I walk into an empty room and it's like walking in on people who've just been talking about me. I want him to tell me I'm not going mad.

'Can you leave now?' I say.

'I missed you.'

'Please.'

'I'm going. Alice.' He puts his hand on my forearm and I feel desire, like liquid silver through my veins. I hold myself as still as I can. 'Be nice to yourself, won't you?' he says. 'It's a big shock.'

I make a noise at the back of my throat. I listen to him walk towards the back door. Open it. Close it. I sense him pause, just inside, and then walk away.

My father is dead. The garden is out of control. The air smells of rain. I bend my legs and lower myself down, my back against the wall, until I am sitting with my legs angled up in front of me. I lean against the house; I let it hold me.

Ten jobs I've held down for more than a month

1) Shop assistant, in a baker's in Preston. I was sixteen.
2) Newspaper round, Broughton. I learnt which houses had a dog waiting in the hallway pretty quickly.
3) Post office sorter, Mount Pleasant.
4) Labourer, south-east London.
5) Gallery invigilator at a place in Soho. I've never been happier.
6) Courier van driver, Leeds.
7) Artists' model, Leeds.
8) Shelf stacker, Sainsbury's, Kentish Town.
9) Office cleaner, White City, London. I remember all those photographs of children and wives and husbands, Blu-tacked to the edges of computer screens.
10) Cab driver, London.

I didn't sleep last night. I should have slept; I can't afford to faint, or end up in hospital, not today. I walked instead — it calms me down, once I'm in a rhythm. It's more of a slow shuffle these days, but it does the job. I circled Hampstead until my legs ached. Every hour or so I'd stop underneath a lamp post, take the scrap of newspaper from my pocket and hold it up to the light: *A family service at Highgate Cemetery, followed by a 1 p.m. service at the Parish Church of St John-at-Hampstead. No flowers. Donations to Marie Curie Cancer Care.*

Once the sun rose, it was as though my energy drained away with the darkness. I found a bench to sit on but I didn't let myself close my eyes. It was too late for sleeping by then. An hour on I still felt as though my limbs were made out of bits of cotton — like some kind of rag doll. So I dragged myself to the supermarket on Heath Street and stood at the exit, trying to catch people's eyes. Any spare change, I asked. I hate doing it, but I needed to eat. I watched people ignoring me. Eventually, a woman holding three white plastic bags stopped and handed over a croissant, still warm. She smiled at me. She was perhaps fifty, one of those women with comfortable bodies and comfortable faces, who you could imagine making you tea, patting your hand, asking questions.

'Thank you,' I said.

'You've somewhere to go?' she asked.

'A funeral,' I answered, and watched her face crease into sympathy.

'Do I look OK?' I asked.

She looked at me and then fumbled around in her bag. 'Look, have some fruit.' She gave me an apple. 'I work for a charity,' she said. 'With the homeless, that is.' I've never liked the term. I let her talk and I took her card.

'I'm sorry, but I have to — ' I gestured to the watch I don't own, and she nodded reluctantly.

I chose an office window — an estate agent's with A4 sheets of photos and bullet-point lists in neat plastic frames — and did what I could with my hair. I ate the apple — all of it: the cool white flesh, the core, the black seeds — and then wiped my hands against my trousers. First impressions are the most important, my dad told me, more than once. It's hard to undo a first impression.

* * *

When I duck through the arched gateway into the churchyard I can hear the strains of an organ. The church doors are open, and a tall, grey-haired man, dressed in white, stands with his hands clasped in front of his stomach, talking to a woman whose shoulders are hunched with age.

I am late. I have already, almost, missed you. No — I'm early, I'm sure of it.

The vicar looks up as I approach and smiles. I have often wished for religion, to be accepted without prejudice, or to at least have people pretend, but I slip past him without saying anything. The inside of the church doesn't match its squat brick exterior. White arches, laced with gold, sweep up above me to where a narrow balcony runs along three walls. The pews are painted the same pale blue as your name. There are maybe twenty people, scattered throughout the church. Most of them are old. Few of them sit together. It is morning prayers. I am not late. I have not missed you. I sit at the back and pick up a prayer book from the shelf in front of me. The pages are like tissue, and smell of dust.

I've never been able to sing; the tune evades me and I find myself sliding about, searching for notes. Even so, I like the feel of it, letting my voice escape from my body without having to think about what I'm saying. And as I sing, I feel it, bubbling at the base of my chest: I have almost found you. My daughter. I am almost there.

I don't speak to the vicar on the way out. I turn right into the graveyard which drops away towards an ivy-covered wall.

My mother's gravestone was smaller than I'd wanted it to be, but money was an obstacle. She'd insisted she should be by Dad. There was a part of me wanted to put her as far away from him as I could, but she'd made me promise. They're not next to each other, we'd have had to be ahead of the game to make that happen, but they're near enough. You can stand by her stone and see over to his. I don't break promises.

I try to go, once a year. I stay there for a day,

sometimes more. I tidy up — pull out the weeds around her headstone and those nearby. I use my penknife to cut the grass as best I can. I collect up stones and twigs and arrange them in patterns. I sit and talk to her. I make sure I'm angled so I can't see my father's grave. I make sure I don't look at him.

It's best, I find, not to imagine what she'd think if she were here now, looking at me with my heart ready to pack in, the hems of my trousers frayed.

I remind myself it's a Thursday: a bright, green day, lifting me up and out of the hollow of the week. It's natural to feel nervous, I tell myself. I have never met you; there is so much to say. I find a bench beneath a tree and am grateful for the shade. I let myself take the picture out of my pocket and lay it across my right thigh. It is wrapped in a plastic carrier bag which rustles at my touch.

* * *

She laughed when I said I wanted to paint her. We were in the café at the National Portrait Gallery. It was the first time we had met by design. I'd thought she wasn't going to come. My tea was already cold, and my heart had sunk down towards my ankles. And then she arrived — in a tumble of wet umbrella, sagging paper bags, wild curls, and a red coat that swirled out from a cinched-in waist.

'You waited,' she said.

She drank Earl Grey tea and ate a slice of

chocolate cake, one tiny forkful after another. I half formed sentences in my mind, but once they reached my lips I saw their stupidity and kept my mouth closed.

'You've had a haircut,' she said. 'It's nice.'

I touched my head, self-conscious. 'Thank you.'

The café echoed with the sounds of teacups on saucers and cutlery on plates, and other people talking.

'You're tongue-tied.'

'I'd like to paint you,' I blurted.

She put her head to one side.

'Naked?' she said.

I felt my heart quicken. 'Well — I mean — '

And then she tipped back her head and laughed, like we weren't in a public place, like no one else mattered.

'I don't want — ' I started, though I did.

'I'm a mother of two,' she said.

'You're beautiful.'

It was the right thing to say. A look of pleasure flashed across her face.

'No one's told me that in a while,' she said.

'Not your husband?' I said and then winced.

She smiled, a little sadly. 'Things get boring, it seems.'

'I think you're very beautiful,' I stumbled. 'I'd like to paint your portrait.'

'You have a studio?'

I shook my head. I could feel my breath tangled up in my chest.

'Are you any good?'

'At what?'

She smiled. 'At painting.'

I shrugged and stared down at my hands. 'I'm OK.'

'Show me.' She reached into one of her bags and drew out a large white envelope and a thin black biro. She laid them on the table between us. 'Go on.' She lifted her chin, pushed her shoulders back, brushed her hair along the line of her face.

I told myself to take it slowly. I told myself it might be my only chance to spend time looking at her like this. I searched for the shape of her bones underneath her skin; the exact angle of her jawline; the detail — a tiny mole on her left cheek, the slight difference in the contour of her eyelids, the almost imperceptible discrepancy between the line of her lipstick and the line of her lips.

'You're not drawing,' she said after several minutes.

'I have to look first,' I said.

'I feel like you're looking inside my brain.'

'I can't do that.'

'Shall I tell you what I'm thinking?'

'Don't move, stay just like that.' I drew her then, in quick confident lines, the tilt of her head, the mischief in her eyes, the slight curl of her lip.

When I was finished I pushed the envelope across the table towards her. She spent longer than I could bear looking at it.

'You don't like it?' I said.

'You've made me look beautiful, and a bit mean.'

'I didn't intend to — the mean bit.'

She smiled then, and went to put the envelope into one of her bags.

'Could I keep it?' I said.

She lifted her eyebrows.

'I'll draw you again,' I said. 'But I'd like to — '

She nodded and handed me the paper. We sat in silence, listening to the clatter of teacups around us.

'Well.' She gave a quick sigh, and smiled. 'It's been nice to see you, Daniel. I'm glad we — ' She shook her head, as though she was trying to get rid of an idea. 'You're a good artist. I'm impressed.' She started to gather up her bags.

'Don't go.' I said it before I could stop myself. It sounded desperate.

She looked at me, a steady glass-green look.

'I mean, would you like to see some of the paintings, maybe?'

'No, not today, I don't think,' she said. 'I've so many bags, and I have to get back for the girls.'

I felt her words sink through my chest. I waited for her to stand, but she stayed in her seat, as though considering how to answer a question. Eventually she released her bags, fished in her handbag and produced the same pen I had drawn with, and a small lined notebook. She wrote quickly, ripped out the page and put it face down on the table. She kept her hand over it for a moment, as if trying to decide whether or not to pick it up again.

'I really must go.' Another flurry of bags, coat, umbrella, hair. I stood too, and tried, ineffectually, to help. She leaned forward, planted a kiss on my cheek, and was gone.

I sat back down and stared at where a red lipstick mark remembered the shape of her mouth on the edge of her teacup. The blood pumped in my veins. I turned over the piece of paper. An address in Bloomsbury. A date — three days in the future, a pearl-white Friday. A time — 3 p.m. Nothing else. No phone number, no message. I looked at her writing, then my drawing. I don't know how long I sat there.

* * *

It's not safe to take it out too often. Ink and paper don't last like you'd hope they might. It's been a long time; it's a miracle, really, I've still got it to look at. The gum along the edge of the envelope turned a dry, dark yellow years ago. The paper itself is soft with age. I push back the plastic so I can see her face. The ink has faded, but not so much that I can't make out the spark in her eye, the lift of her upper lip. Do you look like her, I wonder, do you have the same pale skin, the same pattern of freckles across your shoulders? I bend over the picture so not even a glint of sunlight can reach her. I would like to touch her face, run my fingers along the lines, but I have learnt to think ahead; I have learnt how to keep things safe.

Sometimes, during those afternoons in Bloomsbury, she talked about feeling trapped. Kids ruin your body, and then they ruin your sleep, she'd say. I love them, of course I love them, but sometimes I want to walk out of the house when they're asleep, shut the front door behind me and never go back.

I smooth the plastic bag over her, and fit the picture carefully into my jacket pocket. As I do it strikes me that she might be here, in this graveyard. It is far from impossible.

I comb the whole place, stone by stone. I search for the bright, brash red of her name, but find only a Jennifer, a John, a Juliet, a Joseph.

There's another graveyard just opposite the church. I stand at the corner of it, holding onto the fence, and wait for you.

Two black Mercedes make their ponderous way along the road towards the church. In the back window of the first car there are eight red letters — carnation heads held into plastic shapes: *Granddad*.

Father. Grandfather. I've imagined, of course I have, that you might have had children. It's been long enough. You're old enough.

The cars stop. I am standing absolutely still, but I feel like I'm in the great buffeting chaos of a storm. The driver's door of each car opens, and solemn-faced men wearing smart suits and polished shoes step onto the tarmac. I wonder how many suits they own. I wonder if they have an account at their local dry-cleaners, and whether they take the suits in themselves or have a wife they expect to do it for them. Slow down. I notice the weave of my jacket between my fingers. There's a breeze just got up and I can feel its touch on my cheek. Slow down.

Father. Grandfather.

The drivers open the passenger doors and stand by. The first person out is a man, short and overweight. I can't imagine you with a man like that. After him come three boys. Two are almost as tall as he is; the third is younger. The man puts his hand on the youngest boy's head, and I want — suddenly, desperately — to feel this boy's hair and the shape of his skull underneath my own palm.

I am starting to think it will kill me to see you, after all. But when you step onto the pavement it's like the weight on my chest has turned to dust and blown away. You have her hair. I always knew you would. And you're small, like she was. You hold yourself tight, and I can see from the set of your shoulders that you loved him. It is one of your sisters who walks to the man with his hand on the boy's head.

You turn away from the church, away from all the people waiting there, and as you turn I see your face. It is so like hers it frightens me: almond eyes, small mouth, the bottom lip thicker than the top. You wear your hair coiled up at the back of your head, but I know if you unpinned it it would fall in russet curls across your shoulders. Your eyes skim the streets, as though you are trying to find something to hold onto.

This is it. We are looking at each other. The wind is hustling at the trees and the world shimmers with a dappled, shifting light. We are standing face to face, with only a road and a stretch of pavement between us.

I should know by now that however much I dream something, it doesn't ever turn out that way. When I dream this, you recognise me. When I dream this, I raise my hand, like I'm doing now, and you respond. Sometimes you frown, then laugh; sometimes you know straight away; other times I have to tell you — four words: magenta, ice blue, maroon, pearl white. But your eyes skip over me as though I'm a stranger. I keep my arm raised. I lift my eyebrows and I smile. At you. My daughter.

You turn back to the church and reach for your other sister's hand. My heart can't take this. It's like someone is pressing into the centre of my chest, pulling down at the back of my jaw. *You need to avoid emotional upset*, the doctor told me, *you need to keep yourself away from stressful situations*.

I could let it happen. Maybe you would turn back if I fell to the ground. But you are too far away now. I pull the bottle from my pocket and spray beneath my tongue. Then I cross the street and follow the last black-suited stragglers into the church.

I sit in the same place I sat this morning, careful not to make eye contact with the vicar. He is at the lectern, smiling a smile he must have rehearsed in front of a mirror for these occasions.

I can see the back of your head. You rub the fingers of your right hand against your neck. You glance around and I follow your gaze to a tall dark-skinned man with a thick mop of black hair and a neat beard. He is sitting with his head lowered towards his knees. You look away and I can see a slump of disappointment in your shoulders. I feel a sudden surge of anger towards the man. I try to concentrate on the vicar's words. They flash colours across the backs of my eyes. Intelligent. Professional integrity. Committed father. Three beautiful daughters. Proud.

I wonder what they would say at my funeral, what words they would use — almost; never quite; tried hard. I wonder who would come.

The sister without the husband and children stands up and walks to the lectern. She is introduced as Matilda. I met them both the first time I saw your mother, in the cloisters of the National Portrait Gallery. I wonder if they remember; they were old enough to. I'd been looking at the Dame Laura Knight. I was standing right up close, examining the brushwork on the artist's bright-red cardigan. I like to do that — I like to work out how things are made. Do you know the painting? It's of the artist at her easel, painting a naked woman. The model stands to the right, her left breast just visible, her hands holding the back of her head, a faint blush around her buttocks. The artist isn't looking at the model or at the easel; she gazes into the distance as though she's thinking about something entirely different.

'Mummy, why's that man looking at the woman with no clothes on?'

I jumped back from the painting. It was Cecilia — I only learnt her name later, a wiry girl with brown hair tied into bunches, glaring at me. I looked up and saw her mother, and my heart went into free fall. She held another girl, Matilda — softer, gentler-looking — by the hand.

'I'm terribly sorry,' I said.

'What on earth for?' she said, and smiled, and my heart collided with something hard. 'Darling, it's an art gallery, people are supposed to look at the paintings,' she said to the indignant girl on her right. 'Now let's leave this man to his examination.' She smiled again, with that light in her eyes. I stood rooted to the spot.

'Mummy, why is he staring at us?'

My face burned. The woman hushed her daughter and threw me an apologetic look. 'I'm sorry,' I said again. I was suddenly aware of my arms, useless and awkward, hanging down either side of my body. 'I — um — I couldn't buy you ladies a cup of tea?' I said. It sounded ridiculous, but I couldn't let her go. She pulled herself straight then, looked at me like she was trying to work me out.

'Can I have a hot chocolate?' That was Matilda. I wanted to hug her.

'Of course you can,' I said, 'if that's OK with your mother?'

* * *

They were nice girls, your sisters. I could tell they'd been brought up right. I don't know what I was thinking when I asked her to leave him, to come with me. I thought somehow I could stand in for him, that I could do as well as him.

I watch you gazing up at Matilda. She takes tear-stained gulps halfway through sentences, but she holds it together. Loving father. Dedicated. Always fair.

He knew, your mother told me, he always knew. I hope it didn't make things difficult for you.

I hold your name in my mouth, such an ice-cold blue it makes my teeth hurt.

* * *

I stand with everyone else and we filter towards the door. I keep my head down. You are the only person I want to see. I step out from the cool interior into the bright heat of the day.

But it is Cecilia who greets me. I think, for a moment, that she recognises me, but then I see in her eyes that she's judged me for what I am and wants me to leave. You are turned away, crying. Matilda strokes the space in between your shoulder blades. The man you had looked at during the service stands awkwardly at the gate, as though torn between coming back to take you in his arms and leaving.

'I'm sorry for your loss,' I mutter to Cecilia.

'Thank you,' she says, and lifts her eyebrows just a fraction — waiting.

I don't speak to many people, so words no longer come easily; I have to draw them up, like water from a well. When they reach the top there is always the danger of spillage, a sudden rush into empty space.

'I wanted to come, to say, to give my condolences.'

She looks like someone who diets — her face is slightly drawn and there's an edge of discontent about her.

'Your father.' You are still turned away from me. I cannot lose you.

'You knew him?'

'Malcolm.'

Something softens around her mouth.

'Malcolm,' I say again, like it's some kind of password. 'He was — I just wanted to pay my respects.'

Her chin moves up a little, like the second half of a nod. She wants me to go. You are close enough to touch. She follows my gaze.

'Well, thank you for coming,' she says. The short man walks over, slips an arm around her waist and says something in her ear. She shakes her head, then turns back to me. 'I'm sure you'll understand this is a difficult time for all of us,' she says. 'A time to be together, with privacy.'

'I knew your mother,' I say. 'Julianne.' I haven't said her name out loud for years. Lipstick red.

There is a battle behind her eyes, but my skin and my hair, my clothes and my smell tell her what I am, and I am losing.

The organ has stopped playing. 'Thank you for coming,' she says, and then turns away from me, towards you. I don't know what she tells you, but when you look at me, I see she has ruined it all, and that you too think I'm a tramp with no right to be here.

Matilda leads you towards the car. I don't know where you live. I can't run that fast. The other people are disappearing, turning corners, slamming their own car doors. I don't hear the engine start, but the car you are in is moving. It's back, the weight in my jaw, the crashing through my chest.

Apart from the man who loves you — either that, or he has hurt you and wants to make it better — the other stragglers include an elderly couple, a tiny woman with black hair that looks like a wig, and a family — two kids, the youngest small enough to be lifted up into her father's arms. I choose the woman.

I push my hands through my hair, and run my finger around the edge of my lips. I straighten my jacket, draw my shoulders back, and drag up the accent that I've become so good at hiding it no longer feels like my own.

'Excuse me.'

She turns as though I've frightened her. 'Hello?'

And I know, from the lilt in her voice, from her height and from the blue-grey eyes, that she is Marina. We have never met, but she has been described to me, laughingly, with affection, and there was a photograph in her flat — standing with a furred hood pulled up around her cheeks, against a backdrop of snow-topped trees. Marina and I used to be such free spirits, Julianne had said once.

'I forgot to bring the address,' I say. 'For the house.'

Her eyes narrow. I've got it wrong.

'You're a friend?' she says.

'Of Malcolm, yes. Former colleagues.' I manage to infuse my voice with a rich, coffee-cream sound. That swings it for me. She opens her handbag and pulls out a folded piece of paper.

'Here you are.'

The address is printed in black ink. The words I need are two shades of the same colour: dark navy and a lighter, brighter royal blue.

'I hear Alice still lives there,' I say. It's hard to keep my voice under control.

'Only while she's back, I think. I do feel for them. It's hard when the last parent dies. Can I give you a lift?'

'No, no.' I see suspicion flare in her eyes. 'My car's just on the other side.' I wave behind me. 'I'll see you there.'

'Marina,' she says, and holds out her hand. She wears three gold rings, each glinting with stones.

I swallow and offer her my hand. The skin is thick and callused, my nails are too long. I see she wants to pull back, but she doesn't. I make myself let go, and as I do, I say my name, because it feels like there is nothing to lose now; she is perhaps the only one who might understand. I hold her gaze for a moment, and then I turn and walk away. And even when I hear her voice, turning my name into a call, into a summons, into a question, I keep on walking.

* * *

I know the road. I never took the Knowledge, but I have a memory for where one road branches off to become another. I make myself walk slowly: Heath Street. Perrin's Lane. Gayton

Road. Magnolia, olive green. Royal blue, gold. Purple, chestnut brown. *Avoid emotional upset.* I fix my eyes in front of my shoes. I follow the spaces in between the pavement slabs, register the occasional stubborn smattering of moss or grass. *While she's back*. From where? For how long?

I turn right down Willow Road — sandstone yellow, chestnut brown — because I am not quite ready yet. I need to think. I walk onto the Heath, up above the ponds, then loop west and back towards you.

It will be a big house, I'm sure of it. I imagine pale London brick, tall windows, trees in pots. A grown-up's house, and you so fragile-looking; I couldn't help but think that. I want to take you to a café and put a plate of food in front of you. I want to sit and watch you eat. And when you're finished — when I offer you something else: some cake, or another cup of tea, and you shake your head and say no — then I want to tell you everything.

What first? How I tried to find you both — after she sat across the table from me in that café and told me we had reached the end, that there was nothing she could do, that she was sorry. How I raged and broke things. How I lost my job. None of that would reflect well. Maybe I'd tell you about that summer when I was a kid and all those bees died in our garden, with their soft black-and-orange fur and their delicate wings. I collected them up and made each one a grave, in a long line by the hedge. I picked flowers and made tiny grave-markers from cocktail sticks and cardboard. I sang a song which I considered to be suitably sombre as I buried them.

Cannon Lane. Squire's Mount. Holford Road. Cannon Place. Navy blue, gold. Olive green, black. Magnolia, chestnut brown. Back to navy blue, royal blue.

Number 33.

It is a double door — dark red.

Two narrow panes of rumpled glass, a pattern of twisted ivy around the edges.

A bell, brass, on the left-hand side of the frame.

Tired grey steps, their undersides a mottled black.

A bay tree blocks half the window, but I can see the edges of red curtains, the movement of people inside. A hand holding a wine glass. The back of a balding head.

I have been looking for this house for nearly thirty years.

She moved. He made her — of course he did. The woman I found living at Marina's didn't know where she was. Even if I'd threatened her — and I thought about it, I was desperate enough — I don't think she could have told me.

I stand on the opposite side of the road and imagine pressing the doorbell, an abrupt sound, like a man shouting in the street.

I have come this far.

I cross over and walk slowly up the steps to the front door.

You are standing by the far wall, a glass of red wine in your right hand, talking to the short, bulky man — your sister's husband. Your forehead is creased up; your left hand rubs at your jaw. I do that too, always have, when I am trying not to cry. You catch my eye, I'm sure of it, and then you are walking across the room, towards the hallway. Towards me. I try to smooth down my hair. I run my tongue across my lips so I am ready to speak. My heart strains at my ribs. I wait.

You do not come to the door.

You saw me, I'm sure of it.

I wait. You will come.

You do not come to the door.

While she's back. You are back from somewhere; you must be staying a few days at least. There's a lot to sort out when someone dies. There's time, I tell myself. I can get a haircut, find some new clothes. There's time. And a funeral — it's hardly appropriate, you have enough to be thinking about. At least I know where you are now.

I wait until I am sure you aren't coming, and then I back down the steps and walk slowly away. At the end of the road I find an empty cigarette packet. I pull the silver foil from the inside, and drop the cardboard box into a bin. I met a man, once, who collected pieces of wire — you'd be surprised how many you can find when you look — and twisted them into people's names, into butterflies, into any kind of shape you could imagine. The other thing he did was make flowers from the foil insides of cigarette packets. It's a fernickety business: tearing tiny squares and folding them into petals. It's precise.

Beautiful. It focuses the mind. He taught me how to do it, and I do it now, sitting on this bench in a space carved out from between the roads, studded with black bollards to keep the cars away. The bench has an armrest halfway along, to stop the likes of me from lying down. I arrange the tiny pieces of foil along the length of it and bend over them so they won't blow away. I will make this for you, I tell myself. Then I'll get myself to a shelter and put some food in my stomach, clean myself up, make a plan.

I climb back up to the dark-red door with its brass doorbell. The room is still full of people, but I can't see you. I place the flower on the low wall to the left of the steps, and turn to leave.

Ten things in my father's shed

1) Green wellies, size eleven. I used to love putting my feet in them when I was a kid — all that space to wriggle around in.
2) A lawnmower with a lead long enough to stretch the length of the garden. I don't think I've ever mown a lawn in my life.
3) Eight identical glass jars filled with screws, nails, washers. They used to hold thick acacia honey. He always had honey on almost-burnt toast for breakfast.
4) A spade — the wooden handle cracked along its length.
5) A torch minus the batteries — the weight all at one end: unbalanced. He bought me a head-torch last Christmas. It's in the rucksack I lost.
6) Sixteen dead bluebottles; two dead spiders.
7) A white saucer with a blue rim, grimy with cigarette ash. We never smoked together, except that one time just before he died.
8) Cobwebs. It bothers me that they're so beautiful when they're new, but turn grey and powdery when you touch them; I hate how they stick to your skin and won't let go.
9) His red mug; a chip, like a white glare, out of the handle.

10) A matchbox filled with black seeds. One year, he marked out a neat rectangle in the garden for me to look after. I wasn't interested. I wish I'd at least pretended to be.

It started after the funeral. Tilly saw the first one. A silver flower. Tiny, perfect, sitting on the wall by the front door, in the dip of mortar between two bricks. It was beautiful, folded out of silver paper, the petals delicate paper diamonds. There was even a leaf attached to the bottom of the stem.

'I knew a girl who could make these,' she said, and held it out to me. I thought maybe Kal — But it's not the kind of thing he'd do.

And then nothing for the next couple of days. I almost forgot about it until Tuesday, when I found a pink flower, real this time, in the same place. It had been pushed into a tube made from a Post-it note and secured with a thin nail. There was a bit of gold ribbon tied around the paper, and a scrap of material. Just rubbish, I told myself, but it looked deliberate. I put the flower in a wine glass filled with water. It fell onto its side, and floated on the surface, its petals darkening. The rest of the stuff I threw in the bin.

Yesterday, it was a piece of electric cable, threaded with bottle tops, a circle of worn glass, and some bits of bark. I was coming back from the supermarket with a pile of cardboard boxes, their sharp brown edges digging into my armpit. When I picked up the cable I found a neat square of orange cardboard, punctured by the end of a biro — a pattern of tiny holes with faint ink marks around their edges. Maybe kids, maybe just kids.

I arranged them on the windowsill. It made me feel a bit better, somehow.

Today, when I open the door to the estate agent, I see a glint of gold foil on the wall. The man blocks the doorway. He's earnest-looking, in his twenties, wears an expensive-looking suit and clutches his car keys, mobile, and a blue hardbacked folder like someone is threatening to steal them. I suspect his tan comes from a bottle.

It is way too early for this, but Cee has gone into over-drive. It's her way of coping, Tilly keeps saying. When I pointed out that Cee wasn't the only one trying to cope, Tilly said I should move into hers for a while and let Cee deal with Dad's house. Tilly lives in a one-bed flat in West Hampstead. It's nice, but it's tiny, and it's hers. I'd mooch about on the sofa with the duvet scrunched up at one end, drinking too much coffee, getting in the way. She'd cook for me every night and look concerned the whole time, Toby would pretend not to be annoyed I was there, and I'd have to start temping again, or buy a plane ticket. When I told Cee it felt a bit disrespectful to get the house valued so soon after Dad had died she flushed red and said I was being unfair, and that maybe I should move into hers — God help me — while she sorted things out. And then she made a song and dance about being a working mother of three, the implication being I was a layabout, and so I caved and said that I'd do it. I'd show the estate agents round, I'd sort out the photos and the viewings and whatever the hell else you have to do to sell a house. She pursed her lips and said maybe I was right, maybe we should wait a few weeks, and I stormed off and called the first three estate agents in the phone book. They all offered to come round within the week.

'Michael,' the estate agent says, rearranging everything into his left hand in order to thrust his right hand towards me. 'You must be Alice. Good to see you. Lovely house.' He steps back and looks up. 'Not the best time for the market, but it's a great location.' His eyes flit to each side as he speaks. His teeth are too neat. I wonder if he snorts coke, or grew up with over-demanding parents, or has been threatened with redundancy. I want to see what's on the wall, but instead I shake his hand and invite him in.

'Right, yes, let's get a good gander, shall we?'

He shoves the pile of post strewn across the doormat to one side with his foot. They are all addressed to Mr M. Tanner. I can't touch them. I look up and out of the front door. The sky is so clogged with clouds it's white. A breeze slips into the hallway and makes me shiver.

I follow Michael around the house. He touches the walls, sniffs around the windows, peers at light fittings and electricity sockets. He turns on the shower, flushes the toilets, stamps his feet against the squeaky floorboards. He makes notes with a blue biro, in tiny cramped handwriting. I imagine Dad, watching us with a wry expression on his face. Don't get so worked up, Alice, he'd be thinking, it's business. Just business.

We end up in the kitchen. I can see the sneer on Michael's lips as he takes in the lino floor, the Seventies cupboards, the collection of flowers and bits of rubbish from the front wall that I've arranged on the windowsill. They're my charms, I want to tell him, but he wouldn't understand.

'So, what do you think, then?' I say.

'Yes. Yes.' He nods and forces a smile.

'You don't think it's a bit dark?'

He laughs, nervously. 'Nothing a lick of paint couldn't sort out.'

'I was always a bit — ' and now I laugh at nothing. 'Scared of it, or something.' I shake my head. 'Coffee. Do you want coffee?'

He drinks his black with three sugars. I put chocolate digestives onto a plate; they look a bit pathetic. He eats four. A cluster of crumbs clings to his cheek. I find it hard to concentrate on what he's saying.

'The thing is, Alice, you have to think about the buyer; you have to imagine yourself in their — '

I stare at his shoes. They taper to a gentle point — soft brown leather with pale-blue laces.

' — so I appreciate it might seem like a lot of effort, Alice — '

His hands duck and dive in time with his words. He has thin fingers, cropped nails, no rings.

I found a picture of my mother yesterday, in an unlabelled box in the attic. I'd been trying to convince myself to start sorting things out, and so had pulled the boxes out from the angle of the roof. The first was full of books: *Fahrenheit 451, Do Androids Dream of Electric Sheep?, Brave New World*. The second contained a full set of crockery — scalloped edges, brown glaze. The third revealed a flash of colour. Turquoise silk. Gold thread. I had heard about these cushions — Tilly and Cee used to put them on their heads and pretend to be princesses; they thought Dad had thrown them away with everything else. There were three cushions in the box, and at the bottom, a framed picture of my mother. A line drawing, in fine black ink. Her head is turned a fraction but she is looking straight at whoever is drawing her, smiling. There's no signature.

I told my sisters about the cushions, but not about the picture. It is propped up on the desk in my room, its back edge leaning on the window. The woman at the funeral was right: I have her small, almost snub nose, her almond-shaped eyes, her rounded chin and thick, curly hair. I wonder if that's why Dad didn't seem to want me around, those months after she died, if that's why I'd catch him looking at me so oddly sometimes.

' — so, what do you think, Alice? You're happy to do that?'

'Sorry?' I offer an apologetic smile.

His face falls, and I imagine him as a boy, endlessly disappointed.

'About the painting? And the carpets?'

'The carpets?'

He narrows his eyes. I wonder if he's going to tell me off. Instead he says with exaggerated patience that I need to think about painting the place white, getting new carpets in. It will make a difference, apparently, to the price.

'White?' I say.

'Magnolia, it's a warmer colour, people feel more comfortable with magnolia. Like you say, Alice, it's a bit dark right now.'

I nod. I imagine throwing a tin of white paint across the living-room walls. It makes my heart race.

'So.' He takes a blank piece of paper from his folder and starts to write. 'Painting, as much as you can, really, but definitely the hall and landing, and the living room. Carpets — hall, landings, living room. Get rid of that red and green, put something neutral in. Furniture.' He bites the end of his pen. His eyes flick up to the ceiling. 'I think let's lose the furniture before we get people around. What do you say, Alice?'

I like the idea that something so big and heavy as Dad's furniture could be lost. He would have wanted us to keep it all. I imagine one of his mahogany wardrobes in Cee's house, with its thin walls, its pine and chrome, or the sofa from his bedroom squeezed into the corner of Tilly's flat.

'We can lose the furniture,' I say.

'Great!' Michael claps his hands. I want to punch him. 'You need to think blank slate, Alice. We want the buyer to walk in here and picture themselves coming home from work, opening a bottle of wine, eating dinner. It's just that at the moment it's — well — ' He waves his hand in a way that dismisses the entire house.

I eat a biscuit and then lick the chocolate from my fingers. He watches me, and when I catch his eye he coughs and looks away. 'And then the last thing is the kitchen,' he says. 'It would be worth your while gutting it.'

I tell him I'll think about it — the painting and the carpets, the furniture and the kitchen, and whether we'd like to go with his agency. He looks scared when I say that, tells me again what a reputable outfit they are, how being small allows them to offer a hands-on, personal service, how their rates are very competitive.

I show him to the door. The gold foil isn't there. It's not on the steps either. It must have blown away, or been taken back. Perhaps, I tell myself, it was never there in the first place and I am going insane. I watch Michael walk down to the street, and imagine Dad's house as five photos and a badly written paragraph in an estate agent's window.

They moved here when Mama was pregnant with me. Cee used to tell me about the old house. It was nicer, she said, brighter and happier than this one. She took me there once and we stood at the end of the drive and stared. Pale London bricks; wide windows with white frames; the front garden thick with flowers. Why did we move? I asked, and she shrugged and said she didn't know. The way she said it made it clear she thought it was my fault.

I get myself to the kitchen. I slot bread into the toaster, and watch the elements glow orange and the heat shimmer upwards. I scrape butter across the darkened bread, and slice it into triangles like Dad does. Like Dad did. As I eat, I walk around the kitchen, opening cupboard doors, scattering crumbs. I put the kettle on. It's an old, plastic, straight-edged thing, with stains that look like tomato sauce up one side. It grumbles and rocks, spews steam. I spoon coffee into the cafetière, and breathe in the rich brown smell. The place looks ransacked already, and I haven't moved a thing.

The smell of coffee reminds me of airports. I'll go, I tell myself. As soon as I've done here, I'll go.

I start off OK. I transfer the contents of three cabinets onto the kitchen table, then stand and consider them. The plates are the same white-and-green plates he's had for as long as I can remember. I pick one up, and then put it down. There's no use getting sentimental over crockery. I spray the shelves with disinfectant and rub them free of dust, grains of rice, spilled flour, sticky rings. Then I stand on a kitchen chair to empty the cupboards higher up. The first glass I drop might have been an accident. It doesn't break, just bounces half-heartedly and rolls towards the sink. The second one is thinner — a wine glass with a slender stem — and it shatters dramatically, shards flinging themselves across the floor. The third does the same; the fourth is less satisfying. I empty the entire cupboard, one glass after the next after the next, until I am surrounded. It is quite beautiful, all those edges reflecting back the light.

Ten places I've spent the night

1) In the porch of St Peter's Church, off the Walworth Road.
2) Myatt's Fields Park, underneath the big fir tree, by the greenhouse.
3) On a foldaway bed in the crypt of St John's Church, on Duncan Terrace, Islington.
4) Roundhay Park, Leeds. It's big enough to lose yourself in — miles of manicured grass.
5) Clapham Common, just south of the bandstand.
6) That hostel near Southwark station — I can't remember the name of the road, but I'd recognise it: narrow and a bit claustrophobic, security mesh on the windows.
7) Hampstead Heath.
8) In one of the arches underneath Waterloo Bridge, where there's a wall covered with a backlit picture of another wall.
9) In a concrete pipe casing on the west side of Greenwich Peninsula, listening to the river.
10) Sitting on the edge of Blackfriars Bridge, trying to decide.

The night after the funeral I slept on the Heath, and when I walked back to the house the flower had gone. I imagined you holding it, and it gave me an idea.

Before I met your mother, I spent a couple of years doing labouring contracts on building sites. We'd spend weeks preparing foundations for new houses. You've got to lay the groundwork; if you don't do it properly it's not worth building at all. That is what I am doing — groundwork. It takes time; it is always worth it.

I spent a few days collecting. If you walk far enough and look hard enough, you can find pretty much anything you'd care for. In a skip — filled with broken door frames, cracked glass and concrete rubble — outside a house in Belsize Park, I found an empty blue plastic bag.

I walked across to Kentish Town and on towards Camden. I found a string of fake white pearls curled up on a shop windowsill and four squares of chocolate, wrapped in gold foil, on the ground.

As I queued for soup in a church on Buck Street, I scoured the line of people for Anton, but didn't see him. It wasn't until I lifted the spoon to my mouth that I realised how hungry I was. It was a pale, oily broth, swimming with diced carrot, potato, and bloated barley. I ate three bowlfuls of it, and five slices of white bread.

My mother didn't like to cook. Every meal would start with an apology — the vegetables were overdone or underdone; she hadn't been able to get the gravy to thicken; the white sauce was her second attempt and still lumpy. My father, instead of laughing it off, would nod seriously, and approach his plate with an air of forensic investigation. I always wanted to tell her it was good, she was good, but somehow I couldn't. Once I'd left home, I took to eating standing up. Sometimes I'd just open a can of beans and eat them straight from the tin, perched on the kitchen counter, or leaning against the living-room door, watching the television.

Your mother liked to eat out. We only did it a couple of times. I can't have been much company — terrorised by rows of cutlery and polished glasses. You eat like there's a war on, she'd say, and I'd try my best to slow down. You're making me nervous, she'd say, and I wouldn't know what to do to make it better.

Outside the church I found some broken glass, the kind of thing I'd expect to pick up from a beach, almost the right shade of green for the letter T.

By the end of the day, the blue plastic bag was a quarter full. After three days it was bursting. Bottle tops. Crisp packets. A pink plastic clothes peg. A bright-green paperclip. A length of electricity cable. Sweet wrappers. An orange toy car. An empty silver photo frame.

I began with your name.

I found a piece of pale-blue paper, one of those squares with a sticky strip at the top, for writing messages, or ideas you've just thought of. The stickiness was long gone. I rolled the paper into a tube and pushed through a thin grey nail, so it would keep its shape. I looped a length of gold ribbon round it — the thin papery ribbon people tie round gifts. I found the perfect flower — magenta pink, its petals shaped like hearts — and slipped it into the blue tube. Then I searched for navy blue; found, eventually, a strip of denim, frayed at the edges. It was criss-crossed by orange stitches, which I carefully removed.

I went back to the house, and walked up the steps towards you. I glanced through the window. The table had disappeared. There was a book lying with its pages splayed on the sofa but I couldn't make out the title. I laid the piece of denim on the side wall. My plan was to stand the paper tube upright, like a vase, but it wouldn't balance and so I laid it flat, the flower pointing towards the door.

* * *

Better for her to have no father, than a father like me. I can't get Anton's words out of my head.

* * *

Alice. Daughter.

* * *

The next day I chose a piece of orange cardboard, not quite the right shade, but good enough. I pushed holes through the surface. When you hold it up to the light it will show you the stars. It's a long word: daughter. The more you think about it, the stranger it seems. Most of the letters I found in bottle tops. Pale blue, a warm orange-red, heavy purple. The broken bottle did for the T; the electric cable, coated with magnolia plastic, for the H. The last two letters are ones you can find in trees. The charcoal grey of E, the chestnut brown of R, written out in bark. I threaded everything onto the cable, and carried it to you.

I stood by the front door and looked through the window. The book had gone. I couldn't see anything except the sofa, a dark-red carpet, the curtains tied back with thick velvet bands, and the start of a bookshelf on the far wall. I arranged my gift on the wall and left.

* * *

Better for her to have no father, than a father like me. I can't think like that. It might, after all, just be a matter of appearance. Imagine it: a woman answers her doorbell. A smartly dressed man stands in front of her. She listens to what he has to say. The world shifts. Imagine it: a woman answers her doorbell. A tramp stands in front of her. He has a broken tooth, a scar across his face, and he smells of the street. She closes the door, locks it for good measure.

* * *

Love is the colour of gold. I have never met you, but what other word is there, except love?

Alice. Daughter. Love.

I made a tiny bowl from the gold chocolate wrapper, pressed the foil between my fingers until it hardened into shape. I made a silver ball from another piece of foil and dropped it into the gold curve. I added a lilac flower, smaller than a baby's fingernail, and a sliver of charcoal-grey slate. I walked to you with a light heart and balanced the word Love on the wall outside your house.

* * *

Today, I carry on collecting, despite the rain; wipe what I find against my shirt and hold the top of the plastic bag tight in my fist so everything stays dry. I picture you as I walk, sitting on the striped sofa with your book, your knees tucked underneath you, a cup of tea on the floor, listening to the rain tap against the window. I hope you are warm and dry; it's not a day to be out.

The first night I ever slept out in London it rained. I'd been staying at a friend's place in Camberwell, sleeping on the sofa in the one-bed flat he shared with his girlfriend. I had come back from Leeds, still raging with grief. The girlfriend — I can't remember her name, only that it was tinged through with lilac — was sympathetic for the first week. She made me cups of tea and listened to my ramblings, but soon enough I could see the frustration prickling off her. One night, I went out for a pint, to give them some space. I drank too much. I remember falling out of the pub, my head swimming, and feeling the cold rain on my face. Halfway to their flat I threw up, down my coat and onto my shoes, and knew I couldn't go back. I crawled underneath a bush in Myatt's Fields, or at least that's where I woke up. Everything ached. My bones shook with the cold. My clothes were wet through. Stones and twigs had pressed their shapes into my skin. I remember telling myself I was lucky to be alive, but thinking it might have been better if I wasn't.

I waited until I knew they'd be at work and then slunk back to the flat, ran a bath almost too hot to get into, washed my clothes and put them straight in the dryer. I even polished my shoes. I sat on their sofa and drank a whole pot of tea. I wrote them a thank-you note, and then packed my bag and left.

That's the thing with taboos. Once you've broken them, they don't seem such a big deal any more.

I prefer grass to benches. I prefer corners to open spaces. I like to sleep with the sound of leaves rather than the sound of cars. Sometimes I'll go back to a place: down by the canal where it dips underground near the Angel; the porch behind St Peter's church, tucked off the

Walworth Road. I slept for a while on Clapham Common, just south of the bandstand. What I liked best was the stars. Most of the time you can't see them in the city. I had never learnt the constellations. I still don't know their names, but I can pick them out. I stayed there long enough to see how the earth turned.

The thing is, you lose the rhythms of the everyday. Sleeping, washing, shaving, eating, going out to work. The whole thing disintegrates faster than you'd think. You will ask me why I live like I do. You have every right to. But there is more than one answer.

* * *

Wednesday, I walk west, across the Heath and down through Golders Hill Park, with its spaced-out trees, neat tarmac paths and manicured grass. I take a route past the aviary and watch an egret fly back and forth above the shit-stained concrete.

My heart feels strong today. A young woman smiles at me as she passes. I see a couple embracing by the war memorial opposite Golders Green Tube station, underneath the word 'courage'; he lifts her off her feet and they sway like a tree buffeted by the wind. I walk along Accommodation Road, past the low wooden building covered with painted tiles, past the white fence with its mural of sunflowers and parrots. Black iron fire-escapes curl up the backs of buildings and air-conditioning units spew out discarded air. Hotel workers and shop assistants pull nicotine into their lungs.

I find a conker from last year, dry wrinkled brown. I find an empty purple cigarette lighter and half a dark-grey watch strap. Outside a grocery store, with vegetables piled up in shallow plastic boxes, I find a postcard of a glacier. There is a fast-flowing river heading downhill — milky blue water, the colour of your name. On the back of the card someone has written *Dear* in blue biro. The next word has been scribbled out, and then the same blue biro has dragged a wavering line diagonally across the white space. In the bottom left-hand corner are printed the words: *Franz Joseph Glacier, New Zealand*.

Let's run away, she'd said, and my heart leapt. Just for the weekend, she said, and I did my best not to show my disappointment. Malcolm was taking the girls up to see his parents; she would make an excuse to stay at home. She wanted to go to the sea. Don't you find the sea a sad place, I asked. She called me a silly, sensitive boy, and then kissed me, hard.

We went to Brighton. Our hotel sat on the road that ran the length of the seafront. The window frames were battered by salt air and the wind slipped in under the sash. She threw herself onto the bed — a narrow double, pale-blue sheets tucked tight against the mattress. I feel sordid, she said, and smiled. Come here, she said.

Later, I asked her if she loved me and she said of course she did, and then laughed as though none of it mattered. She called me her 'escape', her ‘naughty secret’. She got cross if I ‘came over all serious’.

I turn up Hoop Lane, past the shock of the cemetery — fields of tombstones jostling for position — and the red-bricked crematorium. I concentrate on the colours. I concentrate on putting one foot in front of the other.

It takes a long time to walk back to you. I stand in Christchurch Passage, and look at the slice of city wedged between the tall brick buildings which reach up over a silent playground. I am sorry, Alice, daughter, love. I am sorry I couldn’t give your mother enough to make her stay. I am sorry I couldn’t be a father. I am sorry I couldn’t find you. I am sorry for everything.

The letter S is olive green. I found an army-style cap on the Heath, hanging on a fence just by the pools. There’s a stain on the peak that I couldn’t get off with soap and water, but I hope you’ll ignore it. I put the letters inside. A broken silver chain for the O, two chestnut-brown leaves for the Rs, and a maroon wheel from a toy truck for the Y.

The curtains are open and the light is on. I walk up the steps and look through the window. You are lying on the sofa. My heart cracks in my chest. You are asleep, your face a mirror image of your mother’s. I stand on the top step and look at you. *Avoid emotional upset*. I could ring the doorbell. I could wake you up. But you look peaceful there, with a jumper underneath your head, your bare feet resting on the sofa arm. And I am not ready, not yet, not quite. I place the cap on the wall and walk away.

Alice. Daughter. Love. Sorry.

* * *

I have one more word to write, and then I'll be ready; you'll be ready. I will go back to Angel, find Anton. He will understand. And if he can't help, then I'll find someone else. A haircut. A shave. I remember my father getting ready for work, how he would stand in front of the hallway mirror and pull down the sleeves of his jacket; jiggle his legs to make sure his trouser seams were straight; lick his forefinger and draw it across each eyebrow; lift his head to check his nostrils were clear. If he saw me watching, he would smile, and pat me on the head. You've got to make an impression, boy, he'd say. Never forget that.

I sometimes think it was the fact my mother refused to be angry with him that was the hardest thing to deal with.

He lied, I said.

He was frightened, she said.

He fucked up.

He always wanted to do the right thing, and there's no need to use words like that.

He threw everything away.

He was lost. I just wish he'd talked to me.

I wish he hadn't done it.

Well there's no use in thinking that, is there?

In the end it got too much for me: her tiny, crummy, rented flat with its worn-out carpet and ugly storage heaters; her face, her eyes without anger, her mouth soft and ready to smile. I hated her acceptance. I hated the tins of cheap sausages and beans, the extra blankets piled onto the beds, the jar of coppers on the mantelpiece. I didn't stop visiting completely, but the gaps between stretched longer and longer; I admit that. She was there for years before her eye-sight meant she had to go into a home. She sorted the whole thing out herself. I have not been a good son.

I wish I'd had the chance to be a good father, but your mother said it was for the best — for you, for her, for me. She had never meant for this to happen, she said. I was supposed to be her escape, she said. I am, I said, I can be, but she shook her head and smiled, except it was too sad to be a smile. She was more trapped than ever now, because of me, because of you: I can see that now.

'You're young, Daniel. You're not even thirty.' According to her there were men who would kill for things to turn out that way.

Not me, not me, I kept saying. We can sort this out, I kept saying.

'There can't be a *we* any more,' she said.

The only way I can explain it to you is that she became a different person. It was like she'd been glazed, there was this new hard sheen across her and I couldn't get through it.

But I love you.

But I want to be a —

But I love you.

She sat across from me, her eyes blank as pebbles. It was a café we'd never been to before.

The tabletops were beige formica circles with thin metal rims. Either the legs were faulty or the floor uneven because every time one of us lifted our cup or put it back down, or knocked the table with our foot, the whole thing tipped precariously, splashing tea into saucers, rattling ceramic. I folded a napkin and jammed it under one leg, gave the table an exploratory prod. No good. I looked around for something else to fold and she put her hand over mine.

'Stop it, Daniel. It doesn't matter.'

Her fingernails were perfect ovals, painted the same colour as her lips, the same colour as her name. I put my hand over the top of hers. She tried to pull away, but I wouldn't let her. I saw a faint rush of colour in her cheeks and it made me feel fractionally better.

'Let go of me,' she said.

'I love you.'

'I've explained, Daniel. I've tried to explain. I don't have a choice.' She fixed her gaze over my left shoulder as she spoke. She wouldn't even look me in the eye.

'You have me,' I said.

She shook her head. 'This wasn't supposed to happen, Daniel. I'm sorry.'

'But I have rights.' I heard the pathetic tilt of my voice.

She raised her eyebrows — neat, plucked lines, a shade darker than her hair. I released her hand then. She started fidgeting with her handbag, and I knew that she'd leave any minute.

'I'll tell him,' I said. I sounded like a spoilt schoolboy.

'He knows, Daniel, that's the whole point. He knows.'

* * *

Alice. Daughter. Love. Sorry. Father.

I take the string of plastic pearls from the bag. The letter F is white, with a pearly sheen. I use white cotton to tie the other letters in the spaces between the beads. A strip of the glacier postcard for the A. A piece of green string for the T. A triangle of creamy plastic for the H. A tiny rose made out of charcoal-grey silk for the E. The conker for the R.

There is a pale-blue jumper draped across the arm of the sofa today, and a thin-necked glass vase filled with overblown daisies on the windowsill. You are not there. I look at the brass doorbell. Tomorrow, I tell myself. Tomorrow. I leave the plastic pearls on the wall and walk away.

Ten things I'm frightened of

1) This house. I don't know why — not because of Cee's ghosts.
2) Staying here and dying of boredom.
3) Leaving here and not knowing where to go.
4) That maybe I do want to get married and have kids — all those things I swore I'd never do.
5) That I'll never see my father again.
6) That I'm erasing him from the house, and I'll never be able to undo it.
7) That I could turn out like Cee, despite everything.
8) The idea of heaven — existing, or not existing.
9) That I've ruined something that could have been good with Kal.
10) That my mother wasn't a very nice person.

Cee likes a family conference, as long as she gets her own way. She called one yesterday, came over with two bottles of sparkling water and a bag of salad. She made a point of collecting all the ashtrays and lining them up by the kitchen sink. Tilly brought quiche, and carrot cake. I served the water in coffee cups. Cee looked unimpressed but didn't comment. Her proposition was that we should get in house-clearance people.

'We can't let strangers go through his things,' I said.

She sighed and drummed her fingers on the tabletop.

'We discussed this,' I said. 'I'm here. I'll sort out the house.'

Cee raised her eyebrows. 'So you're not planning on getting a job, then?'

'I'm OK for a bit,' I said. 'I'm good at living cheaply.'

'Well, I guess it helps paying no rent.'

'Cee,' Tilly said, her eyes wide.

I glared at Cee and then took a cigarette from the packet on the table, which had somehow escaped her attention, and lit it. She sniffed loudly.

'Can we not do this?' Tilly said. I watched her press each fingertip in turn against her thumbnail, over and over.

'OK,' I said. 'In lieu of paying rent on my dead father's house, I will clear it out, paint it, deal with the estate agents. Earn my keep.' Cee screwed up her face — she hates not being in control, but I'd cornered her.

'That's fair, wouldn't you say?' I leant back and blew smoke up towards the ceiling, to give the impression I was making an effort.

And so I spent this morning clearing out his room. I emptied the bathroom shelves of his shower gel, his soap, his shampoo, his shaving foam and his razors. I took the shoes from the bottom of his wardrobe — hard, polished leather — and dropped them into bags, which I had to double up so they could take the weight. I took his clothes off their hangers and bundled them into black bin liners. On the top shelf of the wardrobe I found a cashmere jumper — a woman's — black, with tiny black beads around the neck. I held it to my nose, but all I could smell was dust.

It's a short step from throwing away soap to buying magnolia paint. I get the train to Cricklewood. B&Q is just behind the station. A burger van belches greased bacon breath across the car park. I walk under the low-slung porch, past lines of hopeful-looking bedding plants and jammed-together trolleys. There's a queue at Customer Services, someone starting to raise their voice. I traipse the aisles. Radiators. Lighting. Varnish. Fillers. Tools. Wood. Tiles. Rugs. Curtain rails. Wooden floor samples. Insulation. Paint.

There is an entire aisle of white paint. Stone

White. Bone White. Cream White. Aged White. Brilliant White. Sail White. Soft Linen. Crushed Cotton. Jasmine White. Moonlit Snow. Winterbloom. Magnolia.

Tilly and Cee love to shop. They love great big department stores, warehouses stuffed with choice. Those kinds of places make me nervous. They make me think I'd rather have nothing at all. I have no idea how much paint I'll need. I take two ten-litre tins, suspecting it won't be enough. I buy a roller and tray, a set of paintbrushes, and three plastic dust sheets.

When I was ten, I got to pick the wallpaper for my room. Maybe we came here, I don't know, but I remember all those plastic-wrapped rolls of paper, like sweets somehow, and my dad, more patient than usual. It's your choice, Alice, take your time. I can hear his voice.

When I get back, there is a string of plastic pearls on the wall. Someone has tied bits of rubbish in between the beads — an old conker, a scrap of cardboard, a piece of plastic, one of those roses you used to see people wear in their hair at weddings, and a length of green string. I take it inside and add it to the rest. Gifts. Evidence. I have other things to think about.

Steve was right, the bay tree makes the living room too dark. I leave the paint tins in the hallway and take a pair of secateurs and a roll of bin bags outside. The branches scratch at my arms, but I take no notice. The smell reminds me of Sunday lunches, but I take no notice of that either. I keep at it until the tree is lower than the windowsill, shove the cuttings into the bags and throw them down by the bins.

Then I start on the living room. It's covered in woodchip, painted a dark red both sides of the dado rail. I unpack the dust sheets; they're like cling film, like the thin layers of glue I used to love peeling from my fingertips at school. I heave the sofa, Dad's old armchair, and the coffee table into the centre of the room, and tuck them under the plastic. They seem smaller once I've done this.

I bring a chair through from the kitchen and climb onto it to unhook the curtains. I used to hide behind these curtains, in the space between them and the bulge of the bay window, wrap them around me until I was cocooned in the dusty smell of velvet. They are a bastard to get down. I have to support the weight of the material while I prise the plastic hooks from the plastic hoops. It seems improbable that a few pieces of plastic could hold such a weight. When I drop the first curtain onto the floor, the sun rushes in. The room looks off balance.

I release the roller and tray from their plastic packaging, then get a knife from the kitchen and lever open one of the paint tins. I remember painting the bedroom at Kal's — how proud we'd been when we'd finished. I hate the thought of some other woman waking up inside those walls.

A slash of new white across old red. I stand back and laugh, then turn to look at where the bay tree used to be. It's lighter in here — different. There's something in my throat. I let it out in a kind of hum. And then, because there is no one to hear me, I start to sing: *Alice, Alice, Alice. Don't run down the rabbit hole, I can't bear to see you go. Stay here with me, Alice, Alice, Alice*. I load the roller with more paint, and carry on.

I have to shuffle the chair around the room so I can reach up to the ceiling. I get paint on the skirting boards, and all the way up my arms. It takes me two hours to do one coat, and when I stand in the centre of the room to survey my work, I see how the red paint blushes through the magnolia and the corners are scarred with brush marks. Would he hate me for it? I want to phone someone — Kal — for reassurance. But I won't.

There are four hours to wait until I can do a second coat, so I make a cup of coffee and smoke three cigarettes. I scrub the paint off my hands, forearms, face, then take the key from the nail by the back door and go out into the garden.

My father's shed is tucked into the far right-hand corner, swamped by ivy. Inside, it smells of soil and cigarettes. Cottony spiders' webs cling to the wooden slats. In the bottom drawer of the old dresser, bleached by water and age, I find a matchbox, which rattles when I pick it up. It's full of seeds. Tiny black bullets. They are different shapes: some perfect circles, some narrowed at the end like arrows, others like tiny orange slices. There are paler ones mixed in — like miniature dried peas. In the drawer above the seeds I find four green plastic seed trays, and half a bag of compost.

* * *

I finish the second coat. You can still see the red. Can you still see the red? The paint fumes stir a headache behind my eyes. I sit on the plastic-covered chair and stare at the wall where the map used to hang. Tilly took it. I can imagine it above the fireplace in her living room — *Westminster 1720*, the river bent like a bony elbow, dotted with boats; the city petering out into fields. It feels as though the room is holding its breath, looking at me reproachfully — like I've done something wrong. It's just a room, in a house that's about to go on the market. It is just a room in a house.

You can still see the red — a shadow of it, if you look hard.

I go back to the shed. A light rain has started. I stand for a minute and listen to the quiet tap against the roof, then collect up the matchbox, one of the seed trays and the compost.

I put everything on the kitchen table and sit down. When I empty out the seeds they rush across the tabletop like they're trying to escape. I pick one up and hold it close to my face. It refuses to tell me anything. I get up and pour myself a glass of wine. My eyes are as heavy as piled-up snow. My skin feels numb and my body aches from the painting. Outside, it's almost dark. The rain is setting in, spitting thin steady lines across the windows.

What I need to do is sit down with my father and ask him —

Why did you say you'd kept nothing of Mama's?

Why wouldn't you talk about her?

Did you blame me, for her driving that day?

When will I stop feeling like this? Like I'm walking along a ledge, about to fall off?

Why do I wake in the night and feel as though this house is angry with me?

He'd have no time for questions like that. He was a man who got on with things without thinking or talking too much about them. He'd have given me his confused look. His who-is-this-girl, why-can't-she-be-more-like-the-other-two look. His Alice, you-need-to-get-your-life-on-track look.

I don't plant the seeds in any kind of order. I tip compost into one of the trays, spilling dry brown onto the tabletop and the kitchen floor, then fill an empty wine bottle with water and dribble it in lines across the soil. The water seeps out onto the table, and I mop it up with kitchen towel. I find a newspaper and lay it underneath the tray. Then I press my fingertip into the surface — one, two, three, four, five, until I stop counting. One seed in each hole, and then a layer of compost over the top. I want to be a tiny black seed. I want to tuck down into rich, wet soil and have nothing to do but grow.

I put the seed tray on the kitchen windowsill, next to the flowers — the silver one and the pink one that's dying in the wine glass, the green hat, the string of pearls, and the bottle tops. I want to pour on more water, but I'm afraid of drowning them. I know nothing about gardening. Kal never let me near his plants after I killed a cactus he swore was indestructible. I stand and stare at the dark soil, as if I'm expecting something to happen. I am worried that nothing will happen. Maybe they are too old. Maybe they are already dead.

Ten things I will say to my daughter

1) I'm sorry.
2) Do you have the thing with the colours and the words? Did I give you that?
3) Did he ever tell you, about me?
4) I tried.
5) I don't know how to say all this.
6) I have looked for you, you have to believe that.
7) I don't hate your mother; I can't.
8) Are you OK? Did everything work out for you?
9) I have dreamt you, for your whole life.
10) I'm sorry.

I scan the register for Anton's name, but it's not there, and when I look around the room I can't see him. There are a couple of people I know — Lady Grace with her purple dress and tattered pram; Bob, who always has a smile, regardless — the others I've never seen before. The crypt smells of tomato sauce and instant coffee.

'Do you know a man called Anton?' I ask the girl at the desk. She has a long, thin nose and dark hair scraped back into a bun. She can't be more than twenty.

She frowns and then shakes her head. 'Anton? I don't think so.' Her voice is from Newcastle. I wonder why she's here.

'He's Polish,' I say. 'About my height, but bigger than me, broader.'

She shakes her head again. 'Maybe you can ask around,' she says and gestures to the room.

I move from table to sofa to kitchen. In the end I find someone who knows him. He introduces himself as Hunter — like the posh wellies, he says, and guffaws.

'Anton? The Polish dude?' he says.

'He has a daughter,' I say.

Hunter slaps his thigh. He's wearing dirty white trousers, a size or two too big. 'That's the man. The girl with the pigtails, right?'

'And a blue dress.'

He looks at me sharply. 'Hang on, you're not a paedo, are you?'

'He's my friend. I wanted to ask his help.'

Hunter nods. 'Dude's got a job.' He leans back in his chair and nods again, like he deserves congratulations. 'Dagenham,' he says. 'Building houses. Told me he's saving up for a ticket home. Got some shit to sort out with the missus.' He shakes his head now. He has long grey hair tied back in a ponytail with a piece of string. 'Why people bother with all this marriage bullshit is beyond me.'

I don't know whether to believe him.

'The man's even got a sofa to sleep on,' Hunter says. 'Temporary, like.'

'How do you know all this?'

Hunter narrows his eyes at me. He has wild-looking eyebrows. 'They say if you want to know something, you come to me.' He lifts his shoulders and drops them. 'You take it or leave it.'

I nod. Either way, Anton is not here.

'Now.' Hunter pulls himself out of his chair and slaps me on the shoulder. 'Let's get ourselves some of this fine establishment's hot food, and you can tell me what kind of help you're looking for.'

Dinner is bean stew with tomatoes and slices of white bread. Hunter eats with fastidious neatness, wiping his lips after each mouthful on a piece of kitchen towel.

'So?' he says. 'Knock me out.'

I tear off a piece of bread and dip it into my bowl, watch it soak red. 'I'm meeting my daughter tomorrow,' I say.

'OK.'

'And, well — ' I feel a sudden swoop of panic. 'I mean, look at me.'

'You're a good-looking fellow, Daniel. And you're not a cider man, I can see that.'

'I'm still a tramp.'

'Ah.' Hunter holds up his fork. 'And this is news to the daughter?'

I crumble bread into my stew.

'How old is she?' Hunter asks.

'Twenty-eight.'

He nods, knowingly. 'And you haven't seen her in a while?'

'It's complicated.'

'It always is. She know who you are?'

'I just want to look respectable. I don't want to screw it up before it's started.'

'Of course.' He looks me over.

'I was going to ask Anton.' I laugh. 'I was going to ask him to cut my hair. See if he had a razor.'

Hunter laughs too.

'It's just, I've not bothered with all that for a while now,' I say. I watch Hunter eat. He has three rows of pale wooden beads around his right wrist. He must think I'm a fool.

'I like you, Daniel,' Hunter says at last, laying his spoon neatly across his bowl. 'I've got a good feeling about you. What do we need? Scissors. Razor. A jacket, and a bit of shoe polish. You finish up. I'll be back.'

I make my way through my stew as Hunter works the room. By the time I'm done he's back with a rusty-looking razor blade, a comb, a pair of kitchen scissors, a battered newspaper and a roll of kitchen towel.

'Boss says we're not to make a mess.' He raises his eyebrows and smiles. 'Now. You trust me?'

'I've never met you before.'

'That's not really the point, is it?' He picks up the scissors. 'I'm thinking short back and sides, agreed?'

I swallow.

'Let's get this show on the road.' He pulls my chair out from the table, spreads sheets of newspaper around me, and wraps a length of kitchen towel around my shoulders. Someone brings over a glass of water from the kitchen. Lady Grace rocks her pram and smiles at me. A couple of guys joke about Hunter being a poofter. He shakes the scissors at them and laughs.

Hunter splashes water onto my hair and starts to pull the comb violently through it. I try to keep my head straight. Gradually, it gets easier.

'My mum used to cut my hair,' I say.

'Don't think I'm going to tuck you up and read you a bed-time story too.' Hunter takes hold of a section of hair and I hear the scissors slice through the strands.

'Have you done this before?' I ask.

'It's only hair.'

'It's just — '

'I know.' He's working quickly now. I can feel his fingers on my head, my neck, folding back my ear. I remember my mother. She always coughed when she was nervous and I had to concentrate not to flinch at the sound. She used thin silver scissors; I remember the feel of the cold blades pressed flat against my skin.

Hunter stops cutting. He walks all the way around me. 'I could do with clippers,' he says. 'But it's OK.'

I reach a hand to my head. I realise, as I run my fingers over my cropped hair, that I never really touch my head, not any more.

'You want to look in the bathroom?' Hunter says. 'Or wait till I've shaved you?'

'I can do the shaving,' I say.

'Sure you can, but I'm on a roll, Daniel. Treat yourself. Imagine you're in one of those posh barber shops.' He slaps his cheeks. 'A shave, a moisturise. Hey, look at this lady.'

I turn and see the girl from the reception desk behind me. She is holding a can of shaving foam and a disposable plastic razor. She smiles at me. 'I hear you have an important meeting tomorrow,' she says.

'That's right.'

Hunter dances towards her and takes the foam and the razor. He is camping it up now, having a ball. 'A bowl,' he shouts, waving a hand. 'I need a bowl of warm water.'

Even with the foam and the fresh razor, my skin's so rough and dry it's not a comfortable procedure. Hunter leads me to the bathroom once he's done. We stand next to each other, and I see he's younger than me, by quite a bit. The grey hair's deceptive.

'Good enough?' he says.

I run my hand across my cheek, around my

chin. 'You did a good job,' I say. 'Thank you.'

'We've taken ten years off you.'

I look at myself and can't help but think of sheep when they've just been shorn — all pale and vulnerable-looking. I catch his eye in the mirror. 'You got kids?' I ask.

He drops my gaze. 'We need to sort you out with a clean jacket,' he says. 'And you should wash. I can guard the door if you want.'

'Why are you helping me?' I ask. 'I mean, I'm grateful, I'm really grateful.'

Hunter dips his head to one side. 'That's enough, isn't it? Gratitude.' He leans on each syllable of the word — dark purple, like a bruise.

I undress slowly. I am not used to being naked and it doesn't feel right. The water takes an age to run hot, but eventually I get a sinkful, and coat my hands with soap. It smells of apples. I wash as quickly as I can, trying to avoid the sight of myself in the mirror. It takes a whole stack of green paper towels to get myself dry, and then I use another stack to scrub at the worst bits of my shirt and trousers before putting them back on. The wet patches of cloth press cold against my skin.

When I emerge from the bathroom, Hunter holds me by both shoulders and sniffs approvingly.

'She'll love you,' he says. 'Now, I have to go see a man about a jacket. I'll be back.'

And he is. The jacket is brown cord.

'To match your trousers,' Hunter says, and grins.

It's a bit tight round my armpits. The lining's

ripped, but you can't see that when it's done up.

'It's nice,' Lady Grace says, and then blushes.

'It's fucking perfect,' Hunter says. He spins me around. 'It's fucking perfect.'

'I don't have any — ' I put my hand into my trouser pocket. I have a couple of quid, in silver and coppers, but I don't want to give it up in case I need to buy you something.

'Daniel.' Hunter slaps me on the back. 'It's a gift, man. I wish you well.'

* * *

When I wake up this morning, Hunter's gone.

'He left this,' the girl on reception says, and hands me an almost empty can of deodorant. It's for women. Pink musk. I go into the bathroom, lift my shirt and spray it under my armpits.

I give my old jacket to the girl as I leave, ask her to pass it on to anyone who wants it, or just bin it.

'Good luck,' she says. 'Break a leg.'

* * *

I walk all the way to you. I feel tired right to the centre of my bones, and that knot's back in my stomach. The picture only just fits into the left-hand jacket pocket. The heart spray — which is nearly empty — and my ball of cotton bulge in the other. I'm sweating and I smell like a woman.

When I get to the house it looks different. It takes me a moment to realise it's the tree.

Someone has chopped it back so it barely reaches the windowsill. Black bin bags with branches and leaves bursting through the plastic sit in a pile on the small square of gravel at the front of the house. The place looks exposed. When I walk up to the door I see the furniture huddled in the centre of the room, covered with plastic. The walls are white, but I can still see the red underneath. You are getting ready to go. You have already left. I lean against the wall to steady myself.

* * *

I picture Hunter wielding a pair of kitchen scissors, try to remember the touch of his hands on my face, pulling the skin taut so he could shave me close. Don't waste this.

But I can't ring the bell. Panic pushes at my throat. I have done my groundwork. I am clean and freshly shaved. There isn't much time left.

I have nothing to offer you.

I picture your mother in my tiny flat in Hornsey. It had a green carpet dotted with tiny pink and white triangles. The window frames were rotten and there were burn marks on the kitchen surfaces. I took her there a month or so before that afternoon in the café. A friend lent me his car and I picked her up from the edge of the Heath.

She didn't want to come in. You're my escape, Daniel, she kept saying, don't make this everyday. But I insisted. I had this idea that she'd come and live with me, that we'd wake up together every morning for the rest of our lives.

We drank tea in the kitchen, made love on the fake leather sofa. She was kind, now I think about it, she didn't sneer. Afterwards, she had me drop her off at her house. I'd never seen it before. It must have been intentional — a way of explaining how things were. At the time I didn't care much, because she had chosen me, because I got the best of her, I thought. But later, I understood what she was saying. Why would she give up that for me and a grotty studio flat in Hornsey? I had nothing to offer her, nothing more than we already had.

* * *

But I have come this far. I put my finger on the doorbell and turn to look through the window. The light shifts and I see a shadow of myself overlaid onto the room, and in that moment I realise I can't. I have come this far and I can't do it. I look back to my finger on the doorbell; the skin's still dirty, despite my efforts. I am an old tramp, I tell myself. I have nothing to offer you. I don't even have any proof. You might give me a pitying look; you might — God forbid — reach into your purse for a couple of quid. What else can I expect?

All this, for nothing. I am sorry. Alice. Daughter. Love. Sorry. Father. I am sorry.

Ten things people say to you when your father dies

1) You were lucky to have him, you must remember that.
2) A clever man, Malcolm — he was quiet, but there was a lot going on up there.
3) It's a big job, when the last one goes — a lot of work, a lot of business to sort out.
4) If you need anything, just give me a call.
5) I remember when my father died. I didn't get out of bed for a week. Lost a stone — would you believe.
6) You'll need to make a decision, about the house.
7) The day he married your mother — I've never seen a man look happier.
8) Do you know he was quite a rugby player, in his youth?
9) It wasn't easy for him, your mum gone and three girls to bring up, but it would take more than that to stop a man like your dad. He was proud of you girls, he really was.
10) Are you the one who's always on the other side of the world?

I'll fly straight to Delhi, or maybe Tokyo — somewhere busy, somewhere I can get lost. I bought a new rucksack this week, red with black straps, new hiking boots and a new waterproof coat. I used the money Dad gave me; I hadn't touched it up until now.

This house, at least, will be glad to see me go. I am stripping it back to its shell, to its walls and floors and windows. I am painting it a colour that claims to be the colour of magnolia petals, but looks more like skimmed milk. Next week, the red carpet that walks a line up the stairs, crosses the landing, and bleeds into Dad's study, will be switched for a beige one. The attic floor will change from green to an off-white, flecked with coffee brown. Tomorrow, a man called Shaun and his assistant are coming to start on the kitchen. They will rip out the old cabinets and junk the cooker. They will fill up the space with white IKEA cupboards with long chrome handles, a hob embedded into a stone-coloured surface, an oven at waist height.

Cee hates that she's not in charge. It oozes off her every time she's here. She screws up her eyes and looks for mistakes, she sucks her teeth and folds her arms when I tell her what I'm planning to do next. But she can't deny it looks better; brighter.

Yesterday was the first time I noticed it

sounded different. I walked through the hallway and my footsteps echoed — hollow, like they were coming from a long way away.

Michael is now officially our estate agent. He is 'terribly excited'. There are photos of the living room with its new pale walls, ready to go up on their website. Sometimes I have to stop halfway through a job, press my hand against my chest and close my eyes, so I'm not sick.

It turns out Dad didn't throw away everything to do with Mama. I've found quite a haul: a turquoise evening dress with matching shoes; a postcard of Brighton pier — 'I thought I'd come for the day but it's not the same without you, J.' written in confident black letters; a piece of paper ripped from an envelope with the same handwriting — 'I promise. J.'; three books of poetry — Keats, Shelley, Shakespeare — with her name written on the title page; the necklace with the diamond teardrop she was wearing in the photo I lost; and then the jumper, the cushions, and the picture. Except for the picture, I put everything into a box and presented it to Tilly and Cee. The pair of them went white. Tilly cried, Cee just chewed at her lips.

'I can't believe he didn't tell us,' Tilly said.

Cee fingered the necklace in its faded brown velvet box. 'I suppose we just split it between us,' she said.

'Do you remember that time she tried to make you a birthday cake, Cee?' Tilly said. 'She bought that horrible fondant icing and tried to build you a fairy castle.' Tilly was smiling, but Cee looked unimpressed. 'And then the turrets collapsed halfway through your party.' Tilly laughed. 'God, she was in a state about it.'

I can picture it, Mama all red-faced and flustered, Cee tight-lipped and disappointed.

'She had dress sense though,' Cee said at last, fingering the turquoise silk that spilled from the box. 'She always looked immaculate.'

Tilly nodded. I excused myself and went to the bathroom, sat on the edge of the bath until I figured they'd have finished their reminiscing.

I got the dress. I'm the only one small enough to fit into it. I tried it on once they'd gone, stood in my father's bedroom in front of the wardrobe mirror, with my hair pinned up away from my neck. It's beautiful, lined silk with a low neckline, long sleeves and a cinched waist. Even the shoes fit, give or take. I felt like a ghost.

⋆ ⋆ ⋆

'I know we're not quite ready,' Michael had said on the phone. 'But let's get the sign up, generate a bit of interest, and then we can start viewings in a couple of weeks. There's nothing wrong with whetting people's appetites.'

I asked him about the viewings, what I'd be expected to do. 'Just be there, answer questions,' he said. 'Or don't be there at all if you don't want. Some people find it hard, like they're a stranger in their own home. And often viewers prefer it when the owner's not there.'

'It's not my home,' I said.

⋆ ⋆ ⋆

It's raining again. I lean my forearms on the back of the sofa and look out of the window. The gifts have stopped. The last one — the pearls — was a week ago. Since then, nothing. Kids, just kids, I tell myself; they didn't mean anything. Even so, I find myself opening the front door to look, just in case.

The people with the sign arrive in a white van. I watch them: a youngish man and a slightly older woman. The man holds the plastic part of the sign above his head to keep dry, while the woman fixes the long wooden pole into the ground. They don't ring the bell. They don't look up at me looking down at them.

Someone else will live here. Someone else will put the keys that now sit in my jacket pocket, or Tilly's handbag, or Cee's key cabinet with a picture of a shepherd on the front, onto their own keyring, into their own bag. They will fit them into the lock and let themselves in. They'll shout, honey, I'm home, and someone else will laugh, put down their cup of tea or their paper, and come into the hallway. They will look at the magnolia walls and say, don't you think we should add a bit of colour? They will buy tester pots of green and blue, and paint rough squares on the wall — bicker about the best shade, ask their friends' opinions.

At two o'clock, the doorbell rings. I am not expecting anyone. I'm in Cee's old room. There's nothing much left of her in it — a couple of shells at the back of the top shelf, a rolled-up poster of a man holding a baby. She must have cleared it all out years ago, piled everything into boxes and put them in her loft, or thrown them away — the ballerina books; Barbie dressed in her striped sailor's T-shirt and red mac; the wooden doll's house with the wooden furniture and the tiny wooden fruit bowl which I wanted enough to steal, and then to fight Tilly when she made me give it back. The bell is loud, even this high up in the house. It echoes insistently off the hall tiles. I sit for a moment, balanced on my heels. Kal. His name sneaks into my mind before I can stop it, and I stand and half run down the stairs. I can tell by the shapes behind the glass it isn't him, but even so, I feel a heart-smash of disappointment when I open the door to a couple in their fifties.

'We're very sorry to disturb you.' The man steps towards me. He's bald, his scalp wet from the rain. The woman stays on the step, her eyes sharp with excitement. She holds an umbrella, half closed, its jagged black angles like broken birds' wings. 'It's just that we saw the sign,' the man continues. 'We've been trying to find a property in this area for — ' He looks at the woman and they both let out little breathy laughs. He turns back to me. 'We can't even tell you how long we've been looking. I know we should call the agency, but we were walking past, we were here, and we wondered if you wouldn't mind us having a look around.'

'Just a quick peek,' the woman says, her mouth stretched into a smile. 'We'd be awfully grateful.'

'You're the owner?' the man says. I look down. My jeans are smudged with dust. I'm wearing a cheap green vest top I bought last week.

'It's my — It was my father's.'

He readjusts his features to display sympathy. They are both waiting for me to say something else. I watch the rain falling behind them, listen to it rushing through the gutters. I could call Michael. He'd tell me to pass them over. He'd get me off the hook, but I can't bear the thought of his sugary voice.

'Why don't you come in?' I say.

They both beam at me and advance over the threshold before I can tell them I've changed my mind. The woman holds the umbrella in front of her. It drips onto the hall floor.

'Don't worry about it,' I say. 'Just stick it in the corner.'

The man is twisting his head from side to side, up towards the ceiling, the stairs. He thinks the hallway has always been magnolia. I want to tell him there used to be a painting of my sisters right there, above the little table; I used to stand in front of it, screw up my eyes so the colours blurred, and pretend that I was in it too.

'We're not quite ready for viewings,' I say. 'We're having new carpets put in, and a new kitchen. It should be done by the end of next week.' I am standing between them and the living-room door.

'Not to worry,' he says. 'We're just grateful to have a look.'

He has a neat goatee. He tugs it between his thumb and forefinger and starts asking me questions. How many bedrooms? Bathrooms? Are the fireplaces functional? Have we decided on the asking price? What about the garden? Is it a quiet neighbourhood? What council-tax band does it fall in? He stands in the centre of each room and turns slowly around, nodding, calculating. She touches the walls, the doors, walks to the windows and looks out.

I manage not to panic until we get to Dad's room. I watch them walk around it. The woman is almost purring. It's the master bedroom, of course. They will bring a wide metal-framed bed. She will have a dressing table with three mirrors angled so she can catch her profile. I can see her, sitting on a low cushioned stool, rubbing night cream into her skin. He's in bed, a velvet-trimmed lamp pooling light onto his book.

'Is it for a family?' I ask.

The woman tugs at the hem of her coat. 'No, just the two of us.' She gives me a watery smile.

I nod. 'It's just — I'm not sure it's a house for kids.'

They exchange glances.

'I never felt that comfortable here.'

'It's a beautiful house,' the woman says. She is fingering the edge of the wardrobe.

'If we could have a quick look at the top floor?' he says. 'Literally, a couple of minutes, just so we get the whole picture.'

'You've been so kind,' the woman says. She is wearing a belted cream coat and brown leather boots. She's in good shape.

They follow me up the stairs. I open the door to my old room. I don't want them in here.

'It's important, you're right,' the woman says.

'I'm sorry?'

'To find a house you feel comfortable in. A

real home. I can't think why you didn't like it here.' She gestures towards the desk, my mother's picture, the view of the back garden, the pine shelves with the smattering of things I haven't thrown away yet — kids' books, pebbles, an old teddy bear. 'It's perfect,' she says.

I remember the first time Dad left me at home on my own for an evening. I was fourteen, maybe fifteen, and the idea of being home alone was a luxurious one. I could do anything, eat anything, watch anything on TV. Yet once he'd left, smelling of aftershave and soap, and I'd made hot chocolate with three spoons of sugar and settled myself in the battered leather armchair in the living room that was usually his domain, I heard the deafening silence of the house and started to feel unsure. I turned on the television and upped the volume, but the silence still strained against me. I felt my mouth start to dry out, my heart skip faster. I told myself I was being stupid. It didn't help. I tried asking myself what it was I was frightened of. Burglars, rapists, ghosts, fire, all the lights going out, flooding — or maybe something else, something about the bricks and the plaster and the door frames and the windows, the fireplace with its polished cream tiles and their sinewy green leaves, the hulk of the red-striped sofa and the dark, heavy bookcases. I flicked through television channels but couldn't settle on a programme. I needed the toilet, but there was no way I was leaving that room. By the time Dad got home, my bladder felt like a bag of sharp stones. He held a hand to my forehead and asked if I was OK. I brushed him off, and walked as slowly as I could up the stairs to the bathroom.

Bathroom. Cee's room. Tilly's room. Attic. I run my fingers along the wall all the way back down to the front door. The couple spend an age thanking me. She retrieves her umbrella and I smile and nod, and at last they leave. I close the front door behind them and lean my head against the crumpled glass. I need some fresh air. A brisk walk. Nothing like it, Dad would say — blow the cobwebs away.

The streets are quiet. The air smells of wet tarmac. Cars hiss their way past. On the Heath, there are a few resigned-looking dog walkers. A couple giggles beneath the broad arms of a tree. The wind tugs at my umbrella. I collapse it, and feel the rain lick at my skin.

If my father was here, he would shake his head and tell me to stop being an idiot. Stop fretting about the house, he'd say, it's just a house. And put your umbrella up, or you'll catch a cold. I know you, he'd say, you'll feel good for thirty seconds and then wet and cold for the rest of the day and you'll moan about it. I have tried not thinking about him at all, but I can't seem to manage it.

I leave the umbrella on a bench down by the ponds — someone will be grateful for it. At the top of Parliament Hill I stop and look at the misted-up view of London; the buildings have turned into ghosts of themselves.

If Kal was here he would look at me and laugh. You look like a drowned rat, he'd say, and put his arm around my shoulders, pulling me towards him. I walk down the hill, away from the view. Underneath the trees, the ground is a rich, muddy brown. The water drops in irregular heartbeats.

I take my phone out of my bag — don't — find Kal's number and press call. He answers after one ring.

'Alice?' He sounds wary.

'Are you busy?'

'No, no. Give me a minute.' I hear a shuffling. Paper? Clothes? I imagine him ducking out of a room. 'Alice, how are you? I didn't think you'd — '

'I wanted it to be you,' I say.

'What?'

'The things. The gifts. On the doorstep.'

'Alice, are you all right?'

'I knew they weren't from you,' I say. 'But I wanted them to be. I wanted it to be you.' My voice catches and I stop and swallow hard.

'Alice, are you OK?'

I hold the phone against my ear and stare at the grassy slope in front of me. 'I'm on the Heath.'

'It's hardly the weather for it.'

'Someone came to look round the house today.'

'That's tough.'

'I wish — ' I press my foot into a patch of mud. It curls up around the soles of my trainers.

'Yes?'

'Nothing. You're with someone else, aren't you?'

'Alice, I don't — '

'Do your parents approve this time?'

'You aren't being fair.'

I hate him. I hate her. I hate the way my heart feels squeezed into too small a space. 'Look, I'm going to — ' I can't hang up.

'Do you want to meet? Talk?'

We will sit across a table, in a pub or a café. He won't touch me.

'Alice?'

I want to tell him he's a bastard, but that's hardly fair. I want to tell him it felt like the only option left to me — to finish it; leave.

'We're getting the kitchen redone,' I say. 'Dad's kitchen. It feels wrong.'

'Why don't we go to Dino's?'

We used to go there when we couldn't be bothered to cook. Checked tablecloths. Stone-effect walls. The air thick with garlic.

'I can do tomorrow. Seven?' he says.

He will order pizza Fiorentina. I will have spaghetti vongole. We'll share a green salad and a portion of garlic bread. There will be a red candle in a wine bottle already caked with wax. They'll be playing schmaltzy Italian music.

'It doesn't feel like we're done, Alice.'

'We've been here already.'

'I know we have, but you phoned me, Alice.'

'Don't keep saying Alice, you sound like the fucking estate agent.'

I hear him take a breath. 'Fine. I have stuff to do. Good luck with your travelling, or whatever you're up to next.'

'Seven's good.' I tip my head back so I can feel the rain on my cheeks. He says nothing, but stays on the line. 'Will I see you there?' I ask.

'Fine.' He's sulking.

'Fine,' I say. I wait for him to hang up.

★ ★ ★

When I get back to the house, there is nothing on the wall. There's been nothing there for a week. Whoever it was has stopped. I miss them, which is ridiculous.

Inside, two more letters lie in the hallway. I leave them where they are, head upstairs and run myself a bath. The hot water warms my bones, turns my limbs woozy and tired. When I'm done, I wrap myself in the dressing gown that used to be my father's — I haven't thrown everything away either — and make myself a hot chocolate, in the red mug with the chip out of the handle. The kitchen feels quiet and sad, like it knows its days are numbered. I take my drink all the way up to the attic. I lie on the floor and stare at the skylight, waiting for the stars to come out.

Ten things I thought I'd do with my life

1) Run an art gallery.
2) Be a painter.
3) Get married.
4) Have children.
5) I've always wanted to go to the Arctic, just for the emptiness of it.
6) Be a better son.
7) When I was a kid, I wanted to be an astronaut. I was fourteen when I saw those pictures from the surface of the moon.
8) I wanted to be an architect for a while.
9) Change someone else's life for the better.
10) Avoid turning out like my father.

I think your mother loved me because I could up sticks and go, any time I wanted to — or at least that's how she saw it. You're so young, you're so free, she'd say. Make the most of it, she'd say, and I'd nod and say of course I will, of course I will. I wonder what she'd think of me now. Still free, in her book, but older, with a buggered heart, too tired and too frightened to ring your doorbell.

But I am not one to give up. I don't want you to think I'm a quitter. I don't want you to think I'm a coward. I've been thinking — walking and thinking, and I have come up with a plan.

I am making a place for you. Nothing too fancy. I'll be done in a week. It means I'm back collecting, and that helps calm me a little, keeps my heart from playing up. I know which colours I need. I know what I want to say.

Yesterday I walked north, where the streets are wide and quiet and edged with polished cars. I passed a house with silver balloons in the window. I could see right through to the garden, where children ran about. A group of adults clustered around a long pinewood table, with mugs of tea in their hands. I thought about Anton and his letter. I imagined his daughter tracing the inked flowers with her finger and wishing he had given her an address to reply to. I imagined him in Dagenham, spreading cement onto bricks, building houses and thinking of her.

On a low garden wall I found a pale-blue ring with a white daisy suspended, somehow, in the plastic.

Underneath a bench, at the edge of a triangle of grass, I found a seedpod with a silvery sheen. It reminded me of the mother-of-pearl shells my parents had hanging in the porch. When the wind blew hard they would rattle against the glass.

On a windowsill, next to a pink flowering fuchsia in a thick terracotta pot, I found a navy-blue triangle of plastic.

In the space where a parking meter met the not-quite-circular hole cut for it in the pavement slab, I found a button covered with stained white silk.

By a car tyre, I found a gold star with dog-eared points — one of those stickers teachers lick and attach to children's work, to say well done.

I reached the main road, and everything changed — a roar of hurtling traffic, a hodgepodge of buildings with little to say to each other. The sixth woman I approached to ask for change said, 'I'll buy you a cup of tea,' which meant she thought I was someone who scored crack to take away the emptiness of it all. I followed her into a café with brash green menus, and she bought me tea, watched as I emptied in four packets of sugar. She was too thin, her hair pulled into a tight ponytail. She wore a red coat with big plastic buttons. Earrings shaped like cherries hung as low as the coat's collar. I would have liked to sit with her and drink my tea, but the cup was a cardboard one and she was already holding the door open.

On my way back to the Heath I saw a fire engine pumping great jets of water into a burning office block. The flames kept licking at the bricks, and the air smelt of smouldering metal and burnt plastic. A couple of years ago I slept for a while in a burnt-out warehouse, in Wapping. There were blackened rectangles where windows should have been and the rooms were velvet grey, everything covered in a layer of soft ash. It seeped into my skin until my hands looked like a bird's-eye view of a delta, a map of inky rivers. Living there made me cough like an old man, but it was dry and I stayed until the bulldozers came.

* * *

The place I've chosen isn't far from your house — just a short walk across the Heath. It's five or six feet long, maybe a couple wide, hidden in amongst the rhododendrons. Not exactly a palace, but it's quiet and dry. A man could live here. I clear the ground of leaves and sticks, smooth it flat with the palms of my hands. I empty the plastic bag: a spill of colour. I take the ball of cotton from my pocket and then I pick out the colours, one by one, and tie them to the branches. Alice. Daughter. Love. Sorry. Father. Each piece hangs into the centre of the space, rocking gently from side to side as if there's a breeze. I take a twist of gold foil, loop thread around its centre and tie it up. I choose a scrap of magenta-pink cardboard and use a nail to make a small hole, thread another piece of cotton through that. I feel better now I've started.

Years ago, before my father died, I rented a tiny room in a dirty house. It was like a cell, with cold white walls and a narrow bed. I started to collect colours — bits and pieces I found on the streets, or in the storeroom of the supermarket I was working in at the time. I glued them straight onto the walls. It was against every rule there was, but then the landlord never checked, and I left without a forwarding address. I remember a girl who liked it, who trailed her fingers across its textures. The next morning I woke up and she'd gone, but later that day a hand pushed an envelope under my door and inside was a magpie's feather, a hundred shades of black; a red pencil stub; and a ridged cockle shell, like the ones you pick up as a kid, trailing after your parents along an endless stretch of sand. I glued them carefully in place, imagined her searching them out the next time I saw her, except she never came back.

* * *

I have given myself a week. My hair is starting to grow a little. I don't have a mirror, but I'm hoping I've lost the shorn look. My cheeks, though, are covered in stubble. I don't have a razor and I can't go back to the shelter: not that one, at least. I could tell them you weren't in, that you'd gone away for a while, but I've never been much good at lying.

When I have finished this place it will be beautiful — like nothing you've ever seen. I can picture you, cross-legged in the centre, looking up at the colours, nodding and smiling, because at last you understand.

Ten places I've had sex

1) A hotel room in Irkutsk, with a dirty carpet and a shower that dripped all night.
2) A youth hostel in Singapore. We wedged our rucksacks under the door handle.
3) Cartegena, Columbia. He was younger than me.
4) Boston, Massachusetts. I suspect he was married.
5) A tent by Lake Windermere — I was seventeen. Afterwards we lay and listened to the rain.
6) That time in Greece, on the balcony.
7) On the roof of Kal's flat, overlooking London. I miss the way he'd stroke my hair.
8) In the toilet of a bar in Chiswick, but I'd rather not remember.
9) In the back of a taxi, somewhere in Newcastle. I had drunk way too much.
10) Never here, now I think about it, never in this house.

Cee arrives in her gym kit — silver running shoes, a tan-coloured tracksuit blotched with rain. We pile the bags of Dad's stuff into her car. They look like some kind of overgrown fungi clinging to the seats. The traffic heaves and jerks, fringed with people crouched under umbrellas, sheltering in doorways. The car smells of sweet plastic.

Seven o'clock at Dino's. I could stand him up.

'Do you like being a mother?' I ask Cee as she turns onto the Holloway Road. She drives with frustrating care.

She angles her head to one side, like she's stretching a muscle in her neck. 'Yes. I love it,' she says, straightening herself up again.

I look across at her. She's wearing pale shimmery eye-shadow and brown mascara.

'I don't think you've ever really felt love, until you've had a child,' she says. 'Is it this turn?'

'The next one, just by the pub.' I point.

'When Martin was born it was — ' A flush rises in her cheeks. 'I'd have killed for him, or thrown myself in front of a truck. I still would, for any of them.'

'Just here.' We sit and listen to the tick of the indicator. 'Doesn't it feel a bit wrong?' I say.

'I suppose we're programmed that way. It makes sense if you think about it.' We turn into a side street, between tottering new blocks of flats with coloured balconies like children's toys.

'I mean taking his stuff to the dump.'

'It's a recycling centre. What else would we do with it?'

We follow the signs: left at the roundabout, up a concrete ramp, under a yellow-and-black height restriction. What I want is the kind of rubbish dump you see on television — in Hollywood films, or documentaries about the Third World. I want a pile of rubbish that stretches as far as I can see. I want a cloud-wracked sky and solitary figures stooping to pick out anything of worth. I want wheeling, cawing birds, and the threat of rats. I want it to stink. Instead, I get out of the car into the dim light of a concreted space, like a floor of a multi-storey car park. Six huge skips stand in a line. Metal steps lead to a platform at the side of each. At the far end are smaller bins — for printer cartridges, computers, clothes, shoes. A man wearing a luminous yellow jacket surveys us from a small green Portakabin. Cee and I watch a couple in their early twenties ferry flattened cardboard boxes. The man lobs the cardboard from the concrete floor. The woman runs up and down the steps, holds her arms above the skip and lets go. Four Jamaican men pull a sofa — big enough for all of them — out of a hire van. Their voices rise and dip in the dead space. They loved that sofa. It hurts to see it go, but it's time to move on.

Cee opens the boot and we empty it in silence. There are bags of paper, white corners straining at the black plastic: bills long since paid, receipts for things long since broken, ancient copies of medical journals. Cee and Tilly insisted on sorting out Dad's study, and kept the door closed while they were working. I protested, of course. I can be as stubborn as Cee when I want to be, but the sight of Tilly, all red-faced, with tears in her eyes, stopped me from pushing it. I shrugged and made out I didn't care, but when they'd left, each carrying a plastic bag of paper folders, I opened the door and went inside.

His study has the same dark-red carpet as the one that draws a line up the stairs and then spreads to reach the walls of the landing. There is a corner desk by the curtainless window, with a gold desk light — its hood curved and ridged like a shell. The walls are covered in woodchip, painted off-white years ago. There's a print of a landscape to the left of the desk: something ugly and Dutch, the trees squat and grey, the sky stuffed full of clouds. The room holds the faint smell of his cigarette smoke. I could count the number of times I have been in there on one hand.

I pulled open the filing cabinet drawers one by one. I had tried to do this when I was thirteen or fourteen, and found them locked. Locked doors meant secrets. I had searched and searched for a key, a kind of fury rising through me, but found nothing. This time the drawers opened with a metallic grumble. The top one was still filled with thin green folders, my father's narrow black handwriting on tiny plastic-covered labels. Girls' School Reports. Girls' Music Certificates. Girls' Newspaper Pieces. I pulled out a yellowed newspaper cutting. *Hampstead Girl Runs to Victory* — a picture of Cee in her sports kit, holding up a medal on a thick striped ribbon. I dropped it back into place, and picked out a school report: 'It is difficult to know if Alice abandons things — projects, trains of thought, essays — because she is bored, or because she lacks the confidence to see things through to their conclusion.' Mrs Ward. She smelt of Sugar Puffs. Her front teeth were crooked. I put the report back and slammed the drawer shut. The next drawer was also full of green folders, but they were empty and the labels had been removed from their plastic holders.

* * *

The shoe bank has a metal drawer, like a bank deposit box. The names of the charities that will benefit are painted down one side in cheery green letters. I'm sorry, I'm sorry, I say inside my head, as I listen to the bags of his shoes drop on top of bags of other people's shoes. He used to cover the kitchen table with newspaper on Sunday afternoon and line up his shoes. He'd put the polish on with a soft yellow duster, scrub and shine with a fat wooden-handled brush. Can you see your face in them, Alice? he'd ask. I'd hold them up to my nose and sniff the sharp, chemical scent. Not yet, a bit more, I'd say. A hard taskmaster, he'd call me. Whenever he left the house, even after he'd retired, he'd wear ironed trousers and shoes that shone. I don't think he ever owned a pair of trainers. The lot of them will end up, laces tied together, in charity shops that smell of old carpets, their chipboard shelves crammed with single plates, saucerless cups, ugly cut-glass vases, porcelain animals, dejected-looking dolls.

* * *

'Do you think Dad felt like that?' I ask Cee on the way back. She frowns.

'Like you said about Martin. Do you think he'd have — you know, died for us?'

A kid on a bike sways in and out of the traffic. He wears a grey tracksuit, holds a mobile phone to his ear. I used to feel like that — invincible.

'I'm sure he did,' Cee says. 'He wasn't the kind of person to show it. But it doesn't mean — '

'I always felt he wished they'd stuck with just the two of you.'

'Oh, Alice.' There's something in her tone of voice that makes my stomach dip. I look at her. She knows I'm looking, but she stares straight ahead.

'What does that mean?' I say.

Her jaw tenses. 'That's an awful thing to think. He loved you.'

'You told me they fought when I was born.'

'I did not. When on earth did I say that?'

I shrug. 'Years ago. I must have been six, seven maybe.'

'Well, that hardly counts, does it?'

'I don't see why not.'

'Kids say stuff. We were just kids.'

'You'd have been fifteen, and anyway, Tilly says kids see more than she does, sometimes.'

'Well, I don't think — Look, they fought, it wasn't anything out of the ordinary. I was probably just being spiteful.'

We drive in silence. When we're parked outside the house, Cee switches off the engine and turns to me. 'I'm sorry,' she says. Which is such a remarkable thing for her to say that I can't think of a response.

* * *

We drink tea, sitting at the kitchen table, dunk in ginger biscuits until our fingers meet the surface and then eat them quick, before they collapse. It is hours until seven o'clock, but I want her to go. I need to concentrate.

'Tilly's asked us over tonight,' Cee says. 'She wants to cook for us. And Toby.' She curls her lip at Toby's name.

'I'm going out.' To my dismay, I blush.

Cee narrows her eyes. 'Who with?'

'How are Tilly and Toby?' I say.

'Why she throws her life away on a man she can never have — ' Cee starts, and then meets my eye. Instead of shutting up, she draws back her shoulders and says, 'It's self-destructive, that kind of behaviour. It's like she doesn't really want all the things she says she wants.'

'She loves him,' I say.

Cee shakes her head. 'I sometimes wonder if you two grew up in a different family to me.'

I take another biscuit and snap it in half.

Maybe Kal's changed his mind. Maybe he's decided I am worth it.

'So you're not coming?' Cee says.

'I can't.'

'Alice, have you decided — '

I fold my arms, and lift my eyebrows.

'I mean, once the house is — ' She almost shudders. She is not completely without feeling. 'You'll go back to China?'

'Mongolia.'

'Will you?'

I shrug. She looks at me and I glare back. 'Maybe I'll settle down and get a job,' I say.

Cee laughs and I want to punch her. She picks up our teacups and takes them to the sink.

'What's all this, Alice?' she asks.

Shit.

'I never knew you were green-fingered.'

She is leaning over the sink towards the seed tray that sits on the windowsill, on the newspaper that's turned yellow and dry, next to the gifts. I can't get there fast enough. My heart flips up near my mouth. There in the dark chocolate rectangle of soil are five, no, seven, eight tiny green shoots. They are the height of a baby's fingernail. Each one splits into two green lines. They are growing. I shoulder her away and touch one of the seedlings with my little finger.

Hello. Welcome.

Cee is too close. I can hear her breathing.

'What are they, then?' she asks.

'I don't know.' My voice cracks. I swallow hard. 'They're all different,' I say. 'I found them in the shed.'

I don't know which seeds have grown and which haven't, and I realise that, short of digging them up, I never will know. If I dig them up now I'll kill them. Once they're bigger, once they can survive being uprooted and examined, the seed cases will be long gone.

'It was a stupid thing to do,' I say. 'I've spent all week in this bloody house.'

'You've done a great job, Alice.'

'I feel like I'm erasing him.'

She puts her hand on my shoulder and rubs — like I'm a kid. I find it comforting, despite myself.

* * *

I wear my mother's dress and shoes, paint my eyelids turquoise to match. I put my hair up, pull down a lock on each side to soften my face. We're only going to Dino's. It's too much. But then, if he has changed his mind, I would like to be dressed for the occasion.

The shoes have heels. She must have liked it too — feeling taller than she really was. I arrive ten minutes early, even though I was trying to be late. I take one of the small, square tables along the stone-effect wall, and order a gin and tonic. By the time Kal arrives, I've drunk most of it. The gin makes me feel lighter, more fragile.

I stand. He leans across the table and kisses me on each cheek. I feel the soft scratch of his beard, and breathe in the smell of his aftershave.

'Looks like I need to catch up,' he says, gesturing to my glass. He calls the waiter over and orders a bottle of red wine.

I watch him drape his jacket over the back of his chair, take his mobile and wallet out of his pocket and arrange them on the tabletop. I finish my drink in one mouthful. He settles down and looks at me. I am not going to speak first.

'You look beautiful,' he says.

I rub at my jaw and drop my gaze. I should have worn jeans. He is wearing jeans, and a blue checked shirt I bought for him years ago, though I suspect he didn't think about that when he put it on.

'How are you?' he says.

I shrug.

'You're sorting out the house?'

I nod.

'That must be hard.' His mobile buzzes on the table, a gagged sound. He glances towards it but doesn't pick it up.

'It's not like I ever felt that much at home there,' I say.

'Even so.'

'And your flat? You're still there?'

He gives me a look, and I wonder for a moment if he's seen me, sitting in the gardens, watching. I've only been a few times, four at the most. Maybe five. But he smiles and says, 'Yes. Same as ever. Julie's dog died last month, so things are a bit more peaceful.' Julie lives next door. Her dog used to howl every time she went out.

'Poor Julie,' I say.

'Clouds and silver linings.'

I shouldn't have come.

The waiter brings the wine over and Kal jokes with him about vineyards and soil types. He swills the wine around his glass, sips and nods approvingly. The waiter fills my glass.

'You're ready to order?' he says.

As I predicted: pizza Fiorentina, spaghetti vongole, salad, garlic bread.

I watch Kal take a drink. It always angered me. Booze, fine; sex before marriage, fine; bacon for breakfast, fine — as long as no one who mattered found out.

'So tell me everything,' he says.

I love you. I hate you. I miss you. I don't know who I am any more. 'I went to Russia, then across to Mongolia,' I say.

He purses his lips and nods. 'How was the train?' We had talked about doing it together.

'Good. Long.' I lift my glass to my mouth and drink too quickly. I am not concentrating. Wine spills down my face and onto the dress. I dab at it with my napkin. Kal hands me the salt and I tip it onto the silk, rub it in. I press a napkin against my mouth and concentrate on not crying.

'Dry-cleaners,' Kal says, nodding. 'They'll sort it out.'

'It was my mum's.' My voice wavers.

'Alice.' He takes my hand and I let him. 'I miss you, Alice.'

I look at our hands on the table. His skin is cool, dry, familiar.

'I know we talked about it,' he says. 'I know it was too hard for you. I know what you said.'

'I meant it.'

'I know.'

I wait for him to say he's changed his mind, but he doesn't speak. 'Are you with someone else?'

He lets go of my hand and leans back in his chair. He picks up his fork, and spins it round and round. 'Not really,' he says.

I laugh then, and he looks at me as though I've offended him.

'What about you?' he says.

I slept with a man in Irkutsk, in a hotel room with bevelled mirrors along the length of one wall, and a grey velveteen bedcover. I lit a cigarette afterwards. He said he had asthma and it was a non-smoking room, so I wrapped the bedcover around me and stood on the tiny balcony and smoked my cigarette there. The room looked out over a drab, traffic-clogged road. The noise reminded me of London.

My spaghetti arrives. The clams look tiny and shrivelled in their shells.

'How's work?' I say.

He nods. 'Good.' He cuts a piece of pizza and lifts it to his mouth, the mozzarella stretching into thin strings. 'Great. I'm still at St Thomas's. Had a few things published recently.'

I've always wondered what he's like at work. I imagine he is more decisive, more precise than he is at home.

He offers me some pizza. I stop myself from saying yes.

'How are the Terms and Conditions?' he says.

I smile, I can't help it. 'Same as usual,' I say. 'Tilly's still with Toby. Cee's still a control freak.'

'You're hard on her.'

'She's hard on me.'

'How long are you home for?'

'I'm not sure I am home.'

'In London, then?'

I shrug. 'I don't know.'

'Alice, you look miserable.'

'My dad died. Remember that?' I pick up a clam shell. It is ridged brown on the outside, bruised purple inside. It breaks in two when I bend it back on itself. 'I'm going to go to Delhi, I think. Next week. Tilly and Cee can finish sorting the house. It's pretty much done anyway.'

'I could come with you.'

'You have a job.'

'I get leave. We could try again, Alice.'

'We can barely hold a conversation. And you're seeing someone.'

'It's nothing — '

'Are you allowed to marry this one?'

'I don't want to get married, Alice. I thought you didn't want to get married either.'

'I don't.'

'Then I don't understand what all this is about.'

I can feel the tears crowding at the backs of my eyes. I knead my lips together. 'You know what it's about,' I whisper.

'But we were good together, weren't we?' He reaches across the table and puts his hand over mine. I don't pull away.

'I couldn't answer the phone in our flat,' I say.

He sighs. 'Everyone uses mobiles now anyway.'

'That's not the point. The point is I couldn't.

The point is I couldn't marry you if I wanted to. I couldn't have your kids.'

'I thought you didn't want kids.' He lifts his hand away. I can still feel the heat of it on my skin.

I prise a clam out of its shell. It tastes of garlic and sea-water.

'Why can't we go back to how it was?' he says.

'I'm nearly thirty, Kal.'

'So? We talked about all this. No marriage. No kids. Just you and me, living. It worked. It was fun.'

We never talked about it. Not about what mattered.

'I still love you, Alice.'

'Don't.'

'It's true.' He raises his voice.

Imagine it. Back in his flat. Scrambled eggs on toast for Sunday brunch. Cold beer in the fridge. My days and weeks shaped by his work rota. Saving up and heading off to somewhere new every six months or so; coming back to tell him my adventures. He's right. I don't want to get married. Or have children. I've always known that. And even if I did, there's no one to do it with. And never will be, as long as you waste your time with him, Cee would say. It would be a step backwards. It would be a disaster.

I give up on my spaghetti, lean back in my chair and fold my arms. 'I'll come back if you tell your parents about us,' I say.

He has his mouth full of pizza. When he's done with it, he puts down his knife and fork, either side of his plate. 'You know how it is, Alice,' he says.

We would walk to the river on his days off, buy takeaway coffees and go down to the beach if the tide was out. We would hunt for treasures — a stone shaped like a heart, a silver washer big enough to wear as a ring. We would wake up together. Fall asleep together.

'Then no,' I say.

He lifts his eyes in frustration. 'I don't understand you.'

'No, you don't.' I can't spend the rest of my life living on the sidelines. I can't explain it to him.

'We were together three years, Alice. We were good. We had something. I never tried to change you. I never tried to stop you going off on your trips.'

I shouldn't have called him. This is no easier the second time around.

'If you can't even do that for me, Kal.'

I watch his eyes darken. He says nothing for a long time.

* * *

When he finally speaks, he does so slowly and quietly. 'Do you think it's such a small thing? To lose your family, Alice?' I wince. He carries on. 'All of them, Alice? Would you do that for me? Break their hearts? Never see them again?'

I stare at him. I love his eyes — his thick curled eyelashes. I love the curve of his chin, and the shape of his ears. I finger the turquoise silk at my left wrist. The hem is hand sewn. I have ruined her dress. I think about Dad and the three of us, sitting in the box at the ballet, eating ice-creams out of cardboard tubs, comparing notes on the story so far.

'You're right,' I say.

He frowns.

'You're right,' I say again. I haven't really thought about it before, not properly. 'I wouldn't do it,' I say. Even Cee. Fuck, I wouldn't even give up Cee for him.

He nods. He breaks off a piece of pizza crust and crunches it between his teeth. 'We were fine, just the two of us,' he says, when he's finished. 'We worked round it, didn't we?'

I half smile. 'We were fine,' I say. 'But we're done.'

He licks his lips. 'We don't have to be.'

'I'm sorry I brought all this up again.'

He's leaning towards me. 'We can give it some more time. Meet up. See where we are.'

'I'll be in Delhi.'

'Can I come out and see you?' He holds my gaze. My chest hurts. All of me hurts.

'I should go,' I say. I take a twenty-pound note from my purse. He shakes his head and so I tuck it under my wine glass. As I walk past him his hand moves and I think he'll touch me, but he presses his fingers to his lips instead, and I walk out into the night.

Ten things I'd say about London

1) People drop more things than you'd imagine.
2) It's better when the sun shines.
3) It's both bigger and smaller than you'd think.
4) There is kindness.
5) Get as close as you can to Battersea Power Station, and listen for the starlings in the old cranes by the waterfront.
6) There's a clock in a tree at the edge of London Fields.
7) There's a tank, painted black and white, on the corner of Mandela Road and Page's Walk.
8) There's a mural of a man reading a book by a broken tree, on the corner of Noel Street and Poland Street, not far from Oxford Circus.
9) Often the places that look the least inviting have the most to offer — there's a forest behind the tower blocks of the Heygate estate.
10) It's not a place you can ever really know.

I am careful each time I approach our place. People notice repetition, you might be surprised by that, in a city like this, but it's true. I push back the leaves when I'm sure no one is looking and I bring more colours to make it beautiful.

Step in; welcome. You will lift your eyes to the ceiling and smile. Surprising? Isn't it? Let me talk you through it. Each letter has a colour, you see. You have that too? I always knew you would. But perhaps they're not the same colours as mine? Anyway, let me show you. Here is your name. This pale icy blue for the A; gold for the L; a bright magenta pink for the I; navy blue for the C; and a dark charcoal grey for the E. You're nodding. You understand. Of course you do. Alice. Daughter. Love. Sorry. Father.

I was worried about having something for you, I'll say, and you'll smile and look a little sad, and say I shouldn't have worried — what else could you want but this? You always knew, you'll say, or you always suspected. You've been waiting, you'll say, all this time.

* * *

I go to the house every day, and each time I leave feeling panicked and hurried. The living-room walls are white and the furniture is back in place. The bin bags filled with bits of tree have gone.

You are preparing to leave, but there's still work for me to do. I need it to be perfect. I wonder if you are someone who can wait for things, or if you're more like your mother. She was a whirlwind. She'd pick you up and spin you round and then leave you, breathless and disorientated.

We lasted just over a year. I've always blamed Malcolm for ruining it, but maybe we were finished even before all that. I remember an afternoon in Bloomsbury. She sat at the window — the net curtain bunched in one hand, her forehead against the glass — and stayed there so long I thought she'd fallen asleep. When she finally stirred, I asked what was wrong, and she turned to me with tears on her cheeks.

'I can't bear all this secrecy,' she said. 'All this hiding away.'

I looked at her and thought I'd be happy to spend the rest of my life with her in that tiny flat.

'I feel so claustrophobic, like I can't breathe,' she said.

There wasn't much I could say. I tried. I rubbed her shoulders and kissed her neck. I tried to lure her into a fantasy about running off to Italy, or Scotland, or Australia, but she pulled away from me. 'I've got kids, Daniel, and a husband.'

'I know, I know.'

'You have no idea.'

Later, I bought wine and tiny madeleine cakes, and we sat cross-legged on the bed drinking from Marina's long-stemmed wine glasses. She told me she used to want to be a ballerina, that she would get up before everyone else and practise in her parents' dining room: arabesque, glissade, pas de chat — the words come back to me now. Show me, I said. She laughed and claimed she could barely remember the steps, but she slid off the bed and I watched her glide around the room, her eyes distant and a smile caught on her lips.

'I'd like time to stop,' I said. 'Right now.'

She looked at me and raised her eyebrows. 'If you stopped time, you wouldn't live at all,' she said.

Most of my life, since her, has been slower than you can imagine. It's slowest on the streets, but it matters less there — what day it is, which hour comes next; I sold my watch years ago.

Time was slow when I worked too. I remember those nights driving my cab going on forever. My last job was five years ago: a cash-in-hand number, security for some warehouse over in Bow. They found me asleep on duty and fired me. I am too old and too worn out for employment, it seems, and there came a point when I realised I didn't have all the time in the world, and decided it was more important to search for you.

Except now, time is slipping from me. Today I spent all day collecting colours, and then walked back via the house. When I turned onto your street I saw the sign. *For Sale*. If I had waited there all day, I would have seen someone come, in a van I suppose, with that long white piece of wood and the sign to fix at its top. Seeing it did for my heart; I had to use the spray, though there's barely anything left of it — cold relief on my tongue. I tried to picture the people who put the sign up; it helped me breathe. A man in his twenties — ginger hair, a little greasy. He wore a black sweatshirt, with a hood. His trainers were scuffed, the plastic starting to wear around the soles. The van had a dent in one side and the left-hand wing mirror was missing.

I sat on the bench by the school at the end of your road, and folded a piece of newspaper into a flower. I walked up the steps to your front door and left it on the wall.

It can take a long time to sell a house. I've looked through enough newspapers, walked past enough *Evening Standard* boards, to have some sense of the world. House prices crashing. Walls and roofs suddenly not so stuffed full of money as people had thought. But I feel like the earth has shifted underneath my feet. I feel hurried.

* * *

I work hard, as hard and as quickly as I can. I am almost out of cotton and string. My fingers feel clumsy. Difficult. I spray beneath my tongue, once, twice — but then there is no spray left, and it is still difficult. I can't die here when it's nearly ready, when it's nearly possible.

I concentrate on the colours; list them in my head: ice blue, gold, magenta pink, navy blue, charcoal grey. Breathe. Pale, almost translucent orange, ice blue, warm orange-red, dark purple, magnolia, green, charcoal grey, chestnut brown. Breathe. Gold, silver, lilac, charcoal grey. Breathe.

It is getting easier. My heart feels lighter. Olive green, silver, chestnut brown — twice over, maroon. Breathe. I raise my eyes to the canopy of leaves and the dancing colours. I can see what it will look like when you come here. It will be beautiful. Pearly white, ice blue, green, magnolia, charcoal grey, chestnut brown.

I would like to be able to make you a cup of tea. I would like to pour hot water into a white mug, stir in milk and sugar, squeeze the tea bag against the side with a metal teaspoon. I would like to watch you, sitting with your knees pulled towards your chest, your hands around your cup, the steam rising. I have, instead, the tail end of a bottle of whisky. I've half buried it, and covered the rest with leaves. There's nothing to drink it from. It's not as good as a mug of tea, but at least I have something to offer you.

* * *

This morning I walk to Kenwood House, arrive just as they are unlocking the toilets. I pump liquid soap into my palm, run the tap until it steams hot, and wash my face. The soap smells like sherbet. I splash water onto my hair, and pull my fingers through the knots. It's only a week since Hunter cut it, and it looks fine, I tell myself. When I rub my hands over my cheeks the stubble scratches at my palms. I don't have a razor. Rugged, I tell myself. Confident, I tell myself.

A man comes in. We don't make eye contact, but I register his sideways look at me in the mirror as he washes his hands. I wait until he leaves, and then I drop the empty heart spray into the black plastic bin, and I walk towards you.

Today, I have something for you.

I find the head of a white rose lying by the side of the road. I cup it in my palm all the way to your house.

This time, when I walk up the steps, I know I will ring the bell.

* * *

I might never have found out your mother had died. An out-of-date newspaper, the funeral long since gone. I remember the words slicing me to shreds. I sat in the concrete alcove on the south side of Blackfriars Bridge, with the ripped-out obituary on my lap. The sky was beautiful: hibiscus pink, slashed with dark clouds. The trains carried strangers across the water, and the power station pumped out smoke. I've been back since. There's a red plastic lifebuoy nailed to each alcove with a sign that reads 'To save a life'.

The only thing that kept me from climbing onto the wall, shifting my weight forward, and letting myself go, was your name, listed with your sisters' underneath hers. I am sorry she gave you such a cold, blue name. I would have chosen something warmer, something laced with sunshine. The pink centre of your name drowns in blue and grey. It is a name that makes me think of winter, of someone standing on their own, high up on a hill with no trees to shelter them from the wind and the snow. Even so, it saved me, knowing for the first time who you were.

Ten things that happen when you sort out your father's house

1) You realise how much stuff a person who didn't like shopping can accumulate.
2) You have to deal with a lot of dust.
3) You have to try really hard not to think about where dust comes from.
4) You get exhausted just sitting in one place, barely moving.
5) You get emotionally attached to kitchen cupboards you never even liked.
6) You keep forgetting he's dead.
7) You realise how heavy clothes can be.
8) You forget to eat.
9) You get irrationally excited by the idea that seeds grow into plants.
10) You try to comfort yourself by standing with your body pressed against a wall — it works better than you think it would.

On the way home from the restaurant, I kept my eyes shut for the Tube journey, then walked with my head down back to the house, my mother's shoes rubbing at my heels. I hadn't left any lights on. I stood on the pavement and looked up at it: just a dark house on a dark street, with a *For Sale* sign nailed to a post. There was nowhere else to go, and so I walked heavy steps up to the front door and let myself in. It still smelt of paint. When I took off my mother's shoes the tiles were cold underneath my feet.

I had ruined her dress. I walked up to Dad's room and imagined her standing there, reflected back in the wardrobe mirror, clipping earrings to her ears, reaching to secure her necklace. The stain is in three parts. A large blot, shaped a bit like a leaf, and two smaller drops on either side. I wrestled the zip down, and let the dress fall around my feet. I remembered Kal, running his hands across my skin, telling me I was beautiful.

* * *

This morning I lie in a single bed in the room that used to be my room, in the house that used to be my father's. I feel as though I've been filled up with helium — I might float away any minute. A cry would do me good, that's what

Tilly would say, but I can't even seem to manage that.

I lie and stare at the ceiling. Shaun is coming today. He will pull the kitchen to pieces. I drag myself into the bathroom. The sun seeps through the frosted window glass and turns the tiny blue tiles into shimmering lines. I pull the blind to turn them dull again.

Mama's dress lies on the floor in Dad's room. It's creased, and the stains look bigger and darker than they did yesterday. I must have looked like an idiot last night, all dolled up. I pick up the dress and shove it into a plastic bag.

When I open the front door, I see it. Another flower, bigger than the first, it's made out of newspaper — creased sentences, their meanings disappearing into the folds. It makes my heart lift. Ridiculous. I abandon the dress in the hallway and carry the flower through to the kitchen. It might have been there last night, but I didn't look — I'd given up on the whole thing. I boil the kettle; it growls and clicks itself off, but I don't make coffee. Instead, I sit at the kitchen table and stare at the flower, I don't know how long for. When I've done with sitting I stand up and walk over to my seedlings. They get stronger and taller each day. The paper flower is light enough to place on top without damaging them. I lift the flimsy plastic tray, balance it against my waist with one hand and open the door to the garden with the other.

I kneel by the strip of ground underneath the kitchen window, place the tray at my side, and pull at the weeds and plants already in the bed.

The soil clumps between my fingers and presses into the creases of my skin. When I'm done — the soil clear, a pile of rejected green on the path — I count the seedlings, even though I know how many there are, and then make twenty-three indentations in the ground with my forefinger. I release them from the tray — stark white roots, breakable stems — and transfer them to their new home. There's a moment, as I lower the first one into its hole, when I want to stop, want to return the seedling to the tray and take the whole thing back inside with me. It's too late for that. I carry on until there is an almost straight row of frail green plants. The newspaper flower I leave until the end, push the folded stem into a hole right in the middle of the line of seedlings. It falls to one side and I press at the earth around its base until it stands up straight. I sit back on my heels to look at them, and the tears come from nowhere.

* * *

I am walking up the stairs when the doorbell rings. It stops me, frozen, halfway between up and down.

It will be Shaun, a short, stocky man with an easy smile. He'll be holding a bag full of tools. He is going to gut the kitchen, break it up, rip it out.

It might be Kal. It won't be Kal.

Maybe it's someone else who's seen the sign. I

won't let them in. I'll say I'm sorry but they'll need to call the agency, the number's right there on the sign.

And then, although I know it's stupid, I think it might be my father, his black briefcase in one hand, his long beige coat buttoned up, despite the warmth of the day. I can hear his voice, soft enough to make you pay attention, telling me he's lost his keys. A damned nuisance, I must be getting old, he'll say, and I'll laugh to show I know he's not old at all, he'll last for ever. I walk towards the door. I can see the shadow of a person behind the glass, shorter than him, thinner than him. He never forgot his keys.

I'm about to open the door when the bell rings again. Such a hard, brash sound, it makes me jump. I think of the doorbell Cee bought for Dad, the bell push sitting on the bedside table next to that pink sponge on a stick. Tears sting at the bridge of my nose. He was a stubborn bastard — same as the rest of us.

The man standing on the doorstep is shorter than my father was, and on the unhealthy side of thin. His hair is damp and roughly cut; he needs a shave. His eyes are pale grey, the skin around them thick and creased. I have seen him somewhere before.

'I — ' He speaks quietly. His voice makes me think of moths' wings — a crumble of dust.

I put one hand on the edge of the door frame, and keep the other on the latch, but I don't close the door. I catch the rank, almost sweet smell of unwashed clothes and skin. I've smelt it before: on the Tube, at bus stops, in the corners of libraries, any place you can stop a minute without being moved on.

'I've got — I wanted — ' The man holds out his hand. In his palm is the head of a rose. It's almost dead, its cream petals defeated, their edges browned like burnt paper. He clears his throat, but doesn't speak. I tell myself I'll give him to the count of ten. Dad used to say that: I'll give you to the count of ten, Alice. If you are not down here in one, two, three, four . . .

'I found this,' he says. His teeth are yellowed, and one at the bottom front is broken. 'I was thinking how someone picked it from a field full of roses and pulled off the thorns.' He coughs and flicks a glance at me; there is a hint of blue in his eyes. Of course. I remember now.

'You were at the funeral,' I say.

A flutter of fear moves across his face, like he's been caught stealing. He turns his head and I see a thin white scar drawing a line back from the corner of his right eye.

'Weren't you?' I say.

'Then someone else cut squares of plastic and put six roses in the centre of each piece, tied up the ends and taped one of those packets of flower food to them,' he continues.

He was there, I'm sure of it. At the church, and then at the house, although maybe I've made that up. Maybe he's one of those funeral junkies, who pick names from the newspaper and go along to soak up all that emotion and free booze. All I need to do is close the door. Except I don't really want to.

I look at the flower in his hand, and an image

of Kal flashes into my mind — turning up at my office with a fancy bouquet of red roses. I cut the head off one and pressed it between the pages of a book, like a schoolgirl; I still have it somewhere, or at least I never threw it away.

'You knew my dad?'

He drops his gaze. He's wearing a scruffy cord jacket and even scruffier cord trousers. He has a string round his neck, but whatever's hanging on it is tucked under his shirt. Cee would have slammed the door as soon as she'd opened it. Tilly would have smiled, maybe given him a fiver, closed the door too. But there's something about him that feels familiar, and if I close the door it will just be me and the house, waiting.

'I'd like to show you something,' the man says. 'I'd need you to come with me, if you'd do that?'

I look past the man, down towards the street. Shaun will be here any minute. He'll have a white van and a bag full of tools. He is going to gut my father's kitchen.

'Just to the Heath,' the man says. 'Just to a place on the Heath.' He puts the flower back in his jacket pocket.

We used to go to the Heath with Dad; traipse up Parliament Hill after church, sandwiches packed into a rucksack. Tilly made them. She went through an experimental phase: brie and apple with ginger chutney; ham and tinned pineapple, which seeped sweet juice into the bread. In winter, Dad would take a thermos of coffee; in summer he would fill the same thermos with ice and pour lemon squash into the spaces. It always tasted wrong: stained with caffeine. He would sit on one of the benches facing the sprawl of London, his eyes stretching beyond the horizon. Sometimes it seemed like he was so far away he wouldn't notice if we all disappeared. I would run to him, scramble up beside him and chatter away, raising my voice, asking him questions, forcing him back to earth, to us, to me.

'I thought they grew roses without thorns, these days,' I say.

I see the hope flare in his eyes. 'You'll come?' he says.

I picture it — the view from Parliament Hill, the smell of grass and the wind on my skin. I've been spending too much time in this house. 'I don't know you,' I say. 'And there's a man coming — Shaun. To do the kitchen.'

He scuffs his foot against the top step, and then coughs, like a smoker. I imagine him in a doorway, tucked into a grubby sleeping bag. He's well spoken, though, for a tramp. He looks at me as though he has something so important to say he can't think how to start.

'Did you know my father?' I say.

He flinches.

'Is that why you're here?'

He tips his head to one side as if to say, maybe, it might be. I imagine Shaun ripping out the kitchen cabinets and the thought of it makes me feel sick. I glance down the street again, but it's empty.

'I think maybe they do grow them without thorns,' he says. And then he smiles and his whole face changes, and I can imagine him as a young man — blue-eyed and hopeful.

'We used to go to the Heath on Sundays,' I say.

The man nods, and waits.

I look at the turquoise silk spilling from the plastic bag in the hallway. I should never have worn it. I pull off my socks, push my feet into my new flip-flops, and take the keys from the hook on the wall.

'I need to be back in half an hour,' I say.

'It isn't far,' he says. 'It's important.' The colour is high in his cheeks and he rubs at his jawbone, the same way I do when I'm out of my depth. 'Daniel,' he says, and holds out his hand. He has the same thin fingers as me. Tilly and Cee have Dad's hands — thicker, stubbier. This man's hand has dirt embedded into the knuckles and too-long yellow nails. Shaking it makes me think of crocodile skin.

He walks faster and with more determination than I'd expected. I follow a pace behind, past the cottages, along East Heath Road, across and onto the Heath. A man passes us, and I half want grab hold of him and say, look, look what I'm doing, can't you stop me?

Daniel doesn't speak as we walk, and I'm grateful for it. We follow the dip of the hill towards the ponds, then up again. It's not until we are on a thin path, trees leaning damp branches across our heads, the ground scattered with discarded leaves, that I make myself stop.

'I'm sorry,' I say. 'I don't know what I — I really have to get back, I'm sorry.'

'It's just another minute.' His voice is soft as

bonfire smoke. His grip will be surprisingly strong, I think — I imagine myself describing it to an unimpressed police officer, a polystyrene cup of weak tea on the table in front of us, and me saying, it's just there was something about him, something familiar. I thought I could trust him. No, I can't explain why.

'Another minute? And then go, of course, you must go.' He doesn't touch me.

I keep walking.

He stops. There are trees to the left, long grass to the right, and a view of London truncated by the shallow arc of a hill. A woman pushing a three-wheeled buggy walks past. He waits. When she's gone he looks at me, and then at the trees.

'It's just here.'

I follow him. Along the suggestion of a path, across a thin straggle of a stream, between two rhododendron bushes. The faint wail of a siren calls out from beyond the horizon, and closer, the trill of a bird. He dips left. I stop still and watch him move between the trees. He turns, and his eyes are frightened, like a child lost in a crowd.

'Here,' he says, and makes a gesture with his hand like he's welcoming me to his home. I catch a glimpse of silver foil and pink plastic through the leaves, and step forward.

You could call it a clearing, a space amongst the rhododendrons you'd never really notice. The ground looks as if it's been swept clear of twigs and leaves, and he has tied rubbish to the branches. It makes me think of a church. Blues, greens, browns, purples, flashes of silver and gold in an arch above us.

I think of the gifts on the wall outside the house and my heart batters at my ribcage. He is blocking my exit. He is talking — something about colours and letters — his eyes darting from me to the bits of plastic and metal and paper hanging from the trees, then back to me again. It will be my own fault if I am raped and murdered, left with my blood seeping into the ground. Cee would think as much — though she might not say it out loud — and she'd be right for once.

'It was you who left them,' I say. 'Why did you leave them?' He looks at me blankly. 'And the funeral, why were you at my dad's funeral? And what is all this?' I gesture to the things hanging around us. The man's face tenses, and then sags, as though I've taken something from him. I don't want to hurt him, this quietly spoken man with his half-dead rose and his too-old hands, but I don't understand, and I want, suddenly, to go home.

'There's whisky,' he says. 'I wanted to make you tea, but there's no electricity.' He laughs nervously.

I weigh up my chances. I am smaller than him, but younger and fitter. He doesn't look steady on his feet.

'I'm sorry, I have to — ' I move quickly, aiming to his left. I feel the soft brush of his jacket against my forearm and brace myself. But he doesn't move. He lets me go.

Outside, it's bright, and I feel that same disorientation you get leaving the cinema in the middle of the day — a looping, confused moment when you step outside into cool, bright air, and see that the world has gone on, regardless.

I stand, and wait, though I'm not sure what for. He stays in the clearing. I can see him through the leaves. He looks as old as Dad, but I suspect he's slightly younger. A friend, maybe, a colleague down on his luck.

My mobile rings. *Shaun (builder)*. He'll be outside the house now, with his bag of tools and his assistant. He'll have been ringing the doorbell as I've been standing in a den made by a madman. He'll be irritated, but not too much, not yet. I watch the screen flash. It stops ringing, and then gives a bleep, like an afterthought.

I can hear him. I can see him shouldering his way out from between the branches. I wait until he is standing in front of me, brushing at the leaves and bits of mud on his jacket and trousers. We stand on the narrow path and look at each other.

'I'm sorry — ' he starts to say, and then falters.

'That was Shaun.' I hold up my phone. 'The builder. They're going to rip out my dad's kitchen today, put a new one in. They're at the house.'

He nods. 'Maybe you should — '

'I dropped all his wine glasses on the floor. All of them. And then I put on a pair of his shoes and walked across them again and again.' I have no idea why I'm telling him this. He doesn't say anything. He must think I'm crazy.

To our right, just beyond the trees, a girl dressed in pink runs in swooping circles, her arms out to each side, like she might fly if she tried hard enough. I think about how the kitchen cabinets will end up in pieces, swept up and thrown away like all that glass.

'Can I buy you a coffee? Or a cup of tea?' I say. 'We could go to Kenwood House.'

I think for a minute that he might be about to cry, or to step forward and hug me. But he just shoves his hands into his jacket pockets and nods his head and says, 'Yes, I'd like that, thank you.'

Ten reasons I loved your mother

1) She made me laugh.
2) She had a way of knowing what I was thinking.
3) She had the most beautiful hair.
4) She didn't care that I'd screwed up my degree, that I wasn't quite sure where I was going.
5) She had this energy about her.
6) She reminded me of those porcelain flasks in the British Museum — terrifyingly precious.
7) She said my name like it was something special.
8) When she paid me attention, the rest of the world blurred out; it was just me and her.
9) She thought I was braver than I am.
10) I think she wanted to be with me, I really do.

This time, I follow you. You walk faster than I find comfortable, your shoulders tense under your T-shirt, your flip-flops slapping the ground. You didn't understand. When you left, I had an image of myself — crystal clear — standing on Albert Bridge in the middle of the night, the whole thing lit up like a fairground ride, and me, waiting to fall. But here we are instead, walking.

I knew a man once who could walk along a length of rope suspended in the air. It made me sick to watch him — the tiniest breeze, the smallest distraction, could topple him, force him to remember he was human. I walk, one step, then another, then another. I imagine a thin red line stretching out from you to me, forwards and backwards, to your house — his house — and to all the years we've lost.

When we reach the gravel path up to the white bulk of Kenwood House, you pull cigarettes from your bag and pause to offer me one. I try hard to stop my hands from shaking.

'So my guess is you used to work with Dad,' you say.

The smoke feels good in my mouth; I blow it out in rings. You notice. 'A misspent youth,' I say, and you laugh. 'No, I don't think they'd have ever let me be a doctor,' I say.

'A patient, then?'

I daren't look at you. I stare across the grass

towards the lake and the tiny columned folly on the opposite side. Come on, man.

Your phone cheeps in your pocket. You wait for it to stop, then pull it out and press some buttons. 'He'll be pissed off,' you say. 'Come on.' You start walking again and I follow.

'I used to run away a lot,' you say. I can hardly hear you. 'I got all the way to Finchley Road when I was six.' I imagine you, a tiny, red-haired girl with a defiant look on your face. The thought of it terrifies me, and at the same time makes me proud. 'Dad was furious,' you say. 'I've never seen him so mad.'

I want to offer something in return, but my own tales of running away don't reflect so well.

'It turned into a kind of family joke. You know, the kind that isn't funny — little Alice, always running away, no sense of danger.' You turn and look at me then, and I drop my gaze to the amber pebbles at our feet.

We walk up to the house and through a gap in a tall boxy hedge. The pale gravel stretches out to each side in front of the café. The tables are slatted wood, with herbs in terracotta pots at the centre of each. Kenwood House. It's a long time since I've been here.

You go in to buy tea and cake. You won't let me pay. I have to stop myself from kicking up a fuss — insisting — because I'm not even sure I have enough money, and the thought of emptying my pockets and counting out coppers and five-pence pieces is too much. You ask me to find a table, and when I say 'of course', you look relieved.

I make my way to the courtyard and choose a table at the far end, where two tall brick walls meet. I sit with my back to the corner, hemmed in, but with a view of the whole place. The table has a tiny rosemary bush in a soil-stained plant pot. I pick a leaf and crush its scent into my fingertips. It smells of Sunday roasts and summertime. I see the couple on the next table look at me and then at each other. Further away, a child cranes his neck towards me — blue eyes and blond hair. I looked like that once.

I came here with your mother. The first time, she wore a summer dress with some kind of abstract pattern: summer blues — azure, topaz, cobalt. It sat just off her shoulders, so you could see the clusters of tiny freckles on her back. She wore the same necklace she always wore — a teardrop of a diamond on a gold chain. She played with it as she spoke. It was her mother's, she told me once; she didn't even take it off to sleep.

I try to remember where we had sat, that afternoon with the blue dress, but every time I light on a table I know it's not the one. Our conversation? It was a very long time ago. I pick another rosemary leaf and hold it to my nose. Half of me wishes it was her inside, ordering Earl Grey and carrot cake, because then I could do things differently; I could find enough of the right kind of words; I could be your father.

You step into the courtyard and lift your head to scan the tables, holding the tray as though it might leap out of your hands. I stop myself from standing up, from looking too relieved, too excited. I just lift my hand and you make your way over.

'I got English Breakfast,' you say. 'I hope that's OK. And banana and walnut cake.'

Forgive me.

'My dad always drank Earl Grey when we came here,' you continue. 'I've never liked it much.'

She must have come here with him, too. I won't think about it.

'I brought some sugar. I didn't know if you wanted any.' You push a sprawl of sugar packets across the table towards me. One of them drops through the space in between two slats of wood. You twist your body under the table to rescue it and when you emerge I reach my hand across the table towards you. We both look at it. An old man's hand. A tramp's hand. Not the kind of hand you would want your father to have.

'I'll stir it, shall I?' You lift the hot teapot lid and stab at the swollen bag with a spoon. The steam swirls towards you. 'We had a fight,' you say. 'Me and my dad.'

I withdraw my hand and rest it on my lap; it feels like it belongs to someone else.

'Not so much a fight, as an — I don't know. We didn't leave it well.' You pour the tea. I picture a hillside in India — a rich verdant slope, a woman stooping to pick the leaves.

'Sorry.' You shake your head. 'Have some cake.' You lift one of the plates off the tray and push it towards me. I tear the top off a packet of sugar and empty it into my tea. You are watching me. I tip in another, and then add so much milk the whole thing nearly brims over.

'He died,' you say. 'But then, you know that.'

I stir my tea in slow, gentle circles; it leaks over the edges and pools in the saucer.

'Was it my father that you knew?' you say. 'Or my mother?'

I lift the cup to my lips. Even with so much milk, it is too hot to drink.

'There was a woman at the funeral who knew my mother. I can't remember her name.' You frown. 'In fact, I'm sure she said — '

'Your mother,' I say, too quickly; without thinking. 'I knew your mother.' Marina. Did she tell you? You are looking at me. Do you know, already? You are waiting for me to speak.

'It was a long time ago,' I say.

'Before she met my dad?'

I break off a piece of cake. I can hear myself chewing. Crumbs stick in between my teeth and I run my tongue around my mouth to dislodge them.

'I barely remember her,' you say. 'I was four when she died.'

A car crash. I have imagined it too many times.

You look past me. You haven't touched your cake.

'I was very sorry to hear it,' I say. I am trying my best to keep my voice steady.

'Were you at her funeral?'

I swallow. Shake my head. 'I was — I was out of the country at the time.' Don't start lying, Daniel; that's never got you anywhere.

'I hear it was an accident,' I say, not to hurt

you, just to know a little more.

'She was supposed to be picking me up,' you say. 'I was too young to really understand what was going on, but I know she was going in the wrong direction. The woman at the funeral — I can't remember her name now — she reckoned Mama would have just got an idea in her head and gone after it.'

I lift my teacup, carefully, and take a tiny sip.

'I've always thought that if it wasn't for me she wouldn't have been driving at all. They would have thought that, wouldn't they?'

'No.' I shake my head. 'You can't think like that.'

'And then sometimes I wonder if she was leaving us,' you say. 'I thought there might have been a bag in the boot, with a change of clothes and a toothbrush.' You give a little laugh. 'Maybe there was.'

Maybe you're right. Maybe she'd had enough. I remember walking with her through Bloomsbury once. A crowd of pigeons took off around us and she stood and stared at them. If I could be anything at all, I'd be a bird, she said. I told her she'd be a kingfisher; she said she'd be happy being a sparrow.

I try not to let myself think that perhaps she had changed her mind and was on her way to find me.

'I'm sorry. God knows why I'm telling you all this. Tell me about yourself.' You lean towards me, attentive.

I touch my cheek. I should have found a razor and shaved. It's OK, I tell myself. This is going

OK. 'It's a long story,' I say.

You smile, and I almost say it, right then: I am your father. Four words to unbalance the world. I picture the man I used to know walking across a rope stretched high between two trees, the sheer concentration on his face — the danger of it.

'You're lucky,' I say. You frown, and I blunder on. 'To know your father, to have had a good father.' What am I saying? Why this? 'I didn't really know my old man.'

'He died?'

'No. Well, yes, but a lot later on. It just turned out he wasn't who I thought he was.' I am walking on quicksand. 'It's complicated,' I say. 'I won't bore you.'

'It doesn't bore me.'

We sit in silence. You eat your cake. The couple at the next table leave, and a woman with long black hair in a thick plait takes their place. There is nothing stopping you from looking up, taking your bag from the chair next to you, and saying, 'I really must go,' because what else is there for you to do? I feel the tilt of the earth, and have to hold onto the edge of the table with each hand to stop myself —

'My dad said my mother was difficult.' You push the cake crumbs around your plate with your fork.

'She was beautiful,' I say, and swallow hard. 'And spontaneous, impetuous, I suppose. She liked the unexpected.'

'How did you know her?'

'We met — ' I can't order my thoughts. 'We

both liked art galleries.' You're frowning. 'I met her in a gallery.'

You nod, slowly, like you're not sure.

'She was the kind of person who'd set off to do one thing and end up doing another.' I smile at you. 'And maybe she was a bit frustrated.'

You tilt your head up slightly.

'I don't mean to sound — ' My cheeks are hot.

'It's fine.'

'I just mean it can't have been easy for her,' I say. 'She was a bit of a free spirit, and I guess having kids means you're restricted. Not that she didn't love them — you.'

You rub at your jaw. I want to reach across the table and take your hand.

'Did you ever see her wearing a turquoise dress?' you ask. 'Long sleeves.'

I shake my head.

You pick up one of the sugar packets and fold it in half one way and then the other. Sugar crystals fall onto the table through a tear in the paper. 'They fuck you up, your mum and dad,' you say, and I laugh, and then you laugh, and it feels like there is a little more air to breathe, somehow.

'Do you know, I went out with a man for three years and I never met his parents, his brothers, anyone; they didn't even know I existed. I was so angry for so long, but I don't think I was thinking about it the right way.' You keep folding and refolding the sugar packet. 'It should have made us freer, that's what he said, but it was claustrophobic. I'd sit in the flat and listen to the phone ring, and I couldn't answer it in case it was them, and that made me want to scream.'

I don't know what to say. I can see a bank of clouds, ash-coloured, pregnant with rain, just behind you. To your left the woman with the plaited hair sneaks glances at us. To your right there's a young couple sharing a glass of Coke. They've noticed too — a down-and-out with a beautiful woman. They lean towards each other and speculate, quietly.

'That must have been difficult,' I say eventually.

But I've lost you. You shake your head. 'I'm sorry,' you say. 'I'm just trying to sort some stuff out.' I see for a moment how you might have been as a child. Deer-like, questioning, afraid yet curious. Fleeting. That is the word I would use: fleeting. 'I'm not sure standing the builder up was the right thing to do, either,' you say, and give that half-laugh again. 'I should go back and call him. It's been — It's been nice to meet you.' You smile, as though at a joke, then stand and hold out your hand.

If I touch you I will have to let go, and I'm not sure I'll be able to. I stare at your hand, and I'm struck by how fragile it looks. If I wait too long, there will be nothing to even let go of.

'I need to explain something,' I say.

You hesitate, then sit back down with your bag on your lap, and look at me expectantly. 'I would like to know,' you say, after a pause. 'About the — 'You incline your head towards the Heath.

I rub my lips together. At the other end of the courtyard a dog strains at its lead, barking at nothing.

'The — What I was trying to say — ' I look at you. You are biting your fingernail. What good will it do, any of it? There is enough hurt in your life already, I can see that. 'I have a friend called Anton,' I say. You're listening, but you have the same arch look your mother used to wear when she was suspicious, or bored, or angry. 'He's from Poland. I helped him write a letter to his daughter.' Just saying the word shoots heat across my cheeks. You don't speak. I can see a shadow of a frown on your forehead. 'He thinks his wife has another man, you see?' I'm ruining this. I am saying it all wrong. 'She won't let him talk to his daughter, and now she won't even answer the phone when he calls.'

'Why doesn't he go back and find them?' you ask.

'It's complicated.'

You look at your watch — you have to go back, you have to call the builder. The words are there, in my head; I can hear them.

'I don't know why you left all that stuff on the wall,' you say. 'At Dad's house.'

I want to put my hand over yours. I want to tell you it's OK, that everything is OK.

'Is this just something you do?' You laugh, nervous. 'Did you actually know my mother, or is this some kind of weird joke? You just pick someone and piece together a story? Do other people say yes too?'

I shake my head. 'No, no. No one else.' It is the wrong thing to say. I have lost you again. I watch the fear flash across your eyes. And what else is there for you to think, except that I'm a madman, except that I'm dangerous, crazy, lonely, insane.

'I'm sorry,' you say, 'but I really do have to go.' You stand up. I stay where I am and look at you.

'Your name's blue,' I say. 'A pale, frosted blue.' I am not helping myself.

'Goodbye, Daniel.' You smile, but it's a tense smile — more of a grimace. You turn away from me, your flip-flops scrunch the gravel. I can just see the curve of your heel below the hemline of your jeans.

'Alice.'

You turn back. I love you. I loved your mother. I'm your father. I know it's messy, but it's important. 'Good luck with the builder,' I say.

You smile. You tuck a strand of hair behind your ear. 'Thanks,' you say, and then you turn, and you're gone.

I'm a fool. No news there. I watch you go. You don't look back. You hold one hand tight around the strap of your bag. Your neck is stiff and straight. I want to call out to you again, but I have already blown it. You disappear behind the green wall of the hedge. I have no excuse to be here any more. If it wasn't for the empty teapots and the crumb-scattered plates, I would be asked to leave. I take the rose from my pocket and pull off the petals, one by one, until only the sepals and the stamen are left. Then I reach across the table for your cup and knit my hands around its circumference.

* * *

'I would have liked to be a grandmother,' my mother told me. It was two years before she died. She'd said it before, but this is the time I remember. We were sitting in the living room of the home, a stuffy room crammed with velveteen chairs and doily-covered furniture. All I could think about was sitting in that café, with the word *pregnant* in the air between us.

'I'm sorry to disappoint,' I said.

'No, love, you're not a disappointment. I just — It would have been nice for you too, wouldn't it? Might have settled you down a bit.'

I concentrated on the wallpaper, a tortured pattern of leaves reaching up from the thick green carpet.

'I always hoped you'd meet someone,' she said. 'Your dad did too. We'd have liked that: Sunday lunches, Christmas.' Her sight had almost gone at this point. The whites of her eyes were clouded yellow and there were always tears waiting at the corners to move down her cheeks.

I felt like I was made out of concrete — terrified I wouldn't be able to stand up again, that I would end up like her, in a faded, ugly room, watching the world carry on outside the window. I thought of your mother sitting across the table from me, years before, with you — just a tiny collection of cells: everything starting and stopping at once.

'I should go,' I said.

'You just arrived,' my mother said.

'I'm not feeling so good.'

'I've upset you.'

'No, no, I'm fine.'

'You know I love you, Daniel. You know your father loved you.'

I stumbled out into the soft grey afternoon. I went to the first pub I found — a sparse, sterile kind of a place with an oversized TV screen in the corner. I drank warm, cheap whisky until they asked me to leave.

* * *

I sit for a long time. A waitress approaches, sees the cup in my hand and skirts away.

The rain starts in slow fat drops. The other tea-drinkers jerk into action, as though surprised, though they could have smelt it coming if they'd paid attention. I watch them scatter, rescuing half-eaten cakes and half-drunk drinks, laughing, hurrying. I stay in my seat, holding onto your cup. I watch the rain break the surface of my remaining tea. I watch it soak into the cake crumbs. I sit for a long time, holding on, because I know that once I let go, there will be no coming back to this, not for a long time; not ever.

Ten things you shouldn't do

1) Stalk your ex-boyfriend on Facebook.
2) Accept invitations from total strangers.
3) Anthropomorphise houses.
4) Eat chocolate just before going to bed.
5) Think too hard.
6) Stay in one place for too long.
7) Put your head underneath the water when you're in the bath and consider staying there.
8) Worry so much about the colour of paint.
9) Get attached to plants.
10) Steal a picture of your own mother.

Shaun, the builder, is surprisingly understanding, and surprisingly available. I tell him something urgent came up and I'd left my phone at home. He offers to come tomorrow. I sit on the kitchen floor and drink half a bottle of red wine. I wonder about the man — Daniel — I wonder if he has anywhere dry to go to; if he really did know my mother; how he's ended up the way he has. I try to imagine telling Tilly and Cee about him, but I can't. I think of Kenwood House and all those people drinking tea in the middle of the day. I should have bought two bottles of beer instead, fizzy and cold. I should have asked him more questions.

We used to go to that café as a treat in the school holidays. My dad was the sort of man who always wore a jacket. He had lots of them — they'll all be on donated coat hangers in some Oxfam shop on the other side of London by now. We would walk across the Heath to the café, and spend for ever deciding which kind of cake to have. He would wear the beige cord jacket; the one which, if you stroked it upwards, felt like the skin of an animal, soft and warm. Stroked the wrong way, it ruffled into ugly patterns. I would stand by the central display table on tiptoe to see what was on offer, holding onto the low glass surround with sticky hands. I'd beg Dad to let me drink tea — I didn't like the taste, but it made me feel like one of the grown-ups. He would eat a Florentine and drink a cup of Earl Grey, and sometimes I'd look up at him and his eyes would be faraway and I would know he was thinking about Mama.

Tilly calls me when I'm in bed. 'Alice, I've been talking to Cee.'

I roll over onto my stomach. I haven't eaten any dinner; I couldn't work up the energy.

'We're worried about you.'

I rub my free hand across my eyes. 'There's no need for that.'

'She wants us both to go over.'

Cee lives in an unbearable detached house in Berkhamsted.

'Tomorrow,' Tilly says.

'I can't. The kitchen guy's coming.'

'Didn't you give him a key?'

'Not yet.'

'Well, she doesn't want us until dinnertime.'

'Do I have to?'

'Yes, you do. How is the kitchen anyway? Have they made a good start?'

'It's fine.' I stare at the navy-blue pillowcase.

'Are you all right, Alice? Have you eaten?'

'I'm fine.'

'There's no shame in talking to someone.'

I trace my finger up and down the pillow. 'You know, I realised the other day I'd never give you up, or Cee. Not even Cee. I'm not sure what I think about that.'

'Alice, are you worried about the house, is that it?'

'I'm going to go, Tilly, soon.'

'Where?'

I shift onto my back. 'Somewhere far away. I'm thinking India. Delhi first, and then maybe Varanasi, or Bangalore.' I roll the words around my mouth. Just saying them fills my lungs with oxygen.

'You can't keep running away, Alice.'

I lie and listen to the transmitted silence.

'I'm sorry,' she says at last.

'I don't think it is running away. It's living, that's what it is: living.'

She doesn't say anything for a while. A siren wails outside, close, then getting further and further away.

'Maybe you're a nomad,' Tilly says at last. 'Like those people you told us about, in China.'

'Mongolia.'

'The ones in the tents.'

'That's right.'

'I can see you living in a tent.'

I smile. 'Catching marmot and boiling mutton. Making vodka out of milk?'

'Communing with nature. Waking up in the night and going out to watch the stars.'

Earth beneath my feet. The biggest skies you've ever seen. No one else for miles.

'It's just I miss you when you go away,' Tilly says.

I stare at the ceiling, at the white lightshade, stranded in the middle of an expanse of white plaster.

'Cee does too.'

I snort. 'Surely Cee prefers me on the other side of the world.'

'You should give her more credit, Alice. She loves you, even if you won't see it.'

* * *

Shaun arrives with his assistant at eight thirty on the dot. I check it's him through the living-room window before I open the door.

'This is Geoff,' he says. 'The G-E-O variety, not the J kind.'

Geoff is a tall, skinny man, maybe twenty-five, with pale skin and jet-black hair, an unkempt beard, restless eyes. I can feel the sweat on his palm when I shake his hand. I check the wall outside before I close the door, but it's empty.

'Let's get cracking, then, shall we?' Shaun says. He has a gold tooth at the back of his mouth.

I show them into the kitchen. They stand in the doorway and eye it up. I make them tea, point them towards the packet of biscuits on the table and tell them where the bathroom is. I give Shaun a set of keys and explain about the front door sticking.

'I'll just be upstairs,' I say. 'Shout if you need anything.' And then I flee.

I can hear the noises, even from the attic, even sitting in the rocking chair with my hands clamped over my ears; I can hear them smashing the kitchen to pieces.

Towards the middle of the day, I creep downstairs. The place is already unrecognisable. They have ripped out the cupboards and stacked them against the table. The walls flaunt their scars — deep gouges into the plasterwork. Memories of an earlier colour — a sort of pea green — reveal themselves beneath flaked white paint. The cooker stands stranded in the middle of the room.

I smile at Shaun and Geoff. Geoff has beads of sweat teetering at his temples, balanced along his upper lip. They are both covered in dust, and have scraps of wood and paint in their hair. I manage to walk through the destruction and out into the garden.

The seedlings look lonely. They've grown, but their leaves appear less robust than they did in the safety of the seed tray. I kneel in front of them and touch each one gently. They are starting to look different from each other — some of them long and straight, others growing their leaves broader, with serrated edges. Come on, I whisper, and then check behind me in case Shaun or Geoff has come outside. The newspaper flower has fallen onto its side and drunk up water from the soil. I pluck it from the ground and put it into the wheelie bin.

* * *

When Cee calls, I consider not answering.

'Dinner's at six thirty,' she says.

'I'm fine, thank you for asking.'

'I just wanted to check you're actually coming.'

'Tilly's given me a three-line whip.'

'Right. Steve can pick you up from the station. Which train are you getting?'

'Do you miss me?' I ask.

'What are you talking about?'

'When I go away. I was just wondering if you ever thought about me.'

'Well, of course I think about you. Are you OK, Alice?'

'They're smashing the kitchen up.'

'Are they doing a good job?'

'It's hard to know. The place looks like a bomb's hit it, but I guess that's the general idea.'

'Alice, I've got to take the boys to football practice. Can you text Steve your train times?'

'Tell Max to score a goal for me.'

'You really shouldn't have favourites, Alice, you know that. Kids pick up on that sort of thing.'

The train to Berkhamsted is crowded with shoppers: teenagers comparing new trainers; women clutching huge paper bags with string handles; seats taken up by duvets, food processors, printers. Tilly and I sit on opposite seats. She's distracted by something. Her hands knot around each other and she stares out of the window, her eyes flickering across the landscape.

Steve picks us up at the station. I sit in the passenger seat, even though I'd rather have sat in the back, and look at the tiny purple bag of lavender that swings from the mirror.

* * *

I do my best. I admire the new conservatory: the wicker sofas with their flowered, removable cushions; the wicker coffee table with its glass top; the cacti, like spiked phalluses, in matching brown pots on the long, low windowsill. I sympathise about Martin's school not putting him in the top maths set; listen to the story about Matthew's match-winning goal the previous weekend; admire Max's painting of a space rocket on the fridge. I sit with Tilly, drinking tea on high stools at the breakfast bar, and watch Cee slice chicken breasts into thin pieces. I try not to get annoyed by the fact that, in Cee's kitchen, the teapot matches the cups, which match the sugar bowl, which matches the coffee pot, which matches the tray, which is tucked into a tray-sized space between the fridge and the wine rack.

'Do you two know someone called Daniel?' I ask.

They both look at me.

'Someone who knew Mama. I think he was at the funeral.' I am blushing; I can feel heat splotching my cheeks and neck. 'An older guy, looks a bit like a tramp.'

Cee is pouring tomato sauce over the strips of chicken which sit, fat and pink, in a glass oven dish. 'A tramp?' she says.

'Or whatever you're supposed to say. Homeless.'

'Why would Mama know someone who's homeless?' Cee smooths the sauce over the chicken.

'Forget it,' I say. 'I just bumped into him, on the street. And I recognised him from the funeral. I think he came to the house. And then that woman, Marina — ' I'm right, she'd asked if

I'd met someone called Daniel.

I see Cee and Tilly exchange a glance.

'What?' I say.

Cee turns away, opens the fridge door and pulls out a block of cheese.

'What?' I turn to Tilly.

'Nothing.'

I raise my eyebrows.

'It's nothing.' She twists her saucer round and round.

'Did you talk to him?' Cee asks. She grates the cheese over the dish and I watch it fall.

'A bit.'

'What did he say?'

I lean my elbows on the counter and rest my chin in my palms. 'Nothing much. We had tea. There was something familiar about him. I wondered if I'd met him when I was little, if he was some kind of long-lost family friend.'

'You had tea with a tramp?'

'Cee.' Tilly's voice is unusually sharp. 'Alice, we're worried about you.'

'I'm not five any more,' I snap. 'I can look after myself.'

'We know that,' Tilly says.

I lift my teacup. I would like to throw it at the wall, but instead I take a sip and put it back on the saucer, hard enough to make a noise. 'Cee, can I use your computer?'

'Sure.' She sounds relieved. 'In the study.'

The study is a small rectangular room at the front of the house. There's a bookshelf full of *Reader's Digest* volumes, and Steve's back issues of *Autocar*. I leave the kitchen door open. After a bit of mumbled talking one of them closes it. Fuck them.

I look up flights. Four hundred quid to Delhi. Five hundred to Goa. Eight hundred to La Paz. I try to picture myself with my new rucksack: queuing at a check-in desk; eating hot processed food out of a plastic tray; feeling that flare of adrenalin as we come in to land. I haven't claimed on my travel insurance for having to come home early, to see Dad. It feels callous. But I have savings, and the money Dad gave me, and there'll be money from the house soon.

I look up flights to Marrakesh, Bangkok, Tokyo, Nairobi, then give up and sit back in the chair. It's fake black leather, with wheels and flimsy armrests. I stare at the boys' school certificates hanging on the wall behind the desk. My father's dead, I tell myself. He was as bad as those two in the kitchen, I tell myself. Maybe I would give them up, after all. I think about Daniel, and I wonder if he is homeless, and if he is what it must be like not to have four walls and a roof. I think that maybe I should have given him some money, booked him a night in a hotel. I shortlist three flights to Delhi and email the links to myself.

* * *

After dinner, when the boys have been sent off to bed, and Steve has retreated to the garage, the three of us sit in the conservatory on the new sofas, which squeak whenever anyone moves. Cee opens a second bottle of wine. Her cheeks are flushed with alcohol. Tilly's drinking orange juice. I haven't mentioned Daniel again, and neither have they.

Tilly is bursting to say something — I can sense it, she's been bursting with it all evening.

'What's up?' I ask her.

'I was just thinking you look so like Mama, that's all.'

I notice Cee flick a glance at her. I swallow. 'Do you think that's why Dad — '

'Why Dad what?'

'Nothing.' I fill up my glass. Why didn't he want to look at me after she died? I was young, but I remember that.

'You mustn't think he didn't love you, Alice,' Tilly says.

'Why would I think that?'

Tilly shrugs and chews at her bottom lip. 'I have something else to say, actually.'

We have never been easy together. I remember visiting a schoolfriend in the holidays once — three kids, a full complement of parents; the whole thing had seemed so effortless. I watch Tilly's hands twisting against her stomach.

'I'm pregnant,' she says.

Cee almost spits her wine across the room. Neither of us say anything. Tilly looks from me to Cee, to me again, her eyes wide.

'Well, at least Dad's not around for this one,' Cee says at last.

I watch the tears spring to Tilly's eyes. 'Stop it,' I hiss at Cee.

She folds her arms. 'And what's Toby's take on all of this?' she says. 'He's going to leave his wife?' She says it like it's something that will never happen. She has a point, but Jesus.

'Are you happy about it, Tilly?' I am sitting on the sofa next to hers. I lean forwards and take her hand. It's warm and her palm is slicked with sweat. She looks at me gratefully and I make myself hold her gaze and smile. She nods. A tear dislodges down her cheek.

'You're nearly forty, Tilly,' says Cee.

Tilly kneads her lips together and nods again. 'I didn't think it would work,' she says.

Cee frowns. 'You two planned this? What was he thinking?'

Tilly shifts her weight and the sofa groans like an animal in pain. 'He doesn't know.' She says it so quietly I almost miss it.

'Will you tell him?' I ask.

She shrugs.

'He'll run a mile,' Cee says.

'You don't know what he'll do,' I say.

'Cee's right,' Tilly says. 'Kids aren't part of the deal.'

'So, what? An abortion?' Cee says.

Tilly flinches and squeezes my hand. I listen to the muffled sounds of a television coming from upstairs; the soft metallic tick of the clock in the living room.

'I want it,' Tilly says. 'I'm going to keep it.'

'And lose him?' I say.

She shrugs. 'I meant for this to happen.'

'I'll be an aunty again,' I say, and smile. 'So will you, Cee.'

'Well, I suppose if he pays child support,' Cee says.

Tilly shakes her head.

'It's not easy, Tilly,' Cee says.

'I know that.'

I look at Tilly. She's wearing blue cotton trousers and a loose white shirt. I imagine the baby, small as my finger, or maybe my fist, curled up inside her.

'When — ?' I start.

'I'm two and a half months,' she says.

Cee finishes her wine in one long drink. 'I don't know,' she says.

'There's nothing for you to know, Cee. It's Tilly's business. We're just here to cheer from the sidelines, aren't we?' I glare at Cee until she shrugs and says, 'I'm just worried that — '

'I think it deserves a toast,' I say. I fill Cee's glass, and raise mine towards the centre of the room. 'To Tilly's baby,' I say. 'May it be happy and loved and know that it has the whole of the world at its feet.'

Ten times I've wanted to die

1) My first day at school, when a girl stole my satchel, tipped everything out, and laughed.
2) After the time in the café, when she said no.
3) After I found out about the crash.
4) Before I found out about the crash.
5) When my mother called me to tell me what he had done.
6) That whole winter in Preston.
7) When my mother died. I held a knife to my wrist, but didn't press hard enough.
8) When the gallery went bust and I lost the only job I've ever loved.
9) That time on the beach — not because I wasn't happy, just that it seemed to make sense.
10) I've never really wanted it, because of you, but there are times when it feels like it would be easier than all this.

I am a coward, simple as that, a fucking coward. I come back here because I don't know where else to go. You didn't understand what I was trying to say. Which is fair enough. I take the half-buried, half-empty bottle of whisky, unscrew the cap and drink, straight from the neck. It burns a line down my throat. I am too old to be sitting on the floor. The leaves have kept the worst of the rain away, but water has seeped into the ground; it's like sitting on a damp towel. No matter. I stare up at the colours. Alice. Daughter. Love. Sorry. Father.

Brighton beach. We stood on the shoreline — your mother and I — holding hands, our feet bare on the hard white stones. It was early morning, and the world smelt of salt and seaweed.

'We could fill our pockets with pebbles and walk,' she said. I looked at her blankly, and she told me about Virginia Woolf. She walked into a river, she said, in Sussex, wearing wellingtons and a fur coat with a large stone in the pocket.

I drink some more. It has been a long time since I've allowed myself to, but it feels familiar, this slow sinking.

I filled my pockets — all of them: trousers, jacket, shirt — the stones pulling at the seams, dragging the material out of shape. She watched me, and laughed. I danced around her, rattling my burden, and then I took her hand and walked into the sea. At first she came willingly, almost skipping at my side. I had a moment of hesitation, and then I just kept going, the water pressing my clothes against my skin, the stones weighing me down into the seabed. She hesitated, tried to stop, tried to let go of my hand, but I wouldn't let her.

I was joking, I told her afterwards, I didn't want to hurt her, of course I didn't want to hurt her; it had been her idea in the first place, why did she have to ruin things, it was just a joke. I still remember, though, the panic in her voice, rising up over the water, and the deep sense of peace I found, walking into the sea, holding her hand, with no intention of turning back.

I pull a leaf from the branch just by my head. The bush judders and sends drops of rain into the shelter like tiny, cold bullets. I push my thumbnail into the edge of the leaf, until it slices through and my nail meets my forefinger, then drop the tiny semicircle onto the ground, and cut out another, and then another, until only the spine is left.

I'd known Julianne long enough by then to be able to recognise how things went. First came angry words, coated red, a thick, volcanic roar; and then a blue prickling silence. I had broken the weekend. We'd planned to stay until the sun set, but she folded her arms across her chest and announced she wanted to leave straight away.

We walked back to the hotel in silence. In the bedroom she pulled off her wet clothes and threw them at me. I wrapped my arms around her, buried my face in her hair and told her I loved her. She clawed at me, pummelled my chest with her fists, but her fingers searched out the fastenings of my clothes all the same. Afterwards she rolled away, left me in the empty sea of the bed, listening to the fall of water onto her skin in the narrow ensuite bathroom. She still insisted we left early, and the silence still chilled the inside of the car ice-blue on the journey home.

I think it was that morning that you were conceived. In anger — with the idea of death hovering in the room. That shouldn't have been the case; I'm sorry for it.

I swill whisky like mouthwash, passing it from left cheek to right and back again. I push my forefinger into the damp ground, and feel the soil settle itself beneath my nail.

When the whisky is finished, I screw the top back on and slam the bottle into the ground. It doesn't break. I want something to break.

It is quicker to destroy something than it is to make it. I start slowly, almost reluctantly. I pull at the colours until the branches dip and the cotton strains. I tense my body against each break, the leafy rush upwards, the shake of leftover rain; plastic, string, paper, metal in my hand — nothing but pieces of rubbish. Charcoal grey. Magenta pink. Ice blue. Magnolia. Green. Silver. Maroon. Orange. Gold. I was a fool to think — I never thought. Not really. I drop them out of order onto the ground, until they're just a meaningless collage that crunches beneath my feet.

I could go back to the house. The odds are you'll still be there. But what's the use of it? What good would it do you?

It's all over too quickly. I pace, grinding the colours underneath my shoes, looking for more, but I am done. The lengths of cotton hang like so many snapped nooses, their ends frayed and weak. It is not enough.

When I understand what I'm about to do, I drop to my knees. A sound — abrupt and animal-like — escapes from my lips.

I have carried this picture of your mother since that afternoon in the café, when she traced the line of my cheek with the tip of her finger and it felt like the clean cut of a knife that holds the pain back for later. I have been careful enough that the paper still holds itself together, the ink still curves around the contours of her face. I lift my hand towards my jacket pocket.

Don't.

My heart hurries against my ribs. There is nothing left now. It doesn't matter any more. I take the picture from my pocket, and lift it out of the plastic bag.

Don't.

She looks up at me. Smiling, like she knows something I don't. There is nothing left now. It doesn't matter any more.

The paper is soft with age. It barely resists when I hold its top edge between my forefingers and thumbs and tear a line down the centre of your mother's face. If it had resisted, maybe I could have stopped myself. But once I hold two pieces instead of one, something snaps inside me, and I rip and rip until she is unrecognisable, until I am surrounded by tiny white scraps of paper; like confetti. And I cry — pathetic, childlike sobs, wet breathless sounds I wouldn't want anyone to hear.

It is too much for my heart. Not just the picture, not just the colours, but all of it. I reach for the spray, but it isn't there.

Ten things I'd rather forget

1) The colour of my father's skin before he died.
2) When we were kids, Cee used to hide food under her jumper at dinner, take it to her room, and then creep downstairs to throw it away in the middle of the night. I sussed her and told Dad. I don't think it helped.
3) That Kal and I are over.
4) I went through a shoplifting phase — make-up and chocolate bars and tights.
5) I took the money Dad offered me — out of habit, because it was easy.
6) I cheated on Kal. Just once, and not the whole way. A snog — I kissed a man in a nightclub. Vodka and stress. No excuse.
7) I am an orphan.
8) I used to wish Cee had died instead of Mama — arguably I still do.
9) All the times I was rude to my father.
10) That I can never speak to him again.

Tilly's in Cee's spare room; pregnant. I lie on the sofa bed in the attic, underneath a thick artificial duvet, with a white frill and blue flowers embroidered across its surface. The pillows sport the same design; I can feel the raised petals pressing into my cheek. There's no blind on the skylight and I've been awake since sunrise, thinking about Kal.

I shove the duvet to one side, pull on my T-shirt and jeans and then sit up with my back against the pillows, my legs crossed, my bag — a black Slazenger holdall rescued from Dad's attic — in front of me. I take the gifts one by one from the side pocket of the bag, and lay them out in a line.

He's crazy. It's the only explanation. Except it doesn't quite fit. Old, in need of a wash, probably homeless, yes — but no more crazy than me. I pick up the small pink flower — it has shrivelled into a fragile ball.

The door opens with no knock to forewarn me. I move my hands over the gifts, as though to protect them, and look up to swear at Cee. But it's Max, and he is inside the room and up on the bed before I can say a word.

'Aunty Alice, can I stay here with you and not have to go to church?' His blond hair is still ruffled from the night, and he has sleep like encrusted tears at the corners of his eyes. He wears blue pyjamas dotted with aeroplanes. The top three buttons gape open to reveal the smooth pale skin of his chest. I feel a stab of love. Of course Tilly wants a baby, I think; of course she does. Max scrambles over the duvet until he is on his hands and knees at my side. The gifts lurch about as he moves and I circle my arms to keep them steady.

'What's that?' he asks.

I look down. Rubbish. They're just bits of rubbish. 'I think you'll have to go to church,' I say. 'Or I'll be in trouble with your mother.'

Max pulls a face, raising his upper lip, scrunching his nose, rolling his eyes. He picks up the piece of orange cardboard. I reach out my hand for it. 'Leave that, Max, it's just — '

'Look, it's the stars. That's cool.' He holds the cardboard up towards the ceiling. 'We did Space at school. This one's Orion, he was a hunter. And then here's the Big Dipper. It's got another name too.'

'It's part of Ursa Major. Are you serious?' I take the cardboard from him and look at the pattern of holes punched with a biro, smears of ink around their edges.

Max rolls his eyes. 'In the olden days, they used to lie and look at the stars for so long they learnt all the shapes and how they move round — Miss Jordan said so.'

'Do you like this one?' I pick up the silver flower.

'It's girly.'

'Don't you think it's pretty?'

Max grimaces.

'An old man gave them to me.'

Max looks at me, tips his head to one side and frowns. 'Who is he?'

'I don't know.'

'But he knows you?'

I shrug.

'Mummy says not to talk to strangers.'

'And she's right.'

Max picks up the string of fake pearls. He holds it so the pieces of plastic and cardboard, the string, the conker and the rose swing beneath it. I fidget my hands in my lap. I want him to stop.

'Maybe he's a magician.' Max looks up. He loops the pearls around his wrist. I hold out my hand but he doesn't give them to me. 'We did magicians at school too,' he says. 'We all got to dress up and I was a wizard, except Bradley Stevens had the best hat, it was like this big.' He stretches his arms out to each side of his head and the string of pearls dances through the air. Then he stops and lays them down with a sudden reverence. 'Maybe these are his spells,' he says. He surveys the cluster of gifts, then fixes me with a serious look. 'I hope he's a good kind of a wizard,' he says.

'Oh, I'm sure he is. I don't think you need to worry about that.'

* * *

We all go to church. I sit next to Tilly, behind Cee, Steve and the three boys. I look at my nephews' scrubbed necks, and think about

Daniel and the piece of cardboard pierced with stars. Every time we kneel I'm aware of Tilly, her eyes scrunched, her hands pressed hard together, murmuring intently under her breath. Church is another thing that's more theirs than mine.

We stay for lunch. Cee is all conciliation and care today. She can blow hot and cold; according to Tilly it's something she's inherited from our mother. She's told Steve; he keeps smiling knowingly, and offers Tilly water when he's pouring the rest of us a glass of wine. We are eating Cee's low-calorie chocolate mousse when Max announces that I know a real-life wizard. I feel Cee's gaze rake my face. I try to laugh it away.

'He left her spells,' Max says.

'It's just a joke.' I don't look at Max. 'Just a joke.' I scrape my spoon around my bowl and look at the matching white-and-brown napkins with their silver napkin rings, the place mats with their pictures of fruit. I need to leave. I help clear up, slot plates into the dishwasher, and rinse out the wine glasses. Cee starts to make coffee.

'I'm going to go,' I say. 'See how Shaun's doing.' And then the thought of Dad's kitchen cabinets ripped from the walls makes me have to stop and hold my hand against my mouth.

'Are you pregnant too?' Cee stands with her hip against the dishwasher.

'No.'

'Maybe you should come and stay here for a while. It can't be much fun in that house.'

I look at Cee. She's being serious. 'We'd kill each other,' I say.

But instead of smiling, she looks sad. 'I want you to think of this as your home, Alice.'

What she means is, Dad's dead, Tilly's flat's the size of a postage stamp, and you're a drifter, so this is the base now.

'I'll book a flight this week,' I say.

'Where will you go?'

'Delhi, I think.' Far away. Somewhere I can stop thinking. 'Don't worry, the house is practically done.'

Cee looks towards the dining room. Tilly and Steve are talking quietly. She turns back to me and raises her eyebrows.

I shrug. 'She'll work it out.'

Cee purses her lips.

'I think she'll be a great mum,' I say.

'Of course she will. I just worry — '

I squeeze Cee's arm. 'She can worry enough for the lot of us, Cee. Let's just be — supportive.'

'You're going to be supportive from Timbuktu, then?'

'I'll walk to the station.'

I put my head round the living-room door and say goodbye. I say I've got to rush back; I tell Tilly not to bother rushing too.

* * *

When I get back, Shaun's van isn't there. The house looks tired and empty. I don't want to go in on my own, so I carry on walking. I wish it was winter, that the air was cold against my face, and my limbs were snug inside jeans and jumper.

I wish the sky looked like a smudged-up charcoal picture, rather than a blue-wash computer screen.

The Heath is cluttered with people. I walk quickly, the bag tugging at my shoulder. The wind jostles the trees. I can see the dark, damp soil in between the blades of grass. Sweat starts to dampen my T-shirt, and panic rises like a trapped bird in my throat, beating its wings. I can't find it. I know this place, I tell myself, I should know this place, but it evades me, again and again.

I can't even find Kenwood House, and I've been there a hundred times, a thousand times. I've always prided myself on being happy to get lost, to work things out as I go along. But today I'm on edge. When, finally, I reach the crest of a low hill and see the white form of Kenwood House in the distance, I feel a tug of something closer to disappointment than relief. The café is packed. A long queue snakes towards the ice-cream counter in the far corner. Kids squawk and fuss, high on sugar and sunshine. French, Italian, Spanish, Polish conversations fuse together in the still air.

I buy coffee and find a table right in the centre of the courtyard, then regret sitting somewhere so exposed. I keep glancing up. But he doesn't come. No one comes.

* * *

When I'm unhappy, I hide underneath my duvet. It's a habit from childhood. Your head is the tent pole, and then the duvet makes the walls. It's like a wigwam, only better. I like it best when there's enough light outside to shine through; I like how you can see the pattern of the goose-down underneath the cotton, how it never looks quite the same as the time before. I would like to do that now: sit underneath a duvet, the walls plunging down from the top of my head.

I move as though I am walking in the dark, try to shut off my brain and listen to my body. Right a bit, left a bit, onto a thin path that dips down into green. When I find it — at least I think this is it — I stop and look around. A couple move along a wider path, parallel to the one I'm on, but they take no notice of me. I peer between the leaves. A piece of yellow cloth, a scrap of blue plastic. It is the right place.

Except it's ruined. I duck into the space and look, not up at colours hanging from the branches, but down at the whole random mess scattered across the floor. Lengths of coloured cotton hang, snapped and useless, from the branches. I lower myself to my knees. I pick up a piece of foil folded into a smoothed-out square; a length of green string; the inside of a biro — blue ink like blood in a capillary; a hairgrip, the bright pink paint worn silver at the corners; a pale-blue bottle top; a scrap of paper marked with faded ink; a first-class stamp, its corners crumpled gold. I sift through them, as if touching them will make things right again.

I picture Daniel's face, the thin scar reaching across his cheek, his eyes like a lost child's. He wouldn't have done this. Someone must have found it and thought it would be funny to wreck the place. That's why I need to leave this city: because it's the kind of place where someone would destroy something so obviously crafted, so obviously cared about, just for the hell of it. It could happen anywhere, I tell myself. And it's stupid anyway, to make something so fragile, so vulnerable, so pointless. You're inviting it, really.

At the far end of the space there's an empty bottle of whisky. It isn't a label I recognise. I think that perhaps I can smell it — the whisky — soaked into someone's skin. I imagine him hunched beneath the leaves, drinking.

I smoke two cigarettes, and put the stubs back into the packet. Then I select the hairgrip, reach up and tie it onto a piece of blue cotton. When I let go it sways, as though imagining a breath of wind. I pick up the biro — its nib clogged with dried ink — and tie it up next to the hairgrip. I work slowly, randomly. I find there is some comfort in concentrating on how to connect string and object back together.

There are lots of tiny squares of paper, marked with faded lines. They are the only things in the space that have any relationship to each other. I try to join them together and decide that someone has ripped up a picture of a woman. I make out an eye, maybe an ear, and then I get the idea in my head that it's my mother. It reminds me of the picture I found in the attic. Stupid, really, to get bothered by that. I make a pile of the scraps at the edge of the space, and carry on tying up everything else. I feel like I've been pushed off balance.

It's not right. I stretch myself out on the floor and look up. There was an order to it before, there must have been. I stare at the shapes. There's a lot of blue and brown, an occasional flash of gold and bright pink. What? I ask, breathing out the word so it has just enough shape to be heard.

I lie there and wait, but nothing happens, and so I sit up and pull the bag towards me. I lift out the gifts — his gifts — one by one, and tie them to the branches too. I leave the flowers to the end: the tiny silver one and the dead pink one; the one made from newspaper, which I rescued — stained and misshapen — from the bin, despite myself. I turn it between my fingers and read the fragmented words: *ther, amil, ead, fi, cret, morn*. I make a hole for each, and plant them side by side in the ground.

I'm done. Finished. It's time to leave. I will go to a café and order another coffee. I will drink it, smoke a cigarette, and make myself think. In fact, I will buy a notebook on my way to the café, and a pen — one of those gel ink ones that make writing seem like less work — and I will open the notebook at the first page, sitting in the café with my coffee. At the top of the page I will write 'To do'; no, I will write 'What next?' or maybe 'What now?' and underneath I will write — I have no idea what I will write, but when I'm there, with the book and the pen and the coffee, something will come.

I sit, and listen.

Birds singing — one close by, the other further away, its call fainter than the first. I remember hearing a radio programme about how birds in the Amazon have learnt to imitate the sound of chainsaws; how I'd laughed, and then recounted it to Kal and realised how sad it was.

Leaves — there's barely a wind, but still they shuffle against each other like people in a crowd.

The scuff of footsteps against fine gravel.

The thump of a football.

Another bird, an insistent chirp, broken by impatient silences. I listen for an answer, but there's none.

Time to go. Time to leave. But I stay. I look at my watch: 7 p.m. Cee will be making cheese toasties, slicing a chocolate cake into neat triangles. The boys will be sprawled across the sofas in front of the TV. Tilly will be reading the *Rough Guide to Pregnancy*, or trying to decide about Toby. Daniel — I have no idea where he is or what he'll be doing. I imagine him as a tiny dot on a map of London. There are too many doorways and bridges and corners to know. It is too big for one person.

I don't mean to think about Kal. He'll be with whoever she is. A film and a takeaway, that's what we always did on Sunday nights; hardly original, but I loved it. I miss it: sitting on the deep leather sofa he bought when he passed his exams, which was too big, really, for the room; takeaway cartons on the kitchen counters; the light from the television flickering across our skin.

I get my cigarettes and my phone out of my bag. There are no missed calls. I call Tilly.

'Hi, Alice.'

'Hi.'

'Are you OK?'

'Isn't it a lovely evening?' I lie on my side and balance the phone against my ear.

'Thanks for yesterday, Alice.'

'She'll get used to it. You know what she's like.'

'Are you really going away again?'

'I told you.' The whisky smell has gone, or I've got used to it. Instead I breathe in the metallic tinge of the earth and the fresh summer scent of the leaves.

Dad insisted we all went on holiday together, every year, even when Tilly was at university. We would follow him through ancient archaeological sites — the temple of Knossos, the Acropolis, the Alhambra, variously humouring and berating him. I close my eyes and press my palm into the ground. What I would give now for five minutes of one of those holidays, new sandals burning my feet, the euphoria of walking along pavements laced with unknown smells and incomprehensible words, with Dad walking next to me.

'Do you remember those summer holidays?' I say.

'Where are you? I can hear birds. Are you in the garden?'

'Do you remember that time we all got food poisoning? Where were we then?'

'It was Bruges, wasn't it? We had moules and frites and spent the whole night playing tag team to the toilet.'

'I saw Kal,' I say.

She doesn't say anything. I can hear the TV on

low in the background.

'You were always good about him,' I say. 'I appreciate that.'

'Are you OK?'

'I think what you're doing's really brave, Tilly.'

'Cee thinks I'm being stupid.'

'Ignore her.'

'I'm terrified.'

'Of course you are.' I roll onto my back and look at the pieces of rubbish above me. 'Tilly I keep thinking about that guy. Daniel — the one I told you about.'

She coughs.

'It's like he's trying to tell me something, but I can't understand it,' I say.

'How did you say you met him?'

I think about the gifts on the wall by the front door. 'I just bumped into him,' I say. 'I recognised him.'

'Really?'

'From the funeral. But there's something else, like I used to know him but I've forgotten how.' I pick up the silver flower and twist it between my fingers. 'Anyway, I've lost him. I don't know where he is. I just keep thinking maybe it's important, whatever it was that he was trying to say to me. I keep thinking it might be about Mama.'

'Alice, do you think — '

'What?'

Tilly says nothing. I picture her, lying on her sofa — an overstuffed thing, patterned with ugly yellow flowers.

'Do I think what?' I say again.

'Dad always reckoned some things were better off left unsaid, didn't he?'

'The Tanner family curse.'

'It's just — '

'If Toby leaves you I'll gouge his eyes out. I swear.'

'I didn't mean — ' She pauses. 'Thanks.'

We talk about her twelve-week scan and then I hang up and turn off my phone. I lie and watch the sky darken and the world turn black and white. My hip aches where it presses into the ground. Something inside me is shouting, telling me to get up, to buy myself some dinner, to get myself home. The voice is muted, like it's a long way away, and anyway, I tell it, I've not got a home to go to. It's dangerous, the voice continues — I can tell it's shouting because of the strain behind the words — you're being stupid, it tells me. But I feel safe here. I know I shouldn't, but I feel safe here.

Ten reasons not to jump

1) Someone would have to clean it up.
2) I have a daughter.
3) You might find out, and I wouldn't be there to explain it all.
4) Sometimes you have to trust —
5) I don't want to turn out like my father.
6) I thought he was a coward.
7) I saw what it did to my mother.
8) I'm not one to give up.
9) I love you.
10) And maybe —

Albert Bridge looks like something out of a Victorian pleasure garden: strings of fairy lights; the columns like tiered wedding cakes; a row of golden ironwork flowers spanning the river. I walk along Chelsea Embankment towards it. There's no rush. The river moves stealthily, like an animal slipping through the city, reflecting the bridge and all the other lights back to themselves. If I turned and went the other way, I could walk all the way to the coast. I wonder where the line is between river and sea — or if there's a section where it's both, or neither.

The pavement's narrow. I stop on the north side, in the darkness between two lamp posts, and rest my palms on the cold iron ledge. The river's high. I imagine the water: it will be cold, with a tug like an insistent child. It will push the life out of me. It will insist my heart breaks, once and for all. I look upriver, at the angular tower blocks of the World's End estate, a smattering of windows still glowing yellow; at the dark hulk of Lots Road Power Station; and the river, moving through it all.

I imagine your mother standing next to me and find I can do so without the usual flurry of panic and anger. Look, Julianne, isn't this beautiful? *You're avoiding the issue, Daniel*. But I found her. After all these years I found our daughter. *And did what?* And let her be.

There's a breeze, cool as breath on my cheeks. It doesn't smell like the city here, and the sky feels taller and lighter than it does when you're surrounded by brick and stone. I can still taste the cake you bought me, underneath the whisky.

I don't jump. I've never been one for grand gestures, but you've worked that out already. And it seems my heart's not quite ready to do it for me, not yet at least.

Instead I walk, through the rest of the night and into the dawn, through silent streets and empty squares. This city is more beautiful than ever in the early hours of the morning, when you can hear the sound of your own feet on the pavements; when you can feel the whole world waiting for another day. And dawn — there is something magical in its repetition: always the same, always different. Today the sun enters, stage left, into a clear expanse of sky. Everything it touches, it softens, and the city — our city — reappears, dreamlike, a morning mist turning the concrete baby blue.

I walk north: through the strutting brick terraces of Sloane Street; past the stuccoed embassies on Belgrave Square; over an eerily quiet Hyde Park Corner, and on down glitzy New Bond Street to Marylebone Road. I reach Regent's Park as a man in a high-vis jacket is unlocking the gates. He nods at me but says nothing. To be the first person in Regent's Park on a Monday morning — there is joy in that. I walk all the way across, watching the sky turn pink then fade to blue, scratched with high white clouds. I take the path past the Zoo and walk close to the fence, beneath the trees. Two parrots with bright red feathers sit facing each other. One of them turns and watches me as I walk past.

I am going back to the Heath. I am not sure why. I am not sure I want to. I haven't felt a pull like this for a long time. Perhaps there's a mouthful of whisky left — I could drink that, and then I could lie down and sleep.

* * *

Except when I duck my head into the space I see you, lying on the ground. I throw myself forward onto my knees but find I can't touch you. Your face is pale as marble, your hair spread around you. There's no blood. There are no unnatural angles.

'Alice?' I can barely say the word out loud. You don't move. 'Alice.' Louder now. Nothing. I lean down, propping myself clear of your body with my arms, and lower my cheek towards your mouth. There. A breath; I'm sure of it. I sit back on my heels and steady myself. Alice. My daughter. I watch you sleep, and as I do, the idea that's been crystallising in my head since I met you reveals itself. You are lost, and if I tell you, you'll be more lost than ever. There are other kinds of truths. There are other ways of telling them.

When you open your eyes, you don't seem surprised to see me. You lift your head and then let it fall back onto the ground.

'You came back too,' you say.

'What are you doing here?' My voice falters.

You prop yourself up on your elbow and groan. 'Do you sleep out like this?'

I shrug.

'I feel about a hundred.'

You are here. You might have died. You came back. 'You have the house, don't you? Did something happen with the house?' I say.

'I can't stand it there any more.' You tug your T-shirt down over the waistband of your jeans, and rub at your neck. 'I had the oddest dream,' you say, and then you look away, and I think that maybe you dreamt about me.

'It's dangerous, Alice, sleeping out,' I say.

You lower your eyes and turn your head to one side. 'I'm fine.'

'You mustn't do this again,' I say. 'Ever. You're shivering.' I pull off the brown cord jacket and hold it towards you. You hesitate. 'I'm sorry,' I say. 'Just wear it for a minute, warm yourself up.'

You drape it over your shoulders but don't put your arms into the sleeves. I look down at my shirt. It isn't clean, and there's a button missing. A wave of exhaustion laps at the back of my mind.

'Where did you go?' you ask. There are bits of soil and twigs in your hair.

'I walked.'

You raise your eyebrows, waiting for more. I pick up a leaf from the ground and pull it into ragged pieces.

'Where did you sleep?' you ask.

'I didn't.'

'You look tired.'

'I'll live.'

'I tried to — ' You gesture towards the canopy of leaves and it's only now that I see what you've done. I feel the thrill of it. The colours are all out of order, like a language I've never seen before. 'I came to bring back your things,' you say. I pick them out — the orange cardboard, the pearls, the hat, hanging above us. 'I was trying to — ' You shrug and smile and I want to wrap my arms around you. I feel a stab of pain in my chest. Not now.

'I don't think I got them in the right order,' you say.

'It's beautiful. Thank you.'

I see the pile of ripped paper just to your right, and my heart lurches again. I shouldn't have done it. But maybe, somehow, it brought you back to me. I gather up the pieces, and shove them into my trouser pocket. You watch me, but you don't ask. There are things that don't need to be said. You have enough to deal with — Malcolm, and the man at the funeral.

Your stomach growls, and as if in answer, mine does the same.

'I'm starving,' you say. 'Why don't I buy us breakfast?' You hand me back my jacket.

'No.'

You look up. I've frightened you.

'Do you like blackberries?' I say.

You nod.

'Come on.' As I scramble out of the space, I feel something give beneath my foot. It's the newspaper flower. You have planted it, along with the silver one — and even the tiny, dead, pink one — in the ground, like a child might.

* * *

'I haven't done this in years,' you say. Your fingers are stained purple like mine, and there's a streak of dark juice on your cheek. 'They're kind of tart.'

'They'll be better in a few weeks.'

You nod, and I imagine us coming back here, doing this again.

'I know an apple tree too,' I say.

You lift your eyebrows and then smile. But when we get there the apples are small and out of reach. I watch you, your arm stretched as high as it will go. You catch my eye and grin.

'Do you think you could hold me?' you say. 'On your shoulders?' and then you shake your head. 'Sorry, I don't know what I'm thinking.'

'No, I can do that.' I crouch down, facing away from you.

'Are you sure?'

'Go on.'

I feel your legs around my ears. I start to stand and you grab at my head.

'Are you sure — ' you say, but I'm standing. I haven't felt so strong, so tall, so joyful for years. I want to shout. I want to shout: look at me, with my daughter. Look at us. You lurch a little, and I hold onto your shins. I walk closer to the tree and feel you reach up, your legs pushing against my hands.

'Got one,' you call. 'And another.' I feel the jolt as you pull each apple from the branch. 'I can't hold them all,' you say and you drop one, two, three, four apples onto the ground. They aren't ready for eating. 'OK, OK, down.' I bend my knees, ignoring the pain that stabs along my spine, and you tumble forwards and away, laughing. 'We've got enough for a crumble,' you say, holding up three apples and gesturing to the ones on the ground. I picture it, the two of us sitting at a table, with bowls of apple crumble and custard.

The apples are sharp, acid green. We eat one each, wincing and smacking our lips as we do.

'They're cooking apples,' I say. 'They're not really ready. I'm sorry.'

'They wake you up,' you say, and smile.

'Maybe you can take the rest home.'

You nod and gather them into the crook of your arm. I don't want you to go. I didn't mean that.

'Let's leave them in the — ' You gesture back towards the space. 'I can pick them up later. I'd like to buy you a coffee, in return.'

* * *

I stand outside while you deposit the apples. When you come back out you're wearing the string of plastic pearls around your neck. The bits of cardboard and plastic, the conker and the silk rose hang from it like awkward charms.

Father.

You buy me a cup of tea in a cardboard cu

from a café on Swains Lane — I tell you I don't like all those frothy, fussy coffees, and you laugh, in a kind way. We walk back to the Heath, all the way up to Parliament Hill. We sit on one of the benches looking over the city.

'My nephew thinks you're a magician,' you say, and laugh.

'Your nephew?'

'I have three. The youngest one's kind of my favourite, though Cee says I'm not allowed such a thing.' You rub at a mark on your jeans. 'He's called Max.'

'And you told him? About me?' I can't keep the excitement out of my voice.

'Not really,' you say. 'He just saw the — ' Your hand strays to the pearls around your neck. A seagull swoops across in front of us, crying. 'They always sound so sad, don't you think?' you say. 'Like they're mourning for someone.'

I think about your mother standing on Brighton Beach, her dress soaked to her waist.

'Maybe he's mourning for the sea,' you say. 'I can't imagine why you'd come to London, when you could be out there, on the water.'

'Sometimes I think of London being like a sea.'

You don't say anything. You are staring out over the city.

'Just that it's always changing,' I say. 'It has moods.' I sound like a fool.

You turn slightly, to look at me. 'I'm flying to Delhi,' you say. 'Next week.'

My heart dives.

'I thought about staying, maybe, but — ' You

pull at a strand of your hair. 'I'd like to feel that I could stay.' You lift your feet onto the bench, tuck your knees to your chest and wrap your arms around your legs.

The thought returns. You don't need uprooting — that's what would happen if I told you. You need stability, some kind of connection. I could do that much for you. I could offer you that much, I know it.

Ten reasons to stay

1) My sister is pregnant.
2) My other sister is liable to be a cow about it.
3) I'm tired.
4) Sometimes I feel like I'm going round in circles.
5) I hate hotel rooms.
6) I hate jet lag.
7) I might meet someone. Hell, I might even get married and have a kid myself.
8) Dad would have liked me to; he worried about me, forever flying off to somewhere new.
9) My sisters think I'm always running away.
10) I would like to stop running away.

I smooth the plastic beads against my chest and follow Daniel across the grass, down Parliament Hill. I don't know why I put them on. I must look like an idiot. The conker knocks at my breastbone as I walk. I used to collect conkers as a kid, great glossy piles of them. Every year, I was disappointed when their skins turned dull and wrinkled, even though I knew they would.

Before the running track Daniel veers left, past the tennis courts, the bandstand, the low glass-fronted café, and then right by the lido with its barbed-wire crown, and down towards Gospel Oak station. We stand at the lights and I wonder what the drivers of the passing cars think, whether they even see a young woman — who has slept alone under a tree on Hampstead Heath — standing with a man who is surely a tramp. They won't notice, and even if they do they won't care. I check the piece of cardboard is safe in my jeans pocket.

We pass a brief oasis of brick terraces with neat paintwork, creeping wisteria and controlled privet, before coming up against high-rise flats in dark Seventies brick. Up and over the bridge. Daniel stops midway and we look through the metal mesh fence at the arrow-straight train tracks below.

'Where would you go right now, if you could go anywhere?' I ask.

A train shoots past and the bridge shudders beneath our feet. Daniel runs his finger along the fence — small metallic thuds. 'I'd stay here,' he says, and looks at me.

I dreamt about him — a vivid, disconcerting dream. We both took off our hands, as if we were dolls, and swapped them with each other. Except that when I looked down, I saw my own hands at the ends of my wrists. When I woke up and he was there, I felt strangely at home. There is an idea, at the very back of my mind, that perhaps he and my mother — but it's stupid and I won't think about it. I like him, that's all.

'I'd go to Inverness,' I say. 'Or further north. I'd go right to the top of Scotland and then I'd get a boat to Iceland, or somewhere in Norway. I'd go looking for the Northern Lights. I've seen photos and they never look real.'

He smiles, but it's a sad smile, so I shut up. We walk on, past a lonely-looking building bristling with *To Let* boards, a green sign for a city farm, a road of flats stretching off to the right, with bikes and plant pots and football flags pressed against faded glass balconies. We emerge into the chaos of Kentish Town Road, until he cuts onto the slow sweep of St Pancras Way, left onto Agar Grove. We don't talk much, but in a strange way the rhythm of our feet feels like a conversation. Every so often Daniel stops and picks something up — a gold bottle top; a tiny yellow button with a star cut out of its centre; a nail, bent at a right angle. He looks at them for a moment, and then drops them into his pocket.

'I like your jacket,' I say.

He laughs. 'A man called Hunter gave it me.'

'Hunter?'

'Like the wellies. It was for — ' He looks at me. 'It was for a special occasion.'

On the corner of York Way he stops, and unhooks a small, pale-blue scrap of plastic which has caught on a wire fence. 'You have a blue name,' he says.

A lorry hurtles past us and I feel that slight rush of adrenalin you get when your plane takes off, or when you're standing on a station platform and a train races through without stopping.

'Ice blue, like the water from a glacier,' he says. 'It's a bit like this.' He holds out the piece of plastic and I take it but I don't know what to say. His face falls and he drops his gaze from mine. 'That's just how I see it,' he says. 'I guess you don't have that.'

I smile at him, but it's forced and I'm sure he can tell. We turn onto York Way, walk underneath the bridge where the sounds of the lorries echo against the concrete. Daniel stops by a fence that gives a cross-hatched view onto the back of King's Cross station. A tall, dirty brick wall holds the memory of another building. Buff-coloured Portakabins hunker close to the ground, as if intimidated by all that space in the middle of the city. Further on, we stand opposite the undulating glass of King's Place and look down at a solitary swan swimming in unhurried beats along the canal. A man lifts an empty fishing line from the water, and tosses it in again. Another man sits on a wooden bench watching the man fishing, a gold beer can in one hand. On the wall of the bridge a small toy aeroplane, with a pointed nose and orange wings, lies on its back. Daniel picks it up and hands it to me. It's made of metal and is strangely cold and heavy. I place it on the wall, pointing west, ready to take off.

'Did you meet my sisters, then?' I ask. 'When you knew my mother?'

'Just one time,' he says.

'I asked them about you.'

He puts his hand to his chest and winces as though he's in pain.

'Are you OK?' I ask.

'Fine. Did they remember me?'

I shake my head. 'No. I guess they were too young.'

He turns away and starts walking again. I follow him through the hustle of King's Cross, up along the Euston Road to the scaffolded shape of St Pancras Station. He keeps his palm pressed against his heart.

I walked on a glacier in Canada. One of a group of strangers; we had piled into a coach with tyres the width of my body and then climbed up and up, off the road and onto the slick blue-white ice. We were released for half an hour, and I took slow, careful steps away from everyone else, turned my back on them and the coach so that all I could see was ice, like cracked skin, like dirtied, frozen tears; like nothing I had ever seen.

'So what colour's your name, then?' I ask.

He stops walking, but he doesn't answer. I must have got it wrong. I've upset him. We are standing on Euston Road, the orange and white bricks of St Pancras to our right, a noisy stream of traffic to our left.

'I thought you said my name was blue.' I have to raise my voice to be heard. 'So I just wondered if your name had a colour too?' Crazy, he's crazy. I'm crazy. This is not a place to stand still. We are in the way, bumped into, studiously avoided. This is not a place for a conversation.

'It's orange,' he says at last. His voice is so low I have to lean towards him to make out the words. 'Pale orange, almost transparent, almost not a colour at all.' I wait for him to say something else, but he doesn't. A lorry belches, cars mutter against the tarmac, a mobile phone trills into a jacket pocket, a baby cries.

I think about Dad, lying in that bed with the curtains closed, and those horrible red-carnation letters in the hearse. 'My dad used to look at me sometimes, like — ' Daniel's watching me closely. I start walking and hear him hurry to catch me up. 'We had a bit of a — He wouldn't tell me something, and I wouldn't let it go, and what does it matter, really? Who gives a shit? I mean there's only now, isn't there, there's only the moment.'

'I met a man who told me exactly that, once,' Daniel says. 'He was a Buddhist.'

'Maybe I'm more spiritual than I thought.' I try to laugh it off.

'I'm sure he understood,' Daniel says.

I swallow and walk faster, my head down. Gower Street. Drury Lane. Aldwych. Lancaster Place. We pause on Waterloo Bridge, the concrete blocks of the National Theatre to our right, and Somerset House quiet and majestic to our left. I stare down into the water. It moves more quickly than you'd expect.

'What happened to your friend?' I say.

'Who?'

'I can't remember his name: the Polish man, with the daughter.'

Daniel is leaning on the railings, his chin cupped in his palm. He chews at his bottom lip and says nothing. I turn to watch a dark-haired man with a camera who gestures to his girlfriend — left, more, a bit more. She stands, hands tucked into skintight jeans, shoulders hunched up towards her ears, an embarrassed grin on her face.

'He has a job,' Daniel says at last. 'He'll go home.'

A police boat emerges from the bridge underneath our feet, six men packed into the narrow space, like boys playing at war in a rubber dinghy.

'That's nice.' I watch the boat. The driver stands at the back, his body relaxed, his gaze on the horizon. I have a sudden, strong desire to be held by a man who is taller than I am, to rest my head on his chest and breathe him in. I tug at the beads around my neck. 'So which letter's white then?' I say.

I see him tense his hands into fists.

'I'm sorry. Is this annoying?'

'F,' he says. 'F for father. It's white, sort of mother-of-pearl.'

I scratch at a mark on the railings with my

fingernail, and watch the digital display on the side of the National Theatre, pixelated orange letters chasing each other across the screen. I could ask him again: who are you? How did you know Mama? What are you trying to tell me?

I look at his hands next to mine. We have the same-shaped nails. I glance at his face. He doesn't look well — pale and sweaty, almost grey. He opens and closes his fists. To either side of us clots of tourists congeal around guidebooks and cameras, then peel off in search of something new to see. Birds wheel across the sky. What did he say? London's like the sea.

I tilt my head up so I can take in the whole of the view: Blackfriars Bridge, Southwark Bridge, the Gherkin, St Paul's, the blinking light on top of Canary Wharf in the distance; and I imagine it all turned to water, the bricks and the tarmac, the carved window-surrounds and the sharp metal railings. I imagine the BT Tower wavering then falling, reappearing tall and glistening, wavering, falling again; the whole city rising and falling, row upon row of white-crested, endlessly breaking waves; and underneath it all, a current tugging.

* * *

We turn a corner and see a yellow bulldozer scraping its nose into the edge of a building: old offices — pale-green tiles torn apart like split earth, breaking glass. There's something intimate in the way it moves: whispering sweet nothings into the empty rooms, scraping out rubble with the attention of a lover. I stand and watch. I can feel Daniel looking at me, but I ignore him. The bulldozer nuzzles ineffectually, once, twice, three times, and then a new piece of wall gives in to its touch and crashes down, a flurry of dust swirling in its wake.

We walk past the Old Vic and I remember going there with Kal — his thigh pressed against mine, his fingers tapping an impatient rhythm on my palm all the way through whatever it was we'd gone to see: something with corsets and parasols and white-powdered faces. In the park on the corner someone's barbecuing meat; swirls of smoke rise up through the trees. We walk past the Cuban bar with its wall-high mural: a woman standing on top of the world with her arms raised high. My phone rings. I stand on the pavement and look at the screen flashing blue.

'The builder again?' Daniel asks.

'It's Kal.' The phone keeps ringing.

'The one who made you feel claustrophobic?' Daniel says and I look at him, and then back to my phone. It stops halfway through a ring. I wait. No message. I think about the bulldozer pawing at the broken building.

'You shouldn't go backwards, my dad always said,' I say. 'We were only going to go backwards.'

'What do you want?' He is standing next to me, close enough to reach out a hand and touch my arm, but he doesn't.

'I don't know. I just want to feel — I don't know.'

He smiles, and then he does touch me, briefly.

A fleeting brush of his fingers across my forearm. He snatches his hand back, hides it between his elbow and the side of his body. Then he jerks his head as if to say, come on, let's go, and he starts walking again. We are heading for Elephant and Castle. I can see cranes worshipping the growing shape of the tower block, swathed in blue plastic.

'He lives just down there,' I say. 'I'm not sure I want to — '

He nods and takes a left down a narrow street, loops us back towards the river.

'You can always change your mind,' he says. 'I didn't realise that for a long time.'

'How do you mean?'

He shrugs. 'Just that you might decide that the thing you thought you wanted might not be right after all.' He coughs. 'Just that you can change your mind about things.' He looks at me. 'Like my father, for instance,' he says. 'I've hated him for so long, I thought I'd die hating him, except I've started to think maybe it's more complicated than that. I've started to think maybe he was doing the best he could.'

'So you don't hate him any more?' I say.

He shrugs. 'I don't know. I'm trying.'

We follow the river to Hungerford Bridge. Up the steps, over the heads of the men who blow foot-tapping rhythms from their trumpets in the darkness beneath. The bridge like a metal honeycomb under our feet. A train runs past, sliced into triangles by the metal struts. Thick white wires reach up over our heads and converge in the sky.

'Imagine building a house here,' I say.

'On the bridge?'

I stop. 'Yes, right here, in the middle. Imagine waking up to this each morning.' I lean on the metal railings and look downriver towards Westminster. 'Why are you — ? I mean how did you — ?' I falter.

'Some stuff happened, and then I made some bad decisions, that's all,' he says. He stands next to me. I think about the piece of cardboard in my jeans pocket, punctured with stars. 'And then — well, it turns out it suits me,' he says. 'Not all the time, but — I'd rather sit by the canal and watch the sun set than spend an evening in some of the shitholes I've lived in.'

'Maybe we're the same,' I say. I feel him tense, as though I've startled him. 'I mean, I could buy a flat, couldn't I? We're selling Dad's house, so I could. But it's like I'm in the habit of wandering, and I don't know how to stop. Maybe we're the same like that.'

He says nothing.

'You must think I'm a spoilt brat.'

'No. I'm glad for you. Having a place of your own — that's a good thing.'

'The place on the Heath. Is that, sort of, a home?'

He shakes his head. 'For you — a flat in London, that's a good thing.'

'I was going to book a plane ticket yesterday, at my sister's,' I say. 'To Delhi.'

'You could stay here for a while.'

I look down at the river shifting beneath us. I'm tired. My body aches. I need a shower. 'Shall we keep walking?' I say.

We plunge from daylight into fluorescent light, the walls of the tunnel lined with dirty cream tiles, a bulb shrouded with grimy metal mesh, the rows of pigeon spikes wreathed in dust. Daniel walks ahead of me, his head down. I can see the ragged hems of his trousers, a rip like a knife slash on the left leg, just above the back of the knee. We reach the open platform over Villiers Street, like an Italian balcony, looking out to the park, and beyond it to the river. I almost miss it: the skeleton of a leaf, dyed orange — the kind of thing you would buy in a craft shop to stick on a greetings card. It's broken, the edges frayed like ripped silk. Daniel keeps walking, towards the quiet market perched above the road. I stand and watch him go. When he stops and turns round, even from this distance I can see the panic flare across his face.

I hold out the leaf and walk towards him. 'Here,' I say. 'It's for you.' It weighs nothing, like it doesn't really exist. 'I know it's not quite the right colour for your name, but I thought it was beautiful, so — ' He looks at me and I make myself hold his gaze. A couple walk past and the woman turns back to look. 'So I wanted to give it to you,' I say.

The smile reaches his eyes before it tugs at his lips. He lays the leaf in one palm and covers it with the other.

'Alice,' he says, his voice soft and unsteady. 'I wasn't going to tell you this — '

'Then don't.'

He frowns.

I think about Dad, propped up in bed, a

cigarette trembling between thin fingers. I should have left it. I should have told him I loved him and let the rest of it lie.

'Sometimes it's best just to let things be, don't you think?' I say.

He stares at me for a moment, and then smiles, nods, and turns away.

I follow him down the Strand and out into Trafalgar Square. We skirt the base of Nelson's Column and come to rest by one of the fountains: a serene-faced woman holding onto a dolphin. Two-pence pieces rest on blue tiles, distorted by the water. Tourists flock across the square. To our right rise the columns of the National Gallery.

'My mother used to take us to the National Portrait Gallery,' I say. 'Except I don't remember.' I dip my fingers into the water. 'Seems I don't remember a lot of the good stuff in my family.' Daniel is perched on the side of the fountain, his hands clasped in his lap. 'Is that where you met her?' I say.

'What?' He jolts his head up.

'Didn't you meet my mother in a gallery?'

He looks towards Charing Cross Road. I catch the blue of his eyes, and I can imagine him as a young man again. Good-looking, slim, slightly awkward but with a kind smile. I wonder if he was ever married. I wonder what my mother made of him.

'I had a photo of her,' I say. 'It was in my rucksack and it got lost on the flight home.'

'They didn't find it?'

I flick my hand out of the water, a noisy slosh

of drops across the surface. 'I didn't ask,' I say. 'It's stupid, but I just couldn't. I guess because Dad — ' I give him a half-smile. 'I kind of hope it ended up somewhere interesting, not just in a room at Heathrow with no windows. I was thinking somewhere with good beaches — Jamaica, or Sumatra or Mauritius.'

'You look a lot like her.' He is holding his left hand in his right hand, tight enough to turn the skin white. 'I loved a woman once,' he says. He rubs at his jaw. 'It didn't work.' He lowers his eyes.

'It happens like that, sometimes,' I say.

'I've never quite been able to let go of it.' He says it as though it might not be true any more. 'I started walking,' he continues. 'I used to walk for hours, days, to try and forget. And then I learnt how to look, how to notice things.' He shifts his weight a little. I can smell his skin, the sweat in the weave of his clothes. 'And then I learnt how to stand still.' He looks at me as though he's said something of consequence. 'That's the most important thing,' he says. 'To stand still.'

I watch tourists take the same photograph, over and over. It strikes me that some of the photographs will show the two of us, standing by the fountain, talking. These people will download their images onto computers in France, America, New Zealand, and there we'll be, suspended, ignored, but present.

'If you stand still in a place, for long enough, it will show itself to you. It takes time, but you find the patterns, and once you find them you can start to feel at home,' he says.

I feel tears, quick and unexpected, at the bridge of my nose. I press my lips together and concentrate on a group of teenage girls wearing *I Love London* T-shirts tied into knots above their navels.

When I'm sure I won't cry, I glance at Daniel. He is staring across the square, his face quite serene.

'I'm glad I met you.' I'm not quite sure why I say it.

He turns and smiles. Then he takes hold of my hand, and the rough edges of his skin feel like a surprise, even though I've felt them before. I look down — at my own hand, stacked with silver rings, and at his, a man's hand, callused, but still delicate enough to fold tiny pieces of paper into the shape of a flower.

'Let's watch the sky,' he says, and to please him I tip back my head and look up at the sky.

'No.' He sounds annoyed. 'Not like that.'

He drops my hand, walks a few steps, and lowers himself to the ground until he is lying on his back, in the middle of Trafalgar Square, Nelson's Column rising disdainfully above him. I look about for someone to help; or if not to help, then to react, to tell me what to do. Daniel just lies there, with the orange leaf pressed against his heart. I tug at the beads around my neck. F is white. D is orange. A is blue. I think of the space on the Heath, colours tied to the branches. And then he says something, or at least I think he does, but I can't be sure because the shapes of the words get lost amongst all the other voices, the splash of the fountains, the grumbling traffic. I notice a couple look at Daniel and then at each other. A smirk crosses both their faces, and I feel a swell of anger. There's nothing wrong with it, I want to tell them, he's looking at the sky — no crime in that. I walk towards him and stand with my feet almost touching his thighs. I wait for him to lift his head, to gesture with his hands that I too should lie down in the middle of Trafalgar Square at five o'clock on a Monday afternoon. But he does nothing. I wait, and still he does nothing. I wonder if he has fallen asleep, or died, even, but then he lifts his right arm and shields his eyes with his hand.

Instead of lying next to Daniel, I position myself at right angles: my head by his, my body stretched out and away from him. I am aware of his head next to my own. I can smell him — sweat and dirt and I don't know what. The ground presses hard against my back, and I feel the cracks in between the paving stones through my T-shirt. I imagine a foot, treading the weight of another body into me. I imagine a uniformed arm gripping my shoulder and pulling me up. But nothing happens. Nothing happens at all, and eventually my breath pulls slower and deeper into my lungs and I am able to concentrate on the sky above me.

It's like flying, as though it's me that's moving, not the clouds. If I roll my eyes to the edge of my vision I can see the tops of buildings — South Africa House, Canada House, the National Gallery, St Martin-in-the-Fields — and foreshortened fragments of passers-by. A seagull veers into view and is gone. I follow the slow, silent path of an aeroplane and think about the passengers inside, peering down at us, watching London get smaller and smaller. They'll be able to make out the shapes of the buildings, but the people — me and Daniel and everyone here — will be invisible to them.

I think that maybe it will be a little while before I sit in a plane again, watching the world shrink into patterns beneath me.

People skirt around us; I sense their weight and hear snatches of their words, which hang in the air for a moment before vanishing. It's dangerous to stand still in a city; I can hear Dad saying it, his forehead locked into the frown he reserved for his girls. I stare at the sky and wish for him: the smell of cigarette smoke and suede; the way his eyes lit up when he talked about civilisations who had left behind only carefully arranged stones, a shard of pottery, a hand-crafted tool. And then I think about what Daniel said: *if you stand still in a place, for long enough, you can start to feel at home*. I want to reach out my hand to him. I want to say thank you, but I am not sure what for, and I can't think how to start. Instead, I pull the piece of orange cardboard from my pocket. I cup my hands around it and hold it above me, squint my eyes to focus on the tiny pinpricks of light. Ursa Major. Ursa Minor. Pisces. Orion. I sense Daniel turn his head to watch me, and I move the cardboard back a bit, so that we can both see the stars.

Acknowledgements

Three places have been particularly significant in the writing of *Ten Things I've Learnt About Love*. The idea for the novel came to me on a magical Arvon course at the Hurst in Shropshire, run by Maggie Gee and Jacob Ross in 2007. I am grateful to the Arvon Foundation for the grant they gave me to attend the course, to Maggie and Jacob for their enthusiasm, wisdom and continued support, and to the other course attendees for their early encouragement.

In 2009 I was awarded a Hawthornden Fellowship, and spent a beautiful autumnal month living and writing at Hawthornden Castle in Midlothian, Scotland. I owe huge thanks to all those involved in Hawthornden, and to my fellow writers there for their company and kindness.

Ten Things I've Learnt About Love is, in part, a love letter to London, a city I have spent the last eight years living in, cycling across, loving, hating, and rediscovering. I have been involved in arts projects and writing residencies across the city, all of which have contributed in some way to my writing. Thank you to everyone who has shared their stories, and thoughts on place, with me.

Thank you to Spread the Word, The Literary Consultancy and Evie Wyld for the 'Free Read', and to Arts Council England for supporting the

'Free Read' programme. I am also grateful to Spread The Word for years of support and opportunities, and to the Arts Council for funding a mentoring relationship with Martina Evans during the writing of an earlier, unpublished novel; thank you, Martina, for your sound advice and that bowl of red pepper soup when I really needed it.

I am lucky to have the ongoing support of fabulous friends, many of whom are also fabulous writers. I owe particular thanks to Emma Sweeney, a brilliant writer and the best of readers, and to Emily Midorikawa and Will Francis. Thanks too to Emma Sweeney and Ed Hogan for introducing me to Francesca Main, without whose astute advice, warmth and enthusiasm this book would not be what or where it is today.

Thank you to Andrew Kidd for your calmness and advice, to Andrea Walker for your faith in this book, and to everyone at Picador — especially Francesca Main, and the rights team, who turned a dream come true into more than I had ever imagined.

Finally, thank you to Matt, for your love and constancy; and to my family, especially my parents, for being brilliant, and for nurturing the belief that if I tried hard enough for long enough, I could do anything I set my heart on.

Other titles published by
The House of Ulverscroft:

GOODBYE FOR NOW

Laurie Frankel

Imagine a world in which you never have to say goodbye, a world in which you can talk to your loved ones after they've gone — about the trivial things you used to share; about the things you wished you'd said while you still had the chance; about how hard it is to adjust to life without them. When Sam Elling invents a computer programme that enables his girlfriend Meredith to do just this, nothing can prepare them for the success and complications that follow. For every person who wants to say goodbye, there is someone else who can't let go. And when tragedy strikes they have to find out whether goodbye has to be for ever — or whether love can take on a life of its own . . .

THE NIGHT RAINBOW

Claire King

During one long, hot summer, five-year-old Pea and her little sister Margot play alone in the meadow behind their house, in a small village in Southern France. Her mother is too sad to take care of them: she left her happiness in the hospital, along with the baby. Pea's father has died in an accident, and Maman, burdened by her double grief, has retreated to a place where Pea cannot reach her. Then Pea meets Claude, a man who seems to love the meadow as she does. Pea believes that she and Margot have found a friend — maybe even a new papa. But why do the villagers view Claude with suspicion, and what secret is he keeping in his strange, empty house?

THE COLOUR OF MILK

Nell Leyshon

The year is eighteen-hundred-and-thirty-one when fifteen-year-old Mary begins the difficult task of telling her story. A scrap of a thing with a sharp tongue and hair the colour of milk, Mary leads a harsh life working on her father's farm alongside her three sisters. In the summer she is sent to work for the local vicar's invalid wife, where the reasons why she must record the truth of what happens to her — and the need to record it so urgently — are gradually revealed.

THE TWELVE TRIBES OF HATTIE

Ayana Mathis

When Hattie climbed from a train, her skirt still hemmed with Georgia mud and the dream of Philadelphia sitting round as a marble in her mouth, she couldn't guess that two years later, aged seventeen, she'd be fighting to keep her baby twins alive. Saddled with a husband who will bring her nothing but disappointment, she raises nine children with grit and monumental courage, but no tenderness — she knows the world will not be kind to them and wants to prepare them as best she can. And as her sons and daughters buck against their fates, she feels every one of their triumphs and heartbreaks, for they are all bound together . . .

PHILIDA

Andre Brink

It's 1832. Philida is the mother of four children by Francois Brink, the son of her master. The Cape is rife with rumours about the liberation of the slaves and Philida risks her whole life by lodging a complaint against Francois, who has reneged on his promise to set her free. His father has ordered him to marry a white woman from a prominent Cape Town family, and Philida will be sold on to owners in the harsh country up north. Unwilling to accept this fate, Philida continues to test the limits of her freedom, and with the Muslim slave Labyn she sets off on a journey across the great wilderness on the banks of the Gariep River, to the far north of Cape Town.